Praise for *Imposter Syndrome*

"Brimming with insights while being unputdownable and just plain fun. Simply brilliant!"

—**David Yoon, *New York Times* bestselling author of *Frankly in Love***

"Hilarious, whip-smart, and refreshingly honest—this novel is simply brilliant."

—**Brendan Kiely, coauthor of the *New York Times* bestselling *All American Boys***

"An authentically funny, honest, and real portrayal of the fight to be seen. Magnificent."

—**Ellen Oh, award-winning author of *Finding Junie Kim***

"A dazzling YA debut . . . that is deep, real, and scathingly funny."

—**Gayle Forman, *New York Times* bestselling author of *If I Stay***

"Will give readers the courage to truly define 'imposter' and to smash those definitions that no longer serve us."

—**Jennifer de Leon, author of *Don't Ask Me Where I'm From***

"The joys and travails of Alejandra Kim at Quaker Oats Prep made me laugh one moment and cry the next. . . . I loved this novel!"

—**Marie Myung-Ok Lee, author of *Finding My Voice* and *Hurt You***

"*Imposter Syndrome* is funny and moving, wonderfully earnest and slyly satirical, and an absolute pleasure to read."

—**Benjamin Dreyer, *New York Times* bestselling author of *Dreyer's English***

IMPOSTER SYNDROME
and other confessions of Alejandra Kim

PATRICIA PARK

CROWN
New York

Text copyright © 2023 by Patricia Park
Jacket art copyright © 2023 by Jessica Cruickshank

Visit us on the Web! GetUnderlined.com

Educators and librarians, for a variety of teaching tools, visit us at RHTeachersLibrarians.com

Library of Congress Cataloging-in-Publication Data is available upon request.
ISBN 978-0-593-56337-3 (hardcover) — ISBN 978-0-593-56338-0 (lib. bdg.) — ISBN 978-0-593-56339-7 (ebook)

The text of this book is set in 11-point Bembo MT Pro.
Interior design by Michelle Crowe

Printed in the United States of America
10 9 8 7 6 5 4 3 2 1
First Edition

To my niece and nephew

Part I

CHAPTER 1

Origin Story

WHEN YOU HAVE A NAME LIKE ALEJANDRA KIM, teachers always stare at you like you're a typo on the attendance sheet. Each school year, without fail, they look at my face and the roster and back again, like they can't compute my súper-Korean face and my súper-Spanish first name. Multiply that by eight different teachers for eight periods a day, and boom: welcome to my life at Quaker Oats Prep.

I mean, Alejandra is like the "Jessica" of Spanish girl names—basic as all hell. It's not like my parents named me Hermenegilda or Xóchitl. And yet people still find a million and one ways to butcher my name. I've been called:

1. **Alley-JOHN-druh**
   Mr. Landibadeau, our college guidance counselor, who apparently never took Spanish 101. (Hello, the "j" is pronounced like an "h.")

2. **Alexandra**

    Mr. Schwartz, sophomore year, who ironically "Ellis Islanded" me even though he teaches US history.

3. **Ah-leh-CHHHHHAN-durah!**

    Ms. Sanders, junior-year physics. Technically this is correct—the third syllable is pronounced like the "Chan" in "Chanukah." (Hanukah? Hanukkah? You get my point.) But Ms. Sanders was trying *so* hard to sound muy auténtica, which was almost as bad as if she'd just Ellis Islanded my name in the first place. You know, like those annoying people who go to a bodega and order a "CWAH-sson," when the rest of us commoners just say "cruh-SAHNT."

    But if you're the one ordering croissants from a corner bodega, that's the least of your pretentious problems.

    For the record, I just pronounce it "Ah-lay-HAHN-druh." But I usually tell people to call me "Ally." I say it the easy gringo way: "Alley." As in alley cat, alleyway, back-alley. That's what everyone at Quaker Oats Prep calls me.

    Our school's not actually named Quaker Oats. It's officially Anne Austere Preparatory School, named after a Quaker from the 1600s who was literally burned at the stake for trying to better humanity. But everyone just calls us Quaker Oats. We're not like Brearley or Chapin or Dalton. We're more "progressive" (read: "hippie" and "weirdo"). We're like the minor leagues for the big Quaker colleges like Whyder and Swarthmore and Bryn Mawr. Laurel Greenblatt-Watkins, my first and best friend here, says we're a hotbed of granola crunchiness in the middle of Chinatown. I don't know what to think. I'm just a scholarship kid (90 percent). And Ma never lets me forget about that 10 percent we owe each year.

Back in my neighborhood in Queens, they call me "Ale." Except when Ma gets súper pissed, then it's all, "Alejandra Verónica Kim, ¡andate a tu cuarto!"

Papi always used to call me "Aleja-ya."

If I were Dominican or Puerto Rican or Colombian or Mexican, then at least I'd have some solidarity in New York with "mi gente," *my people.* Which might sound vaguely racist, but it is what it is. But my parents are Argentine, and there aren't a whole lot of us here. Both sets of my *parents'* parents were Korean immigrants who were aiming for America-North back in the day but washed up in America-South.

Sidebar: The Korean name for America is Mi-Guk—*Beautiful-Country.* For South America, it's Nam-Mi—*South-of-Beautiful.* Which is all kinds of linguistically fucked up.

It sounds random, how a bunch of Koreans ended up in Argentina. The short answer is immigrant labor exploitation. They were sent over to farm and "populate" Patagonia, but the land was basically a barren desert. The Koreans were like, yeah, nope, and hightailed it to Buenos Aires, where they settled in a villa miseria called Baekgu and sewed clothes all day.

Every time I get upset about something first-world, like how they forgot the ketchup packet with my fries, I have to stop myself and remember: Papi grew up in literal miseryville. He worked in a sweatshop, forced into child labor by his own parents.

3

That's what happens when you're the kid of immigrants: your whole life is one big guilt trip.

Nothing about my family is "normal." Not even the Spanish we speak, which is all weird and Porteño—aka Buenaryan. Apparently there's a hierarchy within the Latinx community where everyone thinks Argentines are snobby, white European wannabes looking down their noses at the rest of Latin America with their hoity-toity accents and weirder verb conjugations and stubborn refusal to use normal words like "tú"—you. Instead Argentines say "vos," which was súper trending in Spain in the 1500s but has since fallen the way of the pay phone and the postage stamp.

Also, Argentines use the word "che"—hey—a lot, which is how Ernesto Guevara got his nickname.

Anyway, Ma and Papi knew each other as kids back in Baekgu, but they re-met here in New York as adults, and the rest, as they say, is historia.

Che, that was exhausting. What's kind of annoying is how people—adults especially—always expect you to lead with your Origin Story like you're in a Marvel comic, sans the súperpowers. Like, ooh, tell me the exotic story behind your name/face/race/peoples. Walk me through that radioactive spider bite that transformed you into the Súper Freak you are today. (Peter Parker, by the way, is also from Queens.)

I am 94.7 percent sure they wouldn't do that if I looked like my ancestors had stepped off the *Mayflower*.

CHAPTER 2

Quaker Oats

ANYWAY, IT'S THE FIRST DAY BACK at Quaker Oats after the summer break, and everyone is súper excited for Senior Elective in Creative Writing. I'm just medium-whatever. I'm taking this class mostly because I need an elective during Taupe period. Quaker Oats does not believe in numbered periods, lest they create hierarchies in time. As our motto says, "We privilege *all* shades of learners."

Quaker Oats invites experts in different subjects to teach electives to us high schoolers. Usually they're adjunct professors from Columbia or NYU looking for a side hustle. Word on the street is that either we pay handsomely or they're just underpaid.

So we're all sitting in the classroom, awaiting the arrival of our elective lecturer: a novelist named Jonathan Brooks James. I don't know if it's a first-middle-last name situation, two first names and a last name, or two last names. I think about asking Claire Devereaux, who's sitting next to me.

Claire leans over my desk. "God, wasn't *Becoming Brooklyn,* like, perfection? We're so lucky to get him." Before I can answer, she adds, "Oh, right, Ally. Reading's not really, like, your thing."

Everyone at Quaker Oats has a "thing."

For Claire Devereaux, it's being editor in chief of *Ennui,* our literary journal.

For Laurel, it's social activism. She wants to be the next Ruth Bader Ginsburg.

Even my best friend back in Jackson Heights, Billy Díaz, has a "thing." It's "trying to get people to stop acting like assholes on the street." Which I guess translates to "making the world a slightly less crappy place."

I don't have a "thing." I'm "thing-adjacent." Which means I usually just support Laurel's things. We spent the last three years making tons of flyers that people only pretended to pay attention to.

I want to tell Claire I didn't think *Becoming Brooklyn* was *perfection.* It's about a guy who lives above a tortilla factory and is tortured by writer's block, corn odor, and a Manic Pixie barista. I didn't understand why it went on for 734 pages when I kind of got the point by page 2. But what do I know? *Becoming Brooklyn* got nominated for a National Book whatever.

Also, Claire's blond hair keeps whipping my desk, and it smells expensive, like non-drugstore shampoo. I get tongue-tied around her—not because of a girl crush, but in, like, a feudal caste kind of a way. She's tall, waifish, and bland-pretty in the face, like a Madewell model. I'm more like the invisible ethnic assistant at the photo shoot who's supposed to fetch her organic alkaline water.

Claire snaps her attention to the front of the classroom—
"Oh my God, that's him!"—and in walks Jonathan Brooks
James, en carne y hueso. That is, *in the flesh.*

Jonathan Brooks James looks like a Jonathan Brooks James,
or how anyone with those three names might look: preppy
as all hell, right down to the loafers without socks. His skin
and hair are the same sandy color, which only makes his blue
eyes pop—like round bits of glass washed up on Rockaway
Beach.

But the more I look, the more he also seems different from
his boyish author photo. His face is puffier and more ragged,
like he got into a fight with himself.

"Get out your notebooks and pens," he says. No *Good morning,* no *Hello my name is,* no *Welcome to the first day of class.*

Everyone whips out their laptops.

"Anyone who pulls out an electronic device will automatically fail this class."

Claire seems chagrined as she shoves her computer back in
her bag. I'm the only one who already has paper and a pen on
my desk, because I am analog like that. My laptop—a hand-
me-down from my cousin Michael Oppa—is too clunky to
carry on the subway every day and only keeps its charge for
five minutes.

"To write fiction, you must create something from nothing," Jonathan Brooks James says. "You cannot be afraid of the
blank page. So freewrite for twenty minutes. And not some
clichéd bullshit like 'How I Spent My Summer Vacation,' so
don't even ask."

Good, because then I'd have to write about my uneventful

days working at Tía Yoona and Gary Gomobu's dry cleaners on the Upper East Side. Tía Yoona is Papi's older sister. I work at the store to help pay off my tuition and to have extra money for books and field trips and things. While the rest of my classmates spent their summers off volunteering on a blueberry farm in Maine or auditing college classes at Bennington or the Sorbonne or on an anthropological expedition to Cairo or the Orkney Islands. Most days at work I pray to God I won't run into any kids from school.

Being "monied" isn't just about shopping sprees in Beverly Hills or ski trips to the Alps. That would be tacky and gauche—a demonstration of "conspicuous consumption." For us Oatties, it's all about *experiences*. (That's what we call ourselves: Oatties. Cute, right? Kind of not really.)

Claire raises her hand. "Hi, Jonathan Brooks James. I'm Claire Devereaux, EIC of *Ennui*. I'm *such* a fan of your work. We'd love to do a feature interview with you, but let's pin that discussion for later. I just have one clarifying question for this assignment. Is there a more specific writing prompt you could give us? Like, should we write about three objects in the room, or employ poetic imagery . . . ?"

He gives her a blank stare, and she falters. I have never seen Claire Devereaux falter before.

"No, just write," he says.

So we "just write." I write about how my fingers are cramping around my pen. I write about how my shoulders are hunched over as my fingers are cramping around my pen. I start to write about the subway ride to school—but then I cross that out and go back to the hunched-over shoulders and cramped fingers.

Basically, it's a whole bunch of nothing.

Jonathan Brooks James pulls out a stack of typewritten pages from his beat-up leather bag and makes big X marks on the pages and sighs a whole lot. I can hear his sockless feet squelching inside his loafers.

The twenty minutes are up.

Finally, Jonathan Brooks James takes attendance.

Chelsea Braeburn.

Joshua Buck.

Maya Chang.

Claire Devereaux.

He rattles down the list. When Jonathan Brooks James gets to the "K"s, I can feel the familiar tightening in my chest. He stares down at the attendance sheet, pauses. Oh great. It's happening again. I quickly raise my hand to get this over with—

But Jonathan Brooks James doesn't even bother to *say* my name. He just smirks right over it. "Talk about multi-culti. *You'll* have no trouble getting into college," he says, looking straight at me.

Oh *no*, he didn't.

Wait, did he?

My cheeks are on fire.

But he says it in that off-the-cuff, snarky hipster, *Am I rite?* way, which makes me feel uncool if I don't laugh along.

So I laugh along.

Whatever, it's No Big Deal, because people are dying in

Syria and starving in North Korea and there's an opioid epi-demic and there are *much worse* things than a stupid micro-aggressive comment.

And because *I* laugh along, I've basically sanctioned that it's okay. The whole classroom kind of titters. No one speaks out.

I wish Jonathan Brooks James had straight-up bungled my name, like my teachers before him did. Just like every day I wish I had a normal name, like Jane or Anjali or Jiyoung. A name that at least looks like what I'm *supposed* to be.

CHAPTER 3

Kraft on Wonder

AT LUNCH, I FIND Laurel Greenblatt-Watkins. Our spot is the southwestern corner of our rooftop campus, away from the north-end sports kids who say they're applying to the SLACs (small liberal arts colleges, aka the Holy Grail) but are probably secretly applying to the Ivy Leagues. Only at Quaker Oats would applying to the Ivies be something you're embarrassed about—like it's some frank admission of your deepest, darkest capitalist desires. (Brown and Dartmouth being the only acceptable exceptions.)

Laurel and I are kind of on the fringe of the artsy-fartsy kids at the south end, most of whom dress in all black and wear chains on their pants because the whole 1990s-grunge-goth thing is making a comeback. Kids who are applying to the Carletons and Kenyons and Hampshires.

Although *we* don't dress like that. I just wear T-shirts and jeans, and Laurel is súper into sustainable clothing. She usually wears a flowy poncho thing and culottes, hand-sewn by sex trafficking survivors from Bhutan and Nepal.

I haven't seen Laurel all summer. She was away at Middlebury, studying Arabic. Laurel's a polyglot. English, of course, and French lessons since she was a kid, and Latin and Greek at Quaker Oats, and even the Trinidadian Creole she learned from her caregiver. She had to sign a pledge that she would not read, write, speak, or listen to any other language but Arabic all summer. It's kind of funny picturing Laurel doing this on a leafy campus in the middle of lily-white Vermont.

Laurel sent me long letters over the summer, which I promised I'd have translated by Mr. Malouf, who owns the 99-cent store down my block. I didn't tell her I stopped after the first one. I mean, Mr. M's busy, he's got a business to run. I wasn't going to interrupt him so he could translate her letters about the "very good!" classes and the "not so very good!"–smelling dorms.

Laurel has no problem plunking herself down on our Astro-turfed corner, but I put a piece of loose-leaf paper down on the ground before I sit. I mean, this is New York City. There's pigeon poop and smog from all the cars backed up on the Manhattan Bridge and who knows what else. (Not that a sheet of loose-leaf paper will be much help.)

Laurel unboxes her lunch. "Whatcha got today?" I ask.

She shows me. Laurel—or rather, Laurel's family's caregiver—packs her lunch in a glass container, and she schleps that thing in an insulated canvas tote on the train each day. Today it's quinoa with roasted-black-garlic hummus. For dessert she has three kumquats and two squares of Valrhona dark chocolate. For snacks she carries celery sticks in a cloth-mesh bag, which

I don't have the heart to tell her stinks like an unventilated subway car.

I show her mine: Oscar Mayer ham and Kraft American "cheese product" on squishy white bread encased in Saran wrap by yours truly, and a baggie of Utz potato chips, all tossed into a humble white plastic grocery bag that says THANK YOU across the front like ten times. I make my own sandwiches for school now. Papi used to make my lunches for me.

You can tell a lot about an Oattie by what they eat for lunch. You have tennis captain Maya Chang, who alternates between green juice and cauliflower rice. Josh Buck gets McDonald's as an "ironic attempt to connect with the everyman," but by the way he mainlines his Big Macs, it's not ironic at all; it's straight-up love. Chelsea Braeburn, whose moms own the Michelin-starred restaurant Pomegranate, is always complaining about her "leftovers" of braised oxtail or duck confit. (A first-world problem if there ever was one.) But one day in precalc, Chelsea's lunch spilled in her bag and it stunk up the classroom, and I kind of felt bad for her.

Then there's Laurel with her vegan-adjacent boxes prepped by her Trinidadian caregiver, and me with my Kraft cheese on Wonder white.

You are what you eat at Quaker Oats.

"You're so funny, Ally," Laurel says, "with your über-Americana provisions."

According to Laurel, to be "too American" is a bad thing. Funny how all my life that's all I've ever *tried* to be: too American, like I have to prove to the rest of the world that I *am* from here.

13

I guess when you're white, you get to take being American for granted.

"I'm being ironic," I say, and we laugh, but of course it bothers me a little the way Laurel scrutinizes my lunch. She's the only one who knows I'm on scholarship, although I'm sure it's no surprise to anyone else here. Quaker Oats, unlike other "mainstream" prep schools, isn't about owning cool stuff or dressing in name brands. Some kids show up wearing the same tattered rags every day, but then you go over to their house after school for an eco-sustainability project, and it turns out they live in a multimillion-dollar brownstone in Cobble Hill.

"So how was *the* famous Jonathan Brooks James's class?" Laurel asks me, taking a bite of quinoa. She has AP Comp Gov during Taupe period.

"It was okay," I say. "We didn't really do anything." I tell Laurel about his "just write" exercise and how Claire Devereaux thinks we're lucky to get him.

"Hmph, *she* would," Laurel says. We don't like Claire Devereaux. Laurel thinks she's the Upper East Side and the Hamptons all wrapped into one expensive bottle of eau de snob. I think Claire might be from the Upper *West* Side, but I never correct Laurel.

"What'd you think of *Becoming Brooklyn*?" I ask. Laurel reads everything.

"I didn't read it," she says. "I'm not reading anything by white men this year."

"Way to discriminate, Laurel," I tease.

Laurel gives me a Look. "Ally. For centuries, white men have been the only storytellers. My not supporting one generation of them is barely a blip in the bucket."

"Okay, Reverend Laurel."

I always tease her whenever she gets into debate-team mode. A lot of Oatties think Laurel is Intense. But I find it part of her charm. Laurel genuinely believes in the things she says and does. Which is more than I can say for a lot of the "slacktivists" we go to school with.

"Back to business," Laurel says. "What'd you decide on for your Whyder essay?"

Whyder College is Laurel's and my dream. I've wanted to go there ever since freshperson year, when the catalog of its tree-lined campus arrived in the mail. The thought of stepping on a bus at Port Authority and heading north to Maine, leaving behind the chaos of the city and Queens and my mother and everything I've been trying to forget about last year . . .

But I try not to get my hopes up. Whyder College has an 8.5 percent acceptance rate.

"I'm floating a couple of ideas," I say vaguely. "But I haven't settled on anything yet."

Whyder requires both the Common App *and* a special supplement. This year's essay question is "What is 'home' for you?"

I finished the Common App this summer. But I'm still stumped on the supplemental essay.

"I spent all summer working on my Whyder essay," Laurel says. "But it's just not coalescing." Laurel is writing about her struggles to learn Arabic and feel "at home" in the language. She's studying Arabic because she wants to help Muslim women in underprivileged communities, so that *they* can feel "at home."

"Hey, does that mean you broke your Language Pledge at Middlebury?" I ask.

"Of course not!" Laurel is aghast, like I've accused her of cheating. "I wrote my essay in Arabic. I'll work on the English translation this month."

Of *course* she did. That's Laurel for you. "You're such an Oattie," I say to her.

Whyder has been *Laurel's* dream ever since she was a kid. She used to go to Alumni Weekend every year with her mom, sporting her FUTURE WHYDEE! T-shirt. (Laurel's dad is a proud Tiger, aka Princeton grad, and he lives in Connecticut with his new wife and baby. It's kind of a sore point.)

Laurel's got a 99.9 percent chance of getting into Whyder, for several reasons:

1. She's applying ED—early decision.
2. She's legacy.
3. She's bound for the Supreme Court. She fights tooth and nail for every one of her causes.
4. Her GPA. Her grades are a little better than mine—I had a rocky start to freshperson year but hit my stride by year two. It doesn't matter that I did better on the SATs than Laurel; Whyder doesn't care about "statistics." They look at the "holistic picture" because "each Whydee" is "more than just a number." Quoting the catalog here.

"I can't wait till we get to campus," Laurel says. "All the cafeteria food is sourced from the on-campus farm."

"Celery for days!" I say.

"But no Kraft American," she zings back.

We sigh wistfully.

We've been doing this since freshperson year: constructing our new lives at Whyder College. We are dorktastic like that. We talk about Whyder with the same dreaminess that normcore girls talk about boyfriends and the prom.

It could be weird to be vying for the same college as my best friend, but Laurel's great that way—she's súper supportive and not at all competitive. That's also part of the Quaker ethos— helping everyone rise up together as a community.

"Hey," Laurel says as we finish up lunch. "What are you doing this weekend? Come over to my house Saturday and we'll work on our essays together."

"I have work," I remind her.

"Right." She nods, but I know she's forgotten I have my shift at Tía Yoona's dry cleaners. We talk about maybe the following week instead.

I'm not applying early to Whyder because I can't get locked into a financial aid package I haven't seen. I don't have that luxury. That was Mr. Landibadeau's advice when we had our college-counseling meeting junior year. So I'll have to wait until the spring to compare options and see what school is the most affordable. Which sucks because everyone knows it's harder to get in RD—regular decision—than ED. The financial aid stuff is the elephant in the room between Laurel and me.

Laurel smiles, which makes me feel better about not applying early, which she knows, and I know she knows, and she knows I know she knows, but we don't actually talk about it.

It's another reminder to me of how different I am from the other Oatties. I'm the only one I know who has an after-school job, the only one I know who has to worry about how to pay for college. My classmates spend all their energy on getting into the best college first, then worrying about the tuition last to never.

CHAPTER 4

Jackson Heights

AFTER SCHOOL, I WALK with Laurel to the F train at East Broadway. "Why are you going this way?" she asks. "You usually take the 6 to the 4/5 to the 7."

I shrug. "I just want to go a different way."

"But the other way's faster. Remember? You timed it sophomore year."

It's like she's forgotten. I don't want to get into it.

"They're doing track work on the 7."

I feel my face growing hot with the lie. I dart for my subway before Laurel can call me out on it.

Our train tracks literally split apart here—she'll take the F downtown and to Brooklyn, and I'll take it uptown and over to Queens—but it's more than just that. It's like this is where our lives splinter off, and we go back to our separate worlds as if Quaker Oats hadn't brought us together.

When Laurel gets off her F at 7th Avenue, she'll walk past leafy tree-lined streets and rows and rows of beautifully restored historic brownstones. She'll pass farm-to-table restaurants and upscale clothing boutiques where a drab piece of wool sheared straight off a sheep retails for $400. Black nannies push white babies in strollers that cost more than most people's cars in my neighborhood.

I'm on the uptown F, chugging along with the other passengers as we pass Herald Square, Bryant Park, Rockefeller Center. The faces in the train car change, growing darker in complexion as we head east toward Queens. By the time we leave Manhattan, most of the white people are gone.

We head east underground. But if we were aboveground on the 7, we'd see the East River ahead. I wish I could say the vista was inspiring. But it's the wrong view of New York City. The Empire State Building, the Chrysler, the soaring Midtown skyline would all fall behind us.

After "signal problems," "police activity," and "train traffic ahead," I finally get off at 74th Street. Exiting the station, I feel the familiar waves of comfort and dread washing over me. Comfort because I'm back in my hood, and my body can now relax. I guess all day I'm so tense at Quaker Oats, and I don't even realize it until the second I get off the subway and walk home. I don't work out or anything, but holding your body straight and rigid for eight periods a day is probably more tiring than yoga or Pilates. No one here's judging my Wonder bread and Kraft American "cheese product" sandwiches; no one cares if I drink non-fair-trade bodega coffee from a disposable blue paper cup.

But I feel dread because I know what's waiting for me when I get home.

This is Jackson Heights. Everyone is rushing, rushing down

Roosevelt. White people are rare round these parts. Most everyone is Latinx or South Asian, with some East and Southeast Asian people sprinkled in.

Now that I'm back in Queens, the PC terms feel weird and fake. Here we say "Spanish" even though you're not technically from the Iberian Peninsula. We say "Indian" even if someone's from Bangladesh or Sri Lanka. And I'm always "China." It doesn't matter how many times I say, "¡Soy coreana!"—*I'm Korean!* "Chino/a" is one of those charged words—depending on how it's said, it either means *Chinese* or *Chink.*

Imagine if I told people I was "Spanish"; they'd laugh in my face. No one here thinks I count as "Latinx," so I don't check off that box on forms.

This stuff is so confusing.

I pass Mr. Malouf's 99-cent store, the cash-and-carry, the shops selling saris and salwar kameezes in bright pastels. Then the immigration-law offices with signs in Spanish, Bengali, Nepali. Mr. Gómez's bodega, with its yellow-and-red corrugated-metal awning, where Billy Díaz and I used to buy Jolly Ranchers after school for a quarter apiece. The Colombian bakery where Papi would buy guava-filled pastries. I used to *love* those pastelitos, but I haven't touched them in months. The sweet bakery smell follows me down the block before it's replaced by the fry grease from the samosa cart and then the Kennedy Fried Chicken.

I pass María Inez Montoya Park, where Billy and I used to sit on the bench and hurl angry pebbles into the empty fountain, trying to forget the way the kids in junior high would tease us for being nerdy. But I haven't seen Billy since he took off for the Dominican Republic last winter, when his grandmother got sick. We haven't texted, let alone talked, since the night he left.

I turn off Roosevelt, and the bustle dies down. The richer, whiter people have started moving in on the streets just east of us, in the "Historic District." Not so much over here. I pass identical rows of reddish-brown ("shit-brown," according to Billy) brick apartment buildings. One of these buildings is home.

I push open the rickety metal doors of the lobby, and I'm instantly hit with everyone's cooking smells: chilies, curry, frying fish, soy sauce.

Our elevator is a gloppy, dirty beige that's peeling everywhere. Our super should have scraped off all the old layers of exposed paint and started from scratch, but I guess he can't be bothered. He just keeps slathering fresh paint over the old.

Number 2B. My key sticks in the lock of our front door. Papi was the one who always kept the lock greased with WD-40. Now the can sits, rusting, in the cabinet under the kitchen sink. My heart tightens. Inside, a huge black leather couch—a hand-me-down from Tía Yoona—eats up most of our living room. There's still a dip in the beat-up leather cushions where Papi used to sleep all day after he lost his last job, after the fights with Ma that went on all night. It's almost like Papi is still here.

But he's not. It's been eight months since Papi was found dead on the tracks of the 7 train.

CHAPTER 5

Apartment 2B

OUR APARTMENT IS AN illegally converted two-bedroom facing the Q49 bus stop. One day when I was little, Papi and his best friend, Tío Fonsi, came home with Sheetrock and a door frame from The Home Depot, which they smuggled past Julio, our super, while he was on a smoke break. By the end of the day, presto! The dining room nook off the kitchen became my new bedroom.

I don't invite people from Quaker Oats over. Not even Laurel has seen our apartment. Partly because I'm embarrassed, but mostly because I don't want her to feel awkward that her house is so much bigger than mine. She'd go out of her way to make me feel like my house wasn't so bad (*It's so cozy!*), which would only make me feel more uncomfortable.

There's a small framed wedding photo of Ma and Papi in the hallway of our apartment. They're standing in front of city hall. Papi's in a sport jacket, holding Ma's bouquet of bodega carnations. Ma looks so dated: white denim mini, vinyl pumps, teased and hair-sprayed bangs. Still, her beauty is undeniable: heart-shaped face and large dark eyes that catch the light. If she went to my school, she'd get so many guys. I can already hear Laurel correcting me: *That's centering heteronormativity.* She's right. I still think Ma in her prime was equal-opportunity hot.

In the photo, the wind is mussing up Ma's bangs, and she seems fed up as she fixes her hair. Meanwhile, Papi gives a baby-fat, dimpled grin to the camera, like he's the luckiest guy on earth.

I used to think Papi was so happy that day. But on closer look, I see the shadow cast across his face. Maybe it's the angle of the building looming over them, the grainy photography. Or maybe it's something else.

They must have been happy once upon a time, no? Two young, beautiful people in New York City. Cue Erasure or whatever people were listening to back in the 1900s. And the graffiti, broken subway windows, and crime. My parents' marriage wasn't loveless, exactly; Papi clearly adored Ma, would help her into her jacket, hold the door for her, that kind of thing. He'd come home with two roses—one for Ma, one for me—and place them on top of our dinner plates. Ma was never too happy about that—"Why'd you waste our money on something so frívolo?"—and Papi's face would fall right onto his plate. So I'd say, "Papi, I love it!" And his face would brighten again.

Now that I think about it, there was something dried up about their chemistry, like those stale squid crackers Tía Yoona keeps around the house. You grab a fistful from the bowl, and they disintegrate to dust in your palm.

I TOSS MY KEYS on the ledge by Ma and Papi's wedding photo and retreat to my room. It's small, but it's mine. My twin bed is lofted above a set of drawers where I keep most of my clothes. My shelves have books from all across the ages: Little Golden Books, Baby-Sitters Club and Goosebumps, and the dog-eared classics: Austen, the Brontës, Wharton.

I still have the same pink-and-white desk, covered in stupid rainbow-heart and unicorn stickers from when I was a little girl. In junior high I blackened them with permanent marker, so I'm not assaulted by glitter mania each time I study. On my desk is my laptop, covered in Michael Oppa's Transformers decals, and my schoolbooks.

My window looks out onto an air shaft. Still, I can hear the endless honking of car horns over on Roosevelt. I start my homework. AP Calc first, because math is my least favorite subject (I'm only in AB), so I want to get that out of the way. Then AP Geography next.

Before I get started on AP English Lit, I rummage in the kitchen for a snack. Ma's perpetually on a diet, so we have no snacky junk. I find a canister of Planters peanuts in the cupboard above the stove. But the can is sticky with cooking grease and the nuts are stale. I check the expiration date: two years ago. I throw the can away.

I'm dreading dinner tonight because I haven't yet told Ma

that I'm applying to Whyder College. Ma's only letting me apply to colleges she's heard of. Which means if it isn't Columbia or Queens College, then forget it. I probably shouldn't have waited until *September of senior year* to ask her permission. I only told Papi how much I wanted to go to Whyder, and he always encouraged me.

Dream big, Aleja-ya, he used to tell me. *You can be anything you want in this country.*

I guess I was relying on Papi to be the one to persuade Ma. But after Papi passed away, it never seemed like the right time to bring it up with Ma. I kept putting it off, putting it off, like when you start nodding off on the couch and you know you should just get up and brush your teeth and put yourself to bed like a responsible person, but it's like you physically can't.

Dream big. He might as well have said, *Do as I say, not as I do.* Because ever since he took to the couch after he lost his last job, ever since he stopped playing jazz piano altogether, I wonder if Papi ever believed his own words at all.

AFTER I MAKE A big dent in my never-ending homework, I get started on dinner. Today Ma works a double shift—she's a personal-care aide—so it's my turn to cook. Ma hasn't gone grocery shopping yet, so all we have in the fridge besides my lunch stuff is half an onion and three eggs. I find a plastic-wrapped fistful of cooked rice in the freezer, white and icy with burn. Which means I'm making fried rice.

As the rice defrosts in the microwave, I dice an onion, making the crosshatches just as Papi taught me. He loved cooking.

Empanadas were his specialty. Papi filled the dumplings with ground beef, chopped-up hard-boiled eggs, cellophane noodles, olives, and parsley. Instead of baking them the traditional Argentine way, he'd deep-fry them. They were perfect golden parcels of crisp savoriness. If you haven't tried Papi's empanadas, then you haven't lived.

I'm stirring the contents of the pan when Ma comes home. I can tell by the jangle of her keys, by the way she stomps her support shoes on the doormat to get the gunk from other people's houses off the soles, that she's in a bad mood. The elderly patients Ma cares for can't always control their bodily functions. She wears her hair pulled back so she doesn't get bits of food or vomit or excrement stuck in it.

She comes into the kitchen, and I'm momentarily caught off guard by how much she's aged. Her once-jet-black hair is streaked gray, which she covers up with cheap, brassy dye. Her heart-shaped face is pancaked thick with makeup, which does nothing to hide how tired-of-it-all she looks. Her dark eyes are lined with too much worry. She's nothing like her wedding picture at city hall.

"Bad day at work?" I venture when Ma comes into the kitchen.

"Same as every day." Her tone tells me she doesn't want to talk anymore.

This isn't going to be good.

Ma washes her hands in the sink, scrubbing and scrubbing obsessively. When she's done, I can still see a dark red film caked under her nails. I wonder if it's blood.

I set the dining table, pushing aside the mountain of mail

we haven't sorted in forever. The table is a black Formica eight-top, a hand-me-down from Tía Yoona's house that's oversized in our living room. We sit at opposite ends of the table.

"What's all this?" Ma says, suspicion lacing her voice. Usually we eat at the kitchen counter, and Ma scrolls through videos on her phone and I text with Laurel on mine.

"Nothing," I say, placing down our bowls. "Just . . . a change."

We eat. In silence. Well, I eat. The dinner I made is a bland-yet-oily rice concoction. I think about the meals Papi used to prepare for us. He would've taken the same rice, half onion, and three eggs and magically transformed them into something restaurant quality. Maybe he'd have made risotto-style rice, or fried rice balls with a crunchy crust. *Bistro 2B,* he'd have said, flourishing our dinner plates.

I miss Papi's cooking, I think but don't say. Ma doesn't like reminders of Papi. I learned that the hard way.

As I pour soy sauce over my fried rice, Ma frowns.

"Ale, that's too much salt," she tuts.

"It's my food, I can do what I want." My tone comes out sharper than I meant it. But Ma has always made snide comments about what I eat.

She shrugs, lights a cigarette. She was smoke-free during my childhood, but she started up again right after Papi died. I still remember her dressed all in black, huddled at the far end of the funeral home parking lot, lighting up a cigarette. She flicks ash into her bowl of fried rice. The fried rice *I* made for her. She still hasn't eaten a bite.

I wait until she's onto her next cigarette before I tell her the news. "I have something important I need to tell you."

Ma's BS antenna goes off. "Dale, just say it, Ale," she says.

"I decided to apply to Whyder for college. It's a súper-prestigious school."

"Whyder? I never heard of it," she says, wrinkling her nose.

Her tone says: *And I don't want to hear any more about it.*

What I want to say is: *Just because you've never heard of it doesn't mean it's not prestigious.*

What I *do* say is: "It's the number one–ranked small liberal arts college in *U.S. News and World Report.* It's in Maine"—I rush over this part—"and they have a low student-to-faculty ratio, which means small classes, and you get a lot of professor attention." I jam in all the stats and facts.

Ma's no idiot. She latches on to the part I gloss right over.

"*Maine?* Ale," she says. "We already discussed this, ya. You're not allowed to apply to schools outside of New York."

It wasn't much of a discussion. Right after Papi's funeral, Ma said, "Just so we're clear, you're staying in New York for college. End of discussion." She was grieving—*I* was grieving—and it wasn't the right time to bring up Whyder.

But the financial aid forms are due soon.

The wrinkles in Ma's face deepen. She puckers her mouth, like she's been force-fed a lemon. She lets out a stream of yellow smoke.

I cough, loudly. On purpose, of course.

"Aleja," she says, now using her *I'm trying to be reasonable with you* tone. "Your cousins stayed in New York. Michael Oppa went to Columbia. Jason applies there and NYU."

"Whyder ranks higher than *both* of them," I say. Yes, there's an Oattie snobbiness to my voice; I can't help it.

Also, Columbia and NYU are notorious for their shitty financial aid packages. We're not like Tía Yoona's family, who actually have money. So why does Ma even bother to bring up schools we can't afford? Schools I'm not even interested in, anyway?

Ma never graduated from college. Her parents sent her here to the States to study, but the money ran out before she could finish. Blame hyperinflation of the Argentine peso—back then, the price of milk would go up tenfold in the time it took you to check out. People used to carry suitcases full of cash just to buy the day's groceries. There was no plata for Ma to return to Argentina, so she had to make her life here.

I don't get the sense that Ma was ever the studious type, anyway. Papi, who came to America when he was a teen, never even graduated high school, let alone went to college. When I asked why, he just shrugged and said, "Pues." Which is as meaningless as "um" or "uh."

"Alejandra," Ma continues. "What about somewhere like Queens College? Or even Hunter?"

Another flick of ash into her rice bowl. I stare at her in disbelief. Queens College? *Hunter?*

"Somewhere nearby, so you can commute from home," Ma goes on when I don't answer her. "And cheaper, too."

Is Ma for real? "There is *no* way I'm staying here."

She purses her lips again, like she's debating whether to take the bait. She does not.

"Well, you think about it." Ma says it like it's already a done deal, like she's convinced me of her flimsy argument.

"There's not a lot of time to 'think.' The applications are due soon." It's too much: the fried rice, the smoking, Ma's blatant disengaging from this conversation. "Just because *you* never finished college doesn't mean you have to make *me* go to a bad one."

It's mean, but the words leave my mouth before I can stop them.

"Alejandra, I never said that." Ma blows more yellow smoke from her mouth, and her eyes tell me she can't be bothered with this discussion.

This makes me even angrier. What does she want from me? To stay in New York—in this same apartment I've lived in for all my life—and rot away? Ma was ambivalent about my academic ambitions, but ever since Papi's death she's just checked out of momhood in all the wrong ways.

And then I really can't help myself. "Papi would have wanted me to go to Whyder!"

Ma's lips press into an angry white line at the mention of Papi. I know I've gone too far. But she goes quiet, calm—almost too calm.

"Things have changed since your father's accident," she says.

That's what Ma calls it, that's what the witnesses on the 7 train platform said: it was crowded, it was busy, it was just "an accident."

And that's the end of the discussion. Ma stubs her cigarette upright into her bowl of untouched rice. I head to my room, the door slamming shut behind me.

TUCKED IN THE BOTTOM drawer of my desk is a picture of Papi and me at Rockaway Beach. A bucket of KFC grows cold and uneaten between us. Ma's not even in the picture, because she and Papi got into a fight right when we got to the Rockaways. We unloaded our stuff, and Papi realized he'd forgotten the umbrella. Ma thought we'd all burn, Papi said we could rent another umbrella, and Ma threw a fit—"You must think we're just made of money, Juan!"

Their fight was about the umbrella, but I know it was about so much more. Ma ended up staying behind in the car while Papi and I went ahead to the beach. It was supposed to be a happy day—a beach day to celebrate my starting at Quaker Oats in the fall. I wished we hadn't bothered coming at all.

I don't pull out the photo, ever. Looking at it just makes me sad. I thought it would always be Papi and me against the world. Now it's just me.

CHAPTER 6

Montoya Fountain

MA'S PISSY MOOD SPREADS throughout the whole apartment, like skunky water filling up a toilet tank. Like this whole crappy metaphor, I flush myself out of the house, grabbing my keys and heading for María Inez Montoya Park. It's where I go when I just need to get out of my own head for a while.

Calling it a "park" is a gross exaggeration. It's no Central, Prospect, or Flushing Meadows. Montoya Park is a small, fenced-off square with some graffitied benches. The highlight is a dried-up fountain that stopped spewing water ages ago and is now filled with trash. Whoever María Inez Montoya is, I kind of feel bad she has such a lousy place named after her.

I see a familiar figure sitting on the bench across from the fountain: short, dark haired, pudgy. I know it's Billy Díaz.

"Yo, Billy!" I shout, waving my arms to get his attention.

But when I get to the bench, it's not Billy at all. Just some random kid I don't know. He looks at me all funny.

"Sorry," I mumble.

I forgot—Billy's still in Santo Domingo. He left right after Papi's funeral.

I sit way at the other end of the fountain, so this kid-who's-not-Billy doesn't think I'm stalking him.

Billy and I became friends because he doesn't have a dad, and I do. *Did.* In Montoya Park, Papi was trying, and mostly failing, to teach me to play soccer. Billy—back then I knew him only as Guillermo—was the lone kid sitting at the edge of the fountain, watching us longingly.

"That kid looks left out," Papi said.

I shrugged. He was in the second-grade classroom next to mine, but I didn't know him, and he wasn't my problem. Like Ma would always say, *Am I supposed to solve the world's problems?*

Papi pushed me forward. "Go invite him to play with us."

"No!" I protested. "He's going to think I *like* him."

Papi pushed me forward. "Be kind, Aleja-ya."

And so I went, reluctantly. "My *dad* wants to know if you want to play soccer with us."

Billy brightened—but then his smile quickly faded. "That's okay." It was like he sensed that I didn't really want him to play with us but was only being polite. Even back then, Billy had nunchi—which is Korean for Spidey sense in social situations.

I softened. "Come on. We need another player, anyway."

And so the three of us played. I was terrible at soccer—still am—but I managed to have fun. Papi kept losing on purpose, just to let Guillermo—Billy—win a couple of goals. Billy wasn't good at first, either, but he got much better with each kick, each free throw, each headbutt of the ball. After, Papi bought us ice creams from the Mister Softee truck. Soccer in Montoya Park became a ritual, and we'd use our backpacks as makeshift goal posts.

After I started Quaker Oats and I kind of fell out with my old crew in Jackson Heights, my friendship with Billy was my only one to survive. I can talk to him about all the things I can't with Laurel or any other Oattie friends, and vice versa. He "keeps it real," which I know is such a cliché, but it's also true.

Maybe it's because Billy gets me in a way that no one from school does. Maybe it's because he knew Papi. He's wanted out of this barrio, this *world,* for as long as I have.

Or maybe I should say Billy *got* me, past tense.

Because I don't really know where things stand after what he said—gushed—to me at the end of Papi's funeral. I shut it down. Then he was on a plane to the DR. I kept starting and stopping texts to respond. I even thought about asking Mrs. Díaz for Billy's grandma's number in Santo Domingo. In the end, silence seemed safer than words.

The kid-who's-not-Billy gets up and leaves the park.

BEFORE I STARTED SCHOOL at Quaker Oats, I'd never even *heard* of Whyder. All we knew were the Harvards and Columbias of the world. The whole point of getting a university degree was so that you could get a high-paying job that would get you *out* of Queens—and into a penthouse in the city or a mansion on Long Island or both.

Queensites aren't dumb, or even superficial; we're just practical. When you're descended from people fleeing war/famine/

poverty—all the Horribles that make immigrants risk it on the devil they don't know instead of sticking with the one they do—then who has time to worry about what James Wood wrote in the latest *New Yorker*?

Or what Wittgenstein had to say about political systems?

Or what Foucault thought about panopticons?

Also, what the heck is a panopticon?

For most people in my neighborhood, money/food/shelter is the American dream.

But it's not *my* American dream. I long to belong to the people who have *already* arrived. People who get to take money/food/shelter for granted, people whose crisp, polished English is a completely foreign language from the broken-down versions everyone speaks in Queens.

For me, Whyder College is the embodiment of that.

I once tried to explain all this to Papi. But I stopped midway—I didn't want to sound like I was ungrateful for the things I *did* have. Beats Papi's childhood of living in a cement shack in the slums and working twenty-four seven in the family-run sweatshop.

So I kept my feelings to myself.

MORE THAN ANYTHING, I wish I could still hear Papi play jazz on the old Casio. This intense concentration would come over his face as his fingers danced across the keyboard, like he was tuning out the rest of the world. I don't even like jazz that much—it sounds like noisy chaos—but I understood how much the music meant to him.

Ma said Papi used to be, like, a piano prodigy back in Argentina, but, immigration. He never had the chance to pursue his dream of being a músico. He never had the chance to do a lot of things. I thought immigration was all about achieving the American dream. But in my family, immigration just seems to be the American dream killer.

"Papi, I'm sorry," I call to the empty fountain. But my voice echoes hollow across the concrete.

"I'm sorry, I'm sorry, I'm sorry!"

I talk into Montoya Fountain like it's some priestly confessional box. I wait for a penance that never comes. But all the Hail Marys in the world won't bring him back.

I've never admitted this to anyone, but I don't just feel sad that Papi's dead. Because that's what a *good* daughter would feel.

Instead I feel anger. I feel guilt.

I'm mad Papi gave up the fight without a fight.

He taught me not to fight, too.

I talk, I cry, I shout into the fountain. But Papi never answers me.

I REACH FOR MY phone to text Billy. Same old instinct; I stop myself. So I get up from Montoya Fountain and send a text to Laurel instead.

CHAPTER 7

Notorious JBJ

AFTER A WEEK OF "just writing," today Jonathan Brooks James has an actual writing prompt for us on the whiteboard:

Write about a time you received depressing news.

Claire Devereaux's hand shoots up. "How exactly do you define 'depressing'? Do you mean in the clinical sense, which is all kinds of problematic, or do you mean metaphorically—"

He interrupts her. "Depressing like you just found out your life's work amounted to nothing more than a form rejection letter," he says.

His usual manuscript pages are gone. There's something about his face—puffy, red—and the glassy look in his eyes that reminds me of Papi.

Reminds me of the time I came home from school and found out Papi had tossed his Casio keyboard in the trash. He and Ma used to fight all the time about Papi playing jazz, and now they fought about him throwing out the piano:

"Juan, if you were going to get rid of it, then why didn't you at least get some money for it?"

"I couldn't stand the sight of it anymore, okay? ¡Vero, por favor dejame en paz!"

That was junior year.

I pick up my pen, but nothing comes out. For once, I wish Jonathan Brooks James had mailed it in and told us to "just write." Because I can't write to this assignment at all.

AT LUNCH, Laurel is livid.

"Why didn't you tell me what JBJ said to you on the first day of class? 'Talk about multi-culti'? '*You'll* have no trouble getting into college'?"

"Is that what we're calling him now?" I unwrap my sandwich.

"Maya Chang told me during Teal period. Why do I have to hear it from other people and not my own best friend?"

I kind of don't like that Laurel and Maya are talking about me behind my back. And that was week-old news, anyway.

I brush it off. "It wasn't that big a deal."

Correction: it was a medium deal. But whatever. It's not like he called me a "Chink" or anything.

You'd be surprised how quickly people reach for the C-word. Just the other day, I was getting onto a crowded train when I was jostled into the woman in front of me by the man behind me.

The woman turned around and was all, "You fucking Chink!" She raised her fist like she was going to clock me. Everyone just stood around and did nothing, including the guy who'd pushed me into her in the first place. So much for "If You See Something, Say Something," which is only plastered on every subway and bus ad ever. Seriously, you could get stabbed to death like Kitty Genovese, who we learned about in my History of the City of New York class, and most bystanders wouldn't bother to look up from their phones.

I've heard all the variations of the C-word, too. I'll be walking down Roosevelt Avenue and hear "China!," "Chinita!" ("Chink," with sexual innuendo), or "Ching-chong!" (translate that on your own time).

If this is what happens in a city as diverse as New York, can you imagine what it'd be like in the rest of the country? They'd probably come after my whole family. We'd have to sleep with triple-bolted doors *and* an alarm system *and* a starving pit bull, just in case.

No offense to pit bulls. Mrs. González in 4J had one, and Amber was actually a pretty sweet dog.

Wait a minute. How's that any different from saying, *X people aren't so bad, because I have this one friend who's X and they're actually pretty nice!*?

Did I just commit single storyism . . . on a pit bull?

"It *is* a big deal!" Laurel says. "What JBJ said to you is, like, the textbook definition of discrimination. My mom"—Amelia Watkins is a lawyer for the ACLU—"just worked on a case like that. And she *won*. Ally, you should say something to him!"

Sometimes it's easier if you just don't make it a big deal. The more you talk about it, the more it becomes a *thing*. And honestly? I don't need more *things* crowding my brain and my heart than I already have.

As if on cue, Maya Chang comes over to our nook under the tree. She's diplomatic that way, making her rounds across campus from her tennis teammates to the other sub-factions of Oatties. She's drinking her usual lunch of unidentified green juice from a straw.

"Oh my God, Ally," Maya says. "You totally should have said something to JBJ! That was *so* not cool."

Like Maya Chang would have said something to him if our seats had been reversed? Please. She'd have been too worried about ruining her GPA.

I've never been more grateful for the Q train, rattling over the Manhattan Bridge. It temporarily drowns everything out.

"Ally, that was *such* a microaggression!" Laurel fumes. "It's like asking an African American man if he's good at basketball, or a Chinese American if they live in Chinatown." Laurel glances at Maya and quickly adds, "No offense! Oh my God, I'm *so* sorry. It was just . . . a hypothetical example."

"Laurel, you're fine." Maya shrugs it off, but I can tell by the look she gives me over Laurel's head that she's still holding on to a piece of that.

Maya Chang and I are the only two Asian girls in our grade, and at times we have this unspoken thing between us. Call it a sisterhood or shared Spidey sense or whatever. Being Asian is about the only thing we have in common, because Maya Chang is a bubbly, in-your-face athlete whose parents are doctors, and I am none of those things.

But other times it's like there's this unspoken rivalry between us. Because being "diverse" is kind of considered our schtick—it's what makes us "special." So when there are two of us, it ceases to be our schtick, and we're kind of pitted against each other.

Unless it's been *made* to be our schtick by everyone around us.

"Ally," Laurel continues, "if you're not going to talk to JBJ, then you absolutely need to speak with Dr. Van Cortlandt."

"What's the head of school have to do with this?" I say. "Come on, Laurel."

When I started at Quaker Oats, Papi used to say, *You're a guest at this school. Don't make any trouble.* Then he'd remind me of how much money they were giving me to study, and how I should be grateful. I promised Papi I wouldn't make a peep.

Like freshperson year, this junior named Karen Nevins was all, "Welcome! You must be the new diversity student! Let me show you around!" and in my head I was all, *I was in the National Honor Society for three straight years at I.S. 230 and got perfect scores on all my Regents so what the hell are you even talking about please and thank you.* But in reality I just stood there in polite silence. So Karen prattled on about her favorite K-dramas and her family's summer in Riviera Maya and how "sí, se puede hablar español" if I "prefer that to inglés."

Or the time Mr. Schwartz was awarding extra "diversity points" for a group history project. Everyone rushed to claim me and Maya Chang and Colin Okafor—like they were filling up slots on their Diversity Bingo cards.

But whatever.

"Ally," Laurel says, "why are you being so passive?"

Passive? My eyes flash. "That's not fair."

"Sorry, I didn't mean it like that." Laurel backs off.

"I'm just . . . being realistic." I crumple the plastic wrap of my sandwich into a tiny ball so Laurel can't see and give me her usual lip about single-handedly killing the environment with cancer-producing PET.

"If I make a big fuss," I continue, "what's going to come of it? Probably nothing. Honestly, I'd rather just focus on my Whyder supplement."

And finishing up the school year, *and* getting the hell out of New York.

Laurel is deep in thought. She taps a celery stick to her chin.

"I know what we should do," she says. "Ally, can I borrow a piece of paper?"

I am officially the only person left at Quaker Oats who carries around notebook paper like it's still the 1900s. I hand her a fresh sheet.

Right there on the spot, Laurel writes:

Petition to Have Senior Elective Lecturer Jonathan Brooks James Removed. Effective Immediately.

"That's a great idea, Laurel," Maya says approvingly.

I say, "Listen, you guys. Let's just drop it. JBJ doesn't deserve to be fired—"

"Actually, we shouldn't say 'guys' anymore," Laurel interrupts. "It's offensive."

"*Actually,*" Maya corrects, "some lady in the *New York Times* said it's okay to say 'guys.' Because the word is now 'gender neutralized.'"

Laurel's about to retort but switches course. "Well. Then we shouldn't use the word *lady. That's* offensive."

Maya makes another face at me over Laurel's head. The face says, *Whoa, she is so intense, right?*

A lot of Oatties make that face behind Laurel's back. But I never tell Laurel about it because it would only make her feel more self-conscious than she already does.

Laurel continues writing.

We, the undersigned, would like to protest the unfair treatment of one Anne Austere Preparatory School (hereinafter "Quaker Oats") student, Alejandra Kim, by her teacher, Jonathan Brooks James (hereinafter "JBJ"). JBJ does not stand for Quaker Oats's values of diversity, equity, inclusion, and community. By keeping him in office—she crosses out the word "office" and writes "classroom"—Quaker Oats is complicit in sanctioning the otherization as well as discrimination of our students of color.

"Damn, Laurel," Maya marvels. "I can't believe you just came up with that on the fly."

"I'm going to go type this up and print it out," Laurel says. "Maya Chang, I'm counting on your vote!"

"Most def," Maya says, then flits off to rejoin her tennis team. People always know which home base they'll return to, I guess.

"But, Laurel," I say, a final plea. "You weren't even *there*."

"You're my best friend. I got your back." Laurel squeezes an arm around my shoulders. She still smells like celery. "I want to make sure this kind of thing never happens again. It's *not right*."

Then Laurel slings her backpack over her shoulder and rushes to the library before Indigo period ends.

The good thing about Laurel's petitions is that they never really take off. Her last one, to get the cafeteria staff unionized, only garnered four signatures, including ours.

CHAPTER 8

Happy Day

"YOU ABSOLUTELY SHOULD *NOT* say something to your teacher," Michael Oppa says at the dry cleaners that evening. It's slow at work today—we're in a lull between customers—so I tell my cousin about Jonathan Brooks James and what Laurel and Maya said at lunch.

Tía Yoona's store is called, no joke, Happy Day Dry Cleaners. It sounds all broken Englishy, like "Long Time No See" or "Me Love You Long Time." It's basically an open invitation to make fun of the name, like a kid with a KICK ME! sign stuck to his back.

Michael Oppa works full-time at Goldman Sachs, but tonight he's helping me close the store because Tía Yoona and Gary Gomobu had to attend a funeral.

"But you think what my teacher said was . . . okay?"

"Of course not," Michael Oppa says. "For one, it's offensive. For two, it's completely inaccurate. Does he have any idea how hard it is for Asians to get into college? We're considered 'non-underrepresented minorities'—yeah, sit with that one for a minute—so we're all competing against each other like dogs thrown in a pit. Ask any Asian kid I went to Stuy with. It's like we get the worst of both worlds: all the cons of not being white, with none of the pros."

Michael Oppa's first choice for college was Harvard, but he was wait-listed. So he went to Columbia instead. It's still a sore point.

"Then why are you telling me I shouldn't report my teacher?"

"Because if there's one thing I learned in corporate America, it's 'don't escalate,'" Michael Oppa says. "Ale, what's your end game?"

"I don't want to feel uncomfortable in class."

"And?"

"I want to get into Whyder College."

"So let's do the rollback on that. Let's say you say something to Jimmy John—"

"Jonathan Brooks James," I correct him. "JBJ."

"Whatever. Best-case scenario: JBJ goes, *Eureka! Thank you for enlightening me.* He stops making offensive comments, you're happy in class, the end."

"But?"

"But," Michael Oppa says. "What's the worst-case scenario? You say something to him, and all you do is piss him off. He retaliates and gives you a bad grade, and that'll ruin your chances for college."

He loosens his tie; he's still wearing a suit. "Or let's say you go over his head and talk to your headmaster."

"Head of school," I correct him again. "She/her/hers."

"Fine. Head of school. I *guarantee* she'll be annoyed you're this squeaky wheel making her job harder, and even *if* she listens to you—big if—then what? She has a talking-to with JBJ, and he's going to be even more pissed off that you went over his head. He'll *still* retaliate and give you a bad grade, and you're worse off than square one. Nobody likes a whistle-blower, Ale."

Maybe it wasn't a good idea to bring this up with Michael Oppa. Lately, his advice is more numbers than heart. Maybe this is what happens when you become a corporate workaholic.

"So then what?" I argue. "We're all just supposed to stand around and say nothing? My friend Laurel says I should speak out."

"Is she the girl who came here once and wouldn't leave?"

"Yes," I say. I'm still embarrassed by that. Freshperson year, Laurel wanted to come to Happy Day with me. She'd talk to me when I was with customers, and that made the customers annoyed because I couldn't get anything done. So we ended up just talking in the back while Michael Oppa did his work *and* my work.

"Maybe your friend *can* say something," Michael Oppa concedes. "Maybe she's got a dad on the school board, or someone with power. Don't forget, Ale. You're on scholarship."

As if I need yet another reminder.

"I'm just afraid you'll end up worse off than if you said nothing. If your endgame is getting into your dream school, then why don't you just focus your energy on that?"

Michael Oppa sighs. "Besides, you should hear the way

the guys talk at work. It's 'Chink' this and 'fag' that. That's the culture."

"Michael Oppa, can I ask you a personal question?" He nods. "Do people at work know you're out?"

He pauses, then says, "I don't deny that I'm gay. But I don't go out of my way to volunteer it."

"But isn't that the same thing?"

"No, it isn't," he says. "They don't need to know my personal business. I'm there to work."

It doesn't sound right to me. "Couldn't you file a complaint with HR?"

"And then what?" Suddenly Michael Oppa looks very tired. "I speak out, have my five seconds of triumph, catharsis, whatever. Then they get back at me in other ways. I get stuck with all the grunt work. Passed over for a promotion. This is the real world, Ale."

"But—"

"It is what it is. If I have a problem with their culture, then it's on me to leave."

The "real world"—or, at least, Michael Oppa's cynical take on it—sounds miserable. But Michael Oppa's never really had it easy. His mom died when he was a baby, so his dad (Gary Gomobu) remarried, to Tía Yoona. Tía Yoona basically raised Michael Oppa, and he calls her Umma. That's as good as— better than—blood. Especially when his own biological father acts like he doesn't exist.

It's been that way ever since Michael Oppa came out. He only works at Happy Day when Gary Gomobu is not around.

"Michael Oppa," I ask at the next lull. "Why do you still

keep coming to Happy Day? Especially when you and Gary Gomobu are, you know . . ."

"I don't come back to Happy Day for Appa. I couldn't give a shit about him. I come for Umma. So she can get a day—or part of a day—off from *this*."

I know what he's talking about. Once, a lady came to the store to pick up clothes she'd dropped off more than a year ago. Every week we had called and called the number she left and gotten no answer. Most dry cleaners, our store included, have a policy that says if a customer doesn't pick up after sixty days, we donate the clothes. We waited a year. When Tía Yoona told her we didn't have her clothes, the woman said, "Motherfucking Chink."

Here's the thing—there were two other white women in the shop. Both had their Saturday supplements of the *New York Times* and their overpriced coffees. Both women heard but said nothing. But their faces told me everything: *Let them fight it out among themselves*. This wasn't their battle.

THE FRONT DOOR CHIMES open. It's strung up with a stupid red Chinese bell that I'm 98.3 percent sure Tía Yoona got from one of her vendors who thinks we're Chinese and she was too polite to refuse. Another customer staggers in with an armload—no, a mountain—of clothes. It's almost comical, the pile is that huge. She stilts up to us and avalanches the clothes onto the counter.

It's Mrs. Díaz. Billy's mom.

"Mrs. D?"

Mrs. D cleans houses for a living. She works for an agency, so she does jobs all over the city. Including, apparently, on the Upper East Side.

"Ale, ¡mi amor!" she says, and I come around the other side of the counter to hug her. "How come it's so hard to see your face these days?"

I finger the clothes on the counter. They're beautiful: lightweight silks and linens in tasteful pastels. It's after Labor Day, so everyone's dropping off their summer clothes for the season. I know enough about textiles to know these are expensive as hell.

"Oh, you know," I say vaguely. "School, work."

But I know what Mrs. D is getting at. Ever since Billy left for the Dominican Republic, when I'd run into her on the street, I'd always promise to stop by and say hi—the Diazes live over in Building D of our apartment complex—but I never did.

Before she can go into all that, I say, "I didn't know you worked around here."

She spreads out her arms as if to say, *Eh, you know.* "Ah, but I knew. Recuerdo que tu papi trabajaba acá. Hace mucho mucho tiempo de eso."

I knew Papi used to work at Happy Day, back in the day. Ma did, too. But apparently Papi and Gary Gomobu had a falling-out, and then Papi started working for a Korean ajoshi at a fruit-and-vegetable in Flushing, and Ma started as a home aide.

I introduce Mrs. D to Michael Oppa. "I remember you and your son from . . ." Michael Oppa trails off.

"Yes." She nods, not finishing his thought.

I know what they're doing. They're both avoiding the F-word in front of me.

At Papi's funeral, Billy kept rocking back and forth, mumbling to himself. He wore a too-big navy suit he'd borrowed from his cousin Tito. His face was puffy with crying. Mrs. D was rubbing his back, reciting the Ave María.

I get busy tagging the clothes. "When do you need this by, Mrs. D?" I ask briskly. "The day after tomorrow okay?"

"Si puedes," she says. "¡Me puso loca, la señora! Déjeselo bien limpo, ¿eh, mi amor? I don't want trouble."

I promise Mrs. D we'll take good care of the clothes. Just as she's about to leave, she turns and says, "Aleja."

"Yeah, Mrs. D?"

"Billy's coming home."

"Oh, really?" I say, to have something to say. But I figured Billy would have to come back from the DR for the start of the school year.

Her eyes search mine. "Don't be a stranger, m'hija. Okay?"

I nod, tell her I won't.

She pats my cheek. "I see so much of your papi in your face."

I turn, blinking. Mrs. D has the nunchi not to press. She leaves, the Chinese bell clanging behind her.

FOR THE REST OF THE EVENING, Michael Oppa works the front, and I'm at the sewing machine with a pile of clothes to hem. I'm pretty okay at tailoring. Papi taught me. I could hem suit pant legs by age ten; by twelve, I could do the trickier hemming and reattaching of jeans seams. Papi was good at a lot of things: sewing, tinkering with the car, fixing stuff around the house, playing piano. I thought he'd teach me everything he knew how to do.

My eyes start to well up. *No. You do not get to cry.* I press the angry palms of my hands to my eye sockets.

It works. The threat of tears is gone.

CHAPTER 9

"Real" Art

THE NEXT TAUPE PERIOD, Jonathan Brooks James talks about "real art" versus "fad art."

"Real art, *true* art," he says, puffing out his chest, "is writing beyond the vagaries of 'identity politics.' Don't pander to what's 'trending' in the public consciousness, tempting though that may be to garner attention."

JBJ squelch-paces the front of the classroom.

"But aren't *they* the only ones getting published now?" Josh Buck calls out. "'Identity politics' is all I see in the *Times Book Review.*"

"It can be frustrating, yes," JBJ concedes. "But the real question is, Are those fad writers producing works that will stand the test of time?" He wags his finger like, *I don't think so.* "Real art delves into the essential core of the human condition. Real writers write for posterity."

Then JBJ fixes his glass-blue eyes straight at me.

I swear I'm not imagining it.

Am I imagining it?

For the rest of the period, we once again "just write" as Jonathan Brooks James returns to his manuscript pages. New ones, this time.

There's no way I can stay in JBJ's class.

AFTER CLASS, MAYA CHANG says, "So Laurel's out there rocking the vote."

It takes me a second to realize Maya is talking about the petition to get JBJ fired. A cringey feeling twists in my gut.

"So it's now, like, a thing?" I ask her.

Maya nods. "That's pretty cool, what she's doing for *you*."

But the way she says it makes it sound like she thinks *I* was the one who asked Laurel to do it for me.

If I have a problem with their culture, then it's on me to leave. Straight after class I go to the registrar's office. Ms. Kovak, the secretary, searches the schedules on her computer.

"I'm sorry, Alley-HAND-ruh. There are no open spots in any of the other senior electives. Would you like me to add your name to the wait list?"

I tell Ms. Kovak yes, but I think we both kind of know she's just going through the motions. Because spots on the wait list never open up.

* * *

"SO WE'RE UP TO fifteen signatures already!" Laurel announces at lunch.

"Yeah. About that," I say. "I think JBJ *knows*. He was kind of giving me weird looks in class."

"Like pervy looks?" Laurel asks, alarmed.

I shake my head. "No, more like the stink eye." I peel back the film of my sandwich. "I'm just going to transfer out of his class. There's a wait list, but—"

"Why should *you* have to be the one to leave?" Laurel interrupts. "*He* should be the one to leave! You didn't do anything wrong!"

"I know," I say. "But I guess I'm not that much of a Claire Devereaux wannabe, haha."

"This is exactly like when a female employee files a harassment charge, and all they do to 'deal with the problem' is transfer the woman to another department. When they should be firing her boss!"

"Laurel, I don't think—"

"Ugh!" Laurel says. "The way this whole system privileges the patriarchy is straight-up disgusting." She spears her lunch with her fork. Today it's bulgur with broccolini. "And anyway, everyone knows you never get in off the wait list."

A SMALL PART OF ME—once you push past the humiliation that my business is now out there in petition form—is kind of in awe. Okay, maybe it's a medium-sized part. That Laurel had the guts to stand up and say something. For me. When she didn't have to say anything at all.

But she also knew I didn't *want* her to say anything. She knew I didn't want to make a big deal. Especially not senior year, when I need to just keep my head down, get my college apps out, and make it through one last year in New York.

Now word is going to spread about JBJ, and I'm going to have to be the one to deal with the fallout.

Is it possible to feel both thankful to and angry at someone at the same time?

But Laurel's had my back since I started at Quaker Oats. You don't forget a thing like that. This is súper embarrassing to admit, but the first time we officially met, like exchanged names and everything, Laurel found me slumped by the lockers during lunch period, crying. It was freshperson year, and I was ready to drop out.

Before I came to Quaker Oats, being the class nerd had been my thing. At my old school in Jackson Heights, I was voted Most Likely to Be a Librarian. Someone even doodled eyeglasses over my yearbook picture.

But at Quaker Oats, I felt out of my depth. I'd sit in silence as teachers and students alike quoted Kierkegaard and Nietzsche and Schopenhauer. It was all Greek to me.

One morning in English class, I tried to be brave. Mostly because Dr. Shields wrote in my progress notes that my "lack of assertiveness in class was concerning." I raised my hand and said I thought Huck Finn "wore a mask" each time he interacted with a different person in the book. But when another student challenged me, saying, "Define what you mean by that *essentialist* construct," I had no idea what the question even meant. I groped for words, but in the end I was struck silent. I wished I had never raised my hand at all. I wished I had never come to this *school* at all.

When Laurel found me by the lockers, she crouched down to my level and handed me a handkerchief.

"You okay? My mom says it's good to let it out. She says that whenever I catch her crying in the kitchen."

Grateful, I took it from her and blew my snot into it. The cloth felt raw against my skin.

"Keep it," she said, smiling. "By the way, I really liked what you said in Periwinkle period today." I now recognized this girl from English class: frizzy haired, dressed like a modern-day hippie in flowy, flower-patterned clothes. She always had a pencil case with neon highlighters and a Post-it dispenser on her desk.

"Really?" I said between sniffles. "I felt . . . It was kind of stupid."

"It wasn't stupid at all," Laurel insisted. "And I think if you'd just, like, provided a quote from the text, you would have made an even *stronger* argument. There was a line here that perfectly illustrated your point. . . ." She pulled out her copy of *Huck Finn* and showed me. I stared down at her book in amazement. There was no white space anywhere. All the pages were marked with Post-it flags. Whole passages were highlighted in yellow, green, orange, hot pink, blue. Notes were scribbled all over the margins.

I asked her what her different-colored highlights meant. "I was tracking different themes," Laurel explained. "Pink is for poverty. Orange is for Jim. Blue is for whenever Huck has a crisis of conscience. The different colors can be a helpful study tool, especially if you're a visual learner. Even though they've supposedly debunked theories of 'visual,' 'auditory,' 'sensory,' and 'spatial' learners." She closed her book. "I know, I know, it's kind of a silly system."

"It's not." I was amazed. At my old school, we weren't allowed to mark up our books. They were decade-old loaners that smelled like glue and mold.

As she cited other passages in the text, Laurel sounded *so* polished, so confident. She was like a lawyer in a court case, not a high school freshperson. "You sound like one of the DAs from *Law and Order*," I told her.

"I haven't read it yet," Laurel said. Then she saw my expression. "Oh, right. Is that a TV thing? I don't really watch it. I know, I'm weird."

She must have gotten self-conscious with me staring at her mouth all agape. She quickly backpedaled. "But you didn't ask me for my feedback, so, like, never mind. You do you! I know how much I *hate* when my dad is always, like, mansplaining."

I hesitated before asking, "Do you think you can teach me . . . to talk like that in class? Like you?"

I don't know what compelled me to do this, but let the record so reflect that I was the first to ask Laurel for help.

And she did.

It's because of Laurel that I stayed at Quaker Oats. She basically saved my life.

BY THE END OF THE DAY, Laurel texts to say she's up to twenty-two signatures.

That cringey feeling inside multiplies by a hundred. A thousand.

CHAPTER 10

Chivi

AFTER SCHOOL I DON'T head straight home. Ma's off today, and I don't need the third degree from her. We'll just get into another fight, and all of it will come pouring out: the financial strain of going to Quaker Oats and applying to Whyder. And that will lead to Ma's denial about Papi's "accident" and all the what-ifs. There's only so much guilt a body can carry.

So I head to Montoya Park. After all the BS of the day, I just need to zone out for a while, sitting on the green bench and staring into the drained fountain with all the litter people keep throwing into it.

Except I can't. Because some kid's already sitting on the green bench. He's not sitting the normal way, with his butt on the seat. Instead, he's sitting on *top* of the bench, and his feet are where his butt should be.

I don't recognize him from the neighborhood. He's tall and rangy, his arms resting on his legs. He's palming a Gatorade bottle like it's an imaginary basketball. And now this rando is sitting here with his feet on the bench, like he thinks he owns the place? I don't think so.

"Yo, step off that bench!" I call out.

The kid doesn't move.

"I *said*—"

"Ale! Chill. It's just me."

The voice sounds both familiar and not. Its cadence—the rhythms to the words—I recognize. But the tone is low and deep. Not soft and higher pitched like I'm used to.

"Billy Díaz?!"

"What, you forgot me already?"

It's been almost nine months since we last saw each other. Billy looks *nothing* like the short, pudgy, round-faced boy who left New York right after Papi's funeral. This Billy Díaz is tall and lanky, like a ball player. Though there's still a bit of the old baby fat in his cheeks.

"Holy fucking growth spurt," I say. "The hell happened to you, Chivi?"

I deliberately use his old nickname. I haven't called him that in years.

He blushes. "Stop, Ale. I'm exactly the same." His new deep voice cracks as he says it.

Before you start thinking I'm checking him out, I'm not. Billy and I are *so* not like that.

You know what the litmus test is for whether you *like* like someone or not? It's when you're wearing your sweatpants and your hair's in a greasy bun, and you don't care at all because you have, like, zero interest in impressing them. Your heart doesn't race, you have no desire to press your lips to theirs, and the thought of your salivas commingling is kind of gross.

That pretty much sums up how I feel about Billy Díaz.

But he does look *so* different.

We hug—awkwardly. He even smells different, doused in spicy-syrupy cologne.

"Look," Billy says, "about what I said to you last time I saw you. I want to explain. I felt—"

The Awkwardness is starting up again. I shut it down, just like I shut it down before.

"It's all good," I say quickly.

"I didn't mean to put all that on you, Ale. Your dad had just died. I shouldn't have said—"

"I *said,* we're good."

I swat my hand, literally clearing the air between us. "Let's just go back to being normal."

"Normal. Right." He says it flatly, and with his new deeper voice, I can't read his intonations. "Anyway, don't worry. I don't feel like that anymore, so . . ."

Relief floods through me. "Cool."

"Cool," he repeats back.

"So."

"So." Billy passes his Gatorade bottle from hand to hand. He's back to sitting in that ridiculous position on top of the bench.

"Catch me up," I say, putting on my best "normal" voice. "How was living in the DR? I heard from your mom that your grandma was doing much better, thank God."

"Yeah, Abuela's fine now. The stroke was scary, but she recovered pretty quickly after," he says. "But . . ."

"What?"

"It was just *super hard* down there."

"For real?" I ask, alarmed.

"Yeah." Then a sly smile spreads across his face. Classic Billy. "So hard thinking of all you suckers freezing your asses off back in New York, while I was lying on a beach all day."

"Asshole."

"The water's so blue, I'm talking stranded-on-a-fucking-desert-island blue. And there's no trash in it like Doritos bags or used condoms or whatever. It makes the Rockaways look like a dump."

"Double asshole," I say. "Quadruple."

This is Billy's and my dynamic. We talk foul, we curse, we mash our words. I talk differently when I'm at Quaker Oats versus when I'm back home in Queens. At school, I always have to choose my words súper carefully, worrying whether I'm mispronouncing or misusing a word, or misspeaking altogether. (My "fancy" vocab comes strictly from reading. Unlike, say, at Laurel's house, where dinner convo is like an SAT-athon.)

Like, for example, I thought I was hot shit at school for knowing the word "eponymous." In sophomore-year English, I said, "eh-poh-NIM-us," all show-offy. We were reading *Jane Eyre,* and Jane is the *eponymous* heroine of the book. (It's a pretty useless term, but whatever.) Ms. Ingram bit her lip to hold back her laughter. "It's actually 'ee-PAWN-uh-mus,'" she corrected me. "Rhymes with 'hippopotamus.'" The whole class cracked up. It was pretty humiliating.

Now Billy laughs. "I'm just playing. The DR was only all right. Mostly Abuela and I just sat around the house and watched reruns from the aughts dubbed over in Spanish. Once she got better, I think she was just looking for any excuse for me not to leave." He smiles, dimples lighting up. "She said I'm her favorite grandson."

Billy catches me up. He mostly helped his grandmother with chores during the day. In the afternoons, he played dominoes with his grandfather. All his cousins, when they weren't trying to get him to teach them English curse words, made fun of his Spanish.

"I'm glad to be back in New York," he says, "shitty beaches and all."

"You insist on rubbing it in." I give Billy a playful shove—with *just* enough force so he doesn't misinterpret my gesture as anything but sisterly-brotherly.

"You know what was really weird about the past year?" Billy says in his changing-the-subject tone. "I couldn't get over how every single person, on the streets or in the shops or whatever—they were Dominican, like me."

"C'mon, we live in New York," I point out. "You guys literally get your own parade."

"Yeah, but"—Billy grips his Gatorade bottle—"it just felt weird this time, knowing everyone around me and I were all exactly the same. I don't know how else to explain it. Like, here, even if you're Spanish, you might be Colombian, or Mexican—"

I give him a look.

"Sorry, if you're 'Latino.'"

I give him another look.

"What!" He laughs, but I can tell he's exasperated. "I don't go to your fancy prep school. I can't keep up with all your PC lingo."

"Say it with me now: 'Latinx.'"

Why does the word feel so unnatural coming out of my mouth right now? It sounds so normal at Quaker Oats. But outside of school, it feels out of place.

"Okay, Oattie." Billy does this thing where he mocks me by putting his index finger at the bridge of his nose, like he's pushing up a pair of imaginary glasses.

"Eff off," I say.

That's the thing about Queens, or at least our neighborhood in Queens: no one's PC. Being politically correct means you're being corny, and being corny means you're being fake.

An example: Mr. McFadden used to live down the hall from us. He was one of the last white residents in our building, and he always referred to us as "that Chinese family," which was so annoying. Then one morning, in a blizzard, Mr. McFadden shoveled out Papi's Oldsmobile after the snowplows blocked him in. Papi knew it was Mr. McFadden, because he saw the wet shovel outside the door. Mr. McFadden didn't make a show about it, the way some people can be so grubby about trying to get the credit for Doing the Right Thing. Papi nodded thanks, Ma left some fruit outside his door, and Mr. McFadden continued to call us "that Chinese family."

That's being from Queens.

I know this, and Billy knows this, but sometimes I think Billy doesn't think I know this—like ever since I went off to Quaker Oats, I'm some alien in my own home borough. But I know how Queens works, even if I don't always love it. Here, your words may come out all foreign and bumbling, but your intentions are gold.

I once tried to explain this to Laurel, but she just didn't get it. Maybe it's because she's a Brooklynite, and Brooklyn got all gentrified and lost whatever scrappy outer-borough credit it used to have.

I nudge Billy. "Let me get a hit of that."

He passes me his bottle of Gatorade. I take a swig and go *ahhhh*. "Orange is the best."

"Nah, red," he says. "But they were out."

We watch a woman and her kids in the park. They're obvious newcomers; we don't recognize them from the neighborhood. The mom hasn't brushed her hair in *ever*. Her stretchy pants have stains all over, and I can't tell if she's thirty or fifty. I kind of feel bad for her. But not *that* bad, because her kids are sucking on those overpriced squeegee juices that cost more than my lunch.

"Is it just me, or did I leave, and Jackson Heights just got whiter?" Billy asks.

"You're not imagining it," I say.

Ma likes all the white people moving to Jackson Heights. She thinks it's "limpiando el barrio." In other words, *whitewashing the hood*. I tell her that's not a good thing. Then I light into her about Argentina's cruel history of exterminating all the indigenous people, and she puts a cigarette to her lips and tunes me out until I've exhausted myself.

Billy and I watch the family. The mom is holding her older kid's hand while pushing the baby in the stroller. They are taking up the whole walkway, which is the width of at least three persons. Poor Mrs. Nuñez and her kid, coming in the opposite direction, have to stop walking and scoot out of the way to accommodate the woman and her kids and her stroller. But the white woman doesn't say thank you; she's totally oblivious.

These are basic rules in Queens. Billy and I catch eyes and shake our heads.

"I hear they're all priced out of Brooklyn and coming here," he says.

"At least they brought some good coffee shops?" I say.

"I thought your mom doesn't let you drink coffee."

"It was Papi who didn't."

I blurt this out before I can think.

We both fall silent at the mention of my father. We stare into the empty fountain. Then Billy breaks the silence.

"Remember that time you kicked the soccer ball into the fountain? I thought your dad was going to flip."

I remember. Back then, Montoya Fountain actually had water in it, and it spewed gracefully into the air like the fountain in Washington Square. Before it got all dried up and filled with trash.

"Yeah," I laugh, "because it was a brand-new ball!"

"But your pa didn't actually flip. He was mad cool about it."

Papi was the one who gave Billy his nickname: Chivi. It's short for "chivito," which either means *kid goat* or *sandwich* or maybe both. Because Billy's real name is Guillermo, which is Spanish for William, so maybe Papi was thinking Billy-goat? I don't know. That's Papi's humor for you.

"I still think about your pa a lot." Billy's tone is wistful.

"Well, you don't have to."

"Don't be like that, Ale." Billy turns to face me. "I know he's not *my* dad, but . . . He always—"

"You're right. He *wasn't* your dad."

I'm done talking about this.

Because I make it hella awkward by shutting down Billy, we sit in silence and watch the newcomer lady and her kids. The older boy is whining, trying to climb into the stroller.

"We've already discussed this, Draper," the mom says. She sounds like she's talking to a grown-up and not a toddler.

"But, Mama," the boy—Draper—says. "That *my* stroller."

"Draper, sweetie. It *used* to be your stroller. But now it belongs to your sister, Ani. You're a big boy, and big boys walk with their two big-boy legs."

"I wish Ani never born!" Draper says, clawing at the stroller.

The mother doesn't stop him. "This is regressive behavior, Draper," she says, sighing.

Billy and I exchange another look. I didn't know what the word "regressive" meant until, like, last year.

I get a text from Laurel. How's your Whyder essay coming?

I text back a throw-up-face emoji.

Writing date Thurs after school?

Ok! Let the torture begin.

"That your boyfriend?" Billy asks teasingly.

"Nah, it's my friend Laurel." *Boyfriend?* Yeah, right. As if I'm in that headspace. "She's asking about my Whyder essay, which is going *ugh*." I sigh. "This is my one shot. If I have to live one more minute here, with Ma, I swear to God. You're so lucky you got out of here for a while."

"That's one way of putting it." His new voice is deep, gruff. Again, I can't read his tone.

"Yo, how are your college apps going?" I ask. "We can work on them together, if you want."

"Yeah," he says noncommittally. He's looking off into the distance.

The white family strolls away.

"So," Billy says, clearing his throat. "I'm going to the movies with Tito and all tomorrow. *Bikini Car Crash Party III* is out."

I groan. "How do you even say it with a straight face?"

Billy laughs. "Remember when you lectured Tito about 'the objectification of female bodies'? I swear he was going to lose it."

"Why were the women wearing bikinis the whole time?" I argue. "They were in the middle of freaking Siberia!"

"It's just a movie, Ale. Don't take it so seriously," Billy says, which is exactly what Billy's cousin Tito and our old crew, Jessie Gupta, Sandy Liu, Maggie Cisneros, and Sanjay Patel, all said when we went to see *Bikini Car Crash Party I* the summer after freshperson year.

Only Billy came to my defense. But I know that made things weird with everyone. That was pretty much when I stopped hanging out with our old crew from Jackson Heights.

Billy clears his throat. "I know it's not your thing, but you can come, if you want."

"Nah," I say. "It's not my thing. Plus I got my Whyder app to work on. Thanks, though."

"It's all good." Billy's still holding his Gatorade bottle. He traces the sweat lines running down the sides.

"Hey, but maybe we could get coffee or something," I offer. "I saw a new café opened on Thirty-Seventh."

"Get coffee?" Billy mocks my tone. "What, Gatorade not good enough for you, Miss Ale?"

"Eff you, Chivi."

"Touché." Billy holds up his hands. "All right. I'll *get coffee* with you sometime."

"Cool."

"Cool."

I'm glad things aren't so weird between us anymore. Billy's back from the DR, and it's senior year, and hopefully everything can start to feel like normal again.

CHAPTER 11

Study Date

JBJ DOESN'T SHOW UP for our next class. Or the next one, or the one after that. The substitute teacher gives us a free study period. I use the time to try to work on my Whyder supplement. Operative word being "try." The essay question still stumps me.

Claire Devereaux leans across my desk. "I heard JBJ might be leaving the school."

"Where'd you hear that?" I ask.

"Didn't your friend Laurel Greenblatt-Watkins start a petition? I swear, she's—"

Claire stops and flutters her eyelashes, as if it's beneath her to finish her sentence.

"Whatever," I say, which is what I always say when I can't find an actual comeback.

***

LATER, LAUREL CONFIRMS IT: "Ding-dong, the witch is dead! JBJ tendered his resignation. Can you believe it? It's all because of our petition!"

It's Thursday, and we're on the F train to Laurel's house to work on our Whyder supplements.

"You mean, *your* petition," I say. I'm stunned by the news. I didn't believe Claire when she mentioned it in school. "I just thought JBJ was cutting class."

Laurel either ignores or doesn't process my correction. "I sent our petition to Van Cortlandt, and she sent it to JBJ. She told him he needed to get sensitivity training if he wanted to continue teaching here. And you know what he said? He was like, 'No, thanks,' and he quit instead!"

"He lost his job?" I say. "Over this?"

"He didn't *lose* it, Ally! He was the one who up and left. You know what he said to Van Cortlandt? He was like, 'Writers need to develop a thick skin. It would be unethical for me to participate in the coddling of the next generation.' What kind of self-righteous horse crap is that?"

"Wow," I say, softening. "How do you know that?"

"I overheard Van Cortlandt on the phone with Mom," Laurel admits sheepishly. "I was going to tell you sooner."

"Laurel," I say, "the guy lost his job. Over your petition." As awkward as things were starting to get in JBJ's class, I could have just ridden it out for the rest of the year. We could have learned to uncomfortably coexist. Also, honestly, I was looking forward to a "just write" excuse for a free study period, especially with my college apps due in January.

"Uh, that was the whole point of the petition," Laurel says, groaning. "It's like you have Stockholm syndrome, Ally. You were the victim here, okay? And now you don't have to worry about transferring out! We just took a *huge* step for generations of women to come. This is a momentous thing."

For the rest of the train ride, I try to push aside my feelings of unease. Like Laurel said, this is a good thing.

LAUREL'S FAMILY LIVES IN an immaculately preserved brownstone in Park Slope, on a landmarked street. Her family bought it "for next to nothing" back when Brooklyn was considered both dangerous and uncool in the early 2000s and only people who couldn't afford Manhattan moved there. Now, of course, Brooklyn has become an adjective (*That's* so *Brooklyn*), and each time I come over to Laurel's, I see yet another celebrity just doing their daily thing.

Like when we get off at 7th Avenue, a woman in sunglasses and mom jeans pushes a stroller while checking her phone.

I grab Laurel's arm. "Laurel," I whisper, trying not to fangirl. "That's the girl from *Girls*!"

"Who's *Girls*?" Laurel asks in a loud not-whisper.

"Shh! You mean, What's *Girls*?"

Crickets.

I'm not even that into the show—it was about a bunch of twentysomethings in Brooklyn whining about their privileged lives—but still.

"Oh, Laurel," I say.

"Oh, me, indeed," she says.

I continue gawking at the *Girls* girl, but I'm súper subtle as I do it. Native New Yorkers have certain rules about celebrities, since they're as ubiquitous as coffee carts and cockroaches:

1. Ignore them. When eight million people are jammed up in the same tight space, it's all about boundaries.
2. Like you're going to let them think you think they're better than *you*? It's called self-respect.

I watch the girl from *Girls* wheel away.

Laurel and I stop at the corner store and pick out some snacks. This "bodega" looks like a clothing boutique: it has a sleek awning and a window display and clean sparse aisles with shelves that only carry, like, seven things, instead of being crowded with merchandise. We get pre-cut celery sticks and hummus and dark chocolate bars (81 percent). Laurel throws in the milk chocolate bars she knows I like. She waves away my offers to split the bill.

But when we get back to her house, I see we didn't even need to buy the snacks. Her kitchen is stuffed with food.

AT LAUREL'S KITCHEN ISLAND, with our laptops set before us (Laurel lends me her tablet), we get to work. *Clack-clack-clack.*

What is "home" for you?

I type, free-associating: Apartment 2B. Grease-stained kitchen cabinets. Empty fridge. Window overlooking the shaft where the super keeps the dumpsters.

A home that's nothing like Laurel's home, with its stocked pantry and marble countertops and preserved facade on a historic, landmarked street.

I dump what I just wrote in my "Outtakes" file (a study tip I learned from Laurel). I'm pretty sure Whyder does not need a literal inventory of my apartment in Jackson Heights.

Laurel stops clacking. She pushes her laptop across the counter, signaling we're taking a break.

"This is *so* not going," I say, reaching for the milk chocolate.

"Hey, I know what you should write about," she says. "JBJ."

"Laurel," I warn.

"At least consider it, Ally," she urges. "It'd be a whole treatise on race, injustice, and homeland. They *love* that kind of thing. Sometimes"—she pauses—"sometimes you just got to do whatever it takes."

"If you're so obsessed with him," I joke, "then maybe *you* should write about him."

Laurel breathes out deeply. "That's what *I* would write about if I were you." Her tone suddenly turns wistful. "If I could."

ON THE FAR KITCHEN wall is a portrait gallery of the Greenblatt-Watkinses, minus Mr. Greenblatt. (The wedding portrait and family pictures at Rockaway Beach have been taken down since sophomore year.) There are pictures of Laurel and her older sister, Leah, throughout the years. Laurel at her Lower School graduation, braced and bespectacled, her mousy auburn hair pulled back in a frizzy ponytail. Leah at her Princeton graduation, glossy blond hair, makeup flawless.

Laurel glares up at her sister's graduation photo. "If I don't get in early at Whyder, my dad's going to force me to apply to Princeton, just like Leah. To 'make it a father-daughter tradition!'" She says it súper sarcastically, then makes exaggerated retching sounds.

"But Leah turned out all right," I point out. Leah is a junior analyst at PTMT-Warren Wyckoff, with a starting salary of a bajillion dollars a year. She's effortlessly pretty, like a TV actress on her day off. Plus she's really nice, like a friendly Claire Devereaux. She's kind of the whole package.

"Leah is so basic." (In yet another "Oh, Laurel" moment, I actually taught her that word.) "And Dad keeps trying to turn me into her."

I remember last year, when Mr. Greenblatt took us to Grand Central Oyster Bar after Laurel's debate tournament and ordered us steaks. Laurel didn't tell her dad she's mostly plant-based, and he didn't ask.

Instead of congratulating her on her epic win, Mr. Greenblatt kept saying things like:

"Laurel, easy there on the potatoes. You'll never get a boyfriend like that. Have Leah take you to Pilates."

"Laurel, that frizz is out of control. Have Leah take you to her salon."

Mr. Greenblatt also kept telling me he admired how "the Koreans" were "nose-to-the-grindstone immigrants" who "keep their heads down" and "put in the output." He cited the Korean junior analysts at his firm who work long hours all weekend and never complain.

If you couldn't guess, Laurel's dad is kind of an asshole.

The whole time, Laurel stabbed and jabbed her bloody steak like it was a dartboard of her dad's head. I just ducked my head and said, "Uh-huh," because he was the one paying for my sirloin.

Except not really, because Mr. Greenblatt left Laurel to settle the bill as he rushed to catch his train back to Connecticut.

"I'll deposit the money into your account tomorrow morning. Five percent interest," he called out over his shoulder as he left the restaurant.

It's got to be hard on Laurel. She doesn't have the best relationship with her dad. Not since we found the pink thong in the back seat of his car, when he was picking us up from a school function freshperson year. (We don't talk about "Pantygate.") On top of that, Laurel's always had to live in Leah's shadow. As lonely as I felt sometimes as an only child, at least my parents didn't forever compare me to another sibling.

Then again, at least Laurel has *some* kind of relationship with her dad. At least he's still alive.

I bury the thought. It's not fair of me to compare apples to oranges. Misery shouldn't be a contest.

We get back to work. Or rather, *Laurel* works. I keep staring at the blank screen. *Home.* What is home? What *isn't* home?

So I try out Laurel's advice:

Race is an oft-misunderstood thing.

Too basic. I delete that and write:

Navigating identity politics is a tricky thing at my school.

I delete that line, too.
Basic, basic, basic. More basic than Laurel's allegedly "basic"
sister. I start again:

Sometimes your heroes fail you. They can make you feel
"homeless." I learned this the hard way when I met the
celebrated novelist Jonathan Brooks James.

"Looks like somebody's on a roll," Laurel murmurs, leaning
over as I type.
And she's right. *Sometimes you just got to do whatever it takes.*
The words are flowing now; I can't stop them.

THE NEXT DAY, we get an email from the school, informing us
of Jonathan Brooks James's resignation.

We regret any inconvenience this poses to our valued
Anne Austere Prep students. A search will be conducted
immediately for his replacement.

Laurel was right.

CHAPTER 12

Fallen Heroes

Fallen Heroes, Failed Homeland:

A Critical Response to a Critical Moment in Time
By Alejandra Kim
Whyder College Essay Draft #4.3

Sometimes our heroes fail us; they can make us feel
homeless. I learned these lessons the hard way when I met
the celebrated novelist Jonthan Brooks James (hereinafter
JBJ), who came to my school to teach a Senior Elective in
Creative Writing,.

When I first met JBJ, I was in a state of awe. *Becoming
Brooklyn* is a seminal work in the fiction writing field. It isa
bout a writer struggling to make art, but it is also about more
than that. The leaky roof of the protagonist's illegal sublet
"home" symbolizes the "cracks and fissures" of morality
in our society.. The mice that brazenly saunter across the

apt's concrete floors offer a simultaneous portrait of the empowered working-class poor, as well as the increasingly pestilent presence of the "Undesirable"'s that permeate through JBJ's work. ("His murine countenance haunted my dreamless nights, my sleepless days." (646))

Becoming Brooklyn is about thee universal struggle to make meaning in—and of——our post-modern world; it is a masterful tapestry of philosophy, literature, sociology,, politics, history, and humanity.

In short: the fictional "home" in *Becoming Brooklyn* did not feel like home at all. It was a hostile environment. Thorugh JBJ's novel, I came to believe that I had met a writer who understood the universal human condition of alienation—the state of being emotionally "homeless".

Consider my trepidation, admiration, and anticipation in meeting and receiving tutelage from such a staggering and highly—lauded literary figure.

Alas, it twas for naught. On the first day of class, during attendance, JJJ made a remark about the ethncity of my name. It was as if the only lens, or heuristics if you will, through whichhe views the world is a racialized, otherizing one. One could argue that JBJ's remark on both the 'multi-culti'-ness of my name and likelihood of garnering a college acceptance was benign. However, I would assert that it is nonetheless prolbematic and a reminder to, WoCs like myself that we occupy inferior positionalities sin the cultural and societal landscape..

In times like these, we need to lean on the help of our allies, and we are mobilizing to address this issueh ead-on.

My best friend, Laurel Greenblatt-Watkins, has created a petition to have JBJ removed from our school. Said petition has already garnered 20+ signatures, and them movement is only just starting.

I am grateful to have white aliases who champion the rights of the lesser-privileged. Just as I am grateful for each each and every name that has lent its allyship on the petition.

I feel profoundly changed by this movement, and it tis a pivotal moment for me. I fully expect this moment tin time to garner much attention and traction in the coming weeks if not days. I hope to inspire many others in the continual fight against injustice and homeland.

I am looking to shed such instances off feeling made tob be homeless.

I want to come to whyder to search for my home.

OVER THE NEXT FEW weeks, I work on draft after draft of my Whyder supplement. I'm about to email it off to Laurel and Michael Oppa for feedback. They both offered, and Mr. Landibadeau says it's good to get as many eyeballs as we can on our applications. Just before I hit "send," I hear Laurel's voice in my head: *Always print for proofreading!* So I put the document on a flash drive and take it to KopyKatz on Roosevelt, because they're old-school like that.

I print out my essay and am mortified to find all these typos I didn't catch on the computer screen. I fix them, print another copy, and catch *more* errors. It never ends. Finally, I email it off.

Laurel immediately pings me back. This essay is SO good, Ally!!! See? Told you so! They can't NOT accept you!

I'm so relieved by Laurel's reaction. It was like I was holding my breath, waiting for her "Okay!"

MICHAEL OPPA TEXTS ME later that week: I just finished your essay.

I text back: Finally! Jk I know you're super busy so thanks! What'd you think?

> Did you really write it?

>> I didn't plagiarize it if that's what you're implying . . . ?

> Nope. It sounds polished and academicky . . .

>> Thx! I know, I learned a thing or 3 at Quaker Oats.

> But kind of detached? Idk, it just doesn't sound like the Alley-Cat I know.

>> What's that mean?

> . . .

>> That's the way you're supposed to write.

> . . .

>> Things have changed since you applied to college, Michael Oppa. We now have electricity and airplanes!

Ouch. Cheap shot.

Anyway. Ale, you got this. JUST BE YOURSELF!! =)

Why are you shouting?

That's my boss. Ugh. Got to run.

CHAPTER 13

Diversity Assembly

IN MID-OCTOBER, WE HAVE our fall assembly. The whole Upper School reports to the Quaker Meeting House.

I grab a seat in the back so I can do schoolwork in secret. These assemblies are usually snooze fests, culminating with someone from the school's fundraising office soliciting donations—from current students, no less—to "support the next wave of future Anne Austere thinkers, shakers, and Quakers."

Today, though, there's a huge banner draped across the stage of the auditorium:

WE ARE ALL AMERICAN! it says in big, colorful letters. WE *ALL* BELONG. WELCOME TO ANNE AUSTERE PREP'S DIVERSITY ASSEMBLY!

My Spidey sense aka BS detector gets all prickly.

Head of School Van Cortlandt strides across the stage. She runs through the usual "housekeeping" stuff: Repairs to the gender nonconforming bathrooms in the East Wing. Sign-up sheets for the Community Cleanup of Seward Park. Ticket sales for the Holiday Charity Dinner at Tavern on the Green.

Then Dr. Van Cortlandt clears her throat.

"But on to more pressing matters. Today, in our first annual Diversity Assembly, we are here to discuss diversity, equity, and inclusion. At Anne Austere Prep, we pride ourselves—"

Everyone starts booing, until Dr. Van Cortlandt corrects herself.

"All right, all right," she says, holding her hands up like she's under arrest, "Quaker Oats."

Cheers erupt.

"It has recently come to my attention," Dr. Van Cortlandt continues, "that one member of our Quaker Oats community was not treated with the diversity excellence we Oatties pride ourselves on. I'm here to remind all of you that we must treat each and every valued member of our community like they *belong*."

I'm getting that prickly, tingling feeling all over.

"But we're not here to dwell on the past," she goes on. "We're here to look to our bright future ahead. We are gathered in this auditorium because of one student. A student who had the courage to speak out. I can attest she is the textbook definition of an 'ally.'"

Dr. Van Cortlandt crunches her fingers into air quotes, like she thinks she's the first to introduce us to the term when really she's the last to the party.

"Please join me in giving a warm round of applause to . . . Laurel Greenblatt-Watkins!"

Wait, what? *My* Laurel is behind this assembly? She said nothing about it, not even by the lockers this morning. Laurel runs up to the stage. Funny, she's wearing a different outfit than she had on earlier: Leah's black blazer with the sleeves rolled up, and the dark-rinse jeans she only wears on exam days. She pulls her scrunchie out of her hair, which she does whenever she gets anxious. Her hair falls loose and bent.

"My fellow Oatties!" Laurel booms. "We are in an era of *reckoning*. We are gathered today in the Quaker Meeting House to discuss a most urgent matter. I'd like to tell you the story of what happened to a good friend of mine. My *best* friend, who was a victim of cultural insensitivity."

Then, to my horror and humiliation and holy-shit-I-can't-believe-she's-actually-going-there, Laurel tells the whole auditorium about what JBJ said to me in class.

It was bad enough that JBJ had to say it in front of the whole class. Now Laurel repeats his words *to the entire school.*

Dread hits my gut. You know that cringey feeling when you hear a recording of yourself played back at you, and your voice sounds all tinny and whinier than how you hear it in your head? And you can't believe you've lived your whole life sounding tinny and whiny, and suddenly you get súper self-conscious thinking of how you must sound to the outside world?

Multiply that cringey feeling by a thousand, and that kind of sort of approximates what I'm feeling right now.

I've helped Laurel on countless causes. But *I've* never been the subject of her cause.

Nobody likes a whistleblower, Ale.

As Laurel goes on, in her "Reverend Laurel" voice, it feels like a well-oiled performance.

The Meeting House is filled with scandalized gasps. Which is BS, because not a single one of them made so much as a peep when we were actually *in* JBJ's class. Their cries and shouts sound so fake.

Are they performing wokeness—for each other?

You know what would *actually* make me feel "included"? If people spoke out at the times it mattered—like when I or someone like me gets called a slur on the subway or the street. Instead of just sitting there, staring at their phones or those StreetEasy ads. Not just paying lip service to "racial injustice" after the fact, from the safety of a school assembly where it's all just talk, talk, talk and no action.

I've never been more grateful to be way in the back of the auditorium. Far away from the stage and the bright lights.

Laurel's still thundering at the podium. "Are we to sit there, my fellow Oatties, and do NOTHING while my best friend HURTS inside? DOES SHE NOT BLEED?"

Dr. Van Cortlandt snatches the mic from Laurel. "Okay, okay, thank you, Laurel. And with that, it is our great honor to present our inaugural Distinction over Adversity Award to Ale-*ahem!*-dra Kim."

My heart drops. Laurel whispers something into Dr. Van Cortlandt's ear.

"Oh, excuse me. Ale*jan*dra Kim. Please come up to the stage to receive your award!"

Shouts fill the Meeting Room, and a few jeers. But I can't hear them because my blood is pounding in my ears. My face is burning up. My lungs are in my throat. I can't breathe.

All the eyeballs are on me.

Oh God, oh God, oh God. I feel all the things. I kept telling Laurel it was no big deal what happened during Taupe period, to just drop it. I never thought things would escalate to this. All I wanted for senior year was to forget about everything that happened in the past and *move on* with my life.

Laurel, still at the pulpit, spots me and beckons me to the stage.

"C'mon, Ally!" she shouts.

I'm unsteady on my feet. I make my way out the row, into the aisle. The chants grow louder, booming in my ears.

Everything goes numb. My legs shake, but they do as told. And then suddenly I'm onstage. Suddenly Dr. Van Cortlandt hands me the award, suddenly there's a photo opp. All the flash-bulbs. All the spotlights. Laurel standing beside me, looking like it's the happiest day of her life.

WHEN YOU LOOK BACK at those photos, now framed front and center in the lobby of Quaker Oats, Laurel and Dr. Van Cort-landt and I are standing together onstage.

All three of us are smiling for the camera.

One of us is completely faking it.

CHAPTER 14

Queensboro Plaza

AS SOON AS I'M off the stage, I take off running. To the exit, onto the street, across Canal, and down to the subway below.

Anger is a funny thing. Actually, it's not funny at all. It's red-hot and white-cold at the same time; it's solid and liquid and gas. It's all the contradictions. It sits heavy in my gut and rises up, burning the back of my throat and blazing through my temples. My eyeballs, no joke, feel like they're about to explode.

I've never felt so put on display. I've never felt so humiliated—like everyone thinks I'm the Girl Who Played Victim. Like I'm the world's biggest imposter.

Talk about multi-culti. You'll have no trouble getting into college.

You totally should have said something to JBJ!

You'll end up worse off than if you said nothing.

You're a guest at this school. Don't make any trouble.

DOES SHE NOT BLEED?

All the voices swirl in my head. All I want to do is go home. I don't even know what home *is* anymore.

Which is ironic, because I just wrote my whole Whyder essay on it.

I rush onto the train, the memories peeling sharp like an onion, the sting forcing me to tears. I blink them back.

The pamphlet for Anne Austere Preparatory School sitting on the kitchen counter. The picture on the front looking so inviting: a bunch of kids of *all* colors, sitting in a circle on a lush green campus. One of the kids was talking animatedly while the others were smiling and listening attentively. I couldn't believe a school like this could exist in the city, and I wanted so badly to go to there.

Believe it or not, it was actually Ma's idea to send me to Quaker Oats. Technically, it was Tía Yoona's idea first. She was thinking of sending Jason there, but it turned out his grades—surprise, surprise—weren't good enough to qualify. Tía Yoona gave the pamphlet to Ma. (I have been the beneficiary of countless cousin castoffs.) I was actually all set to go to Bronx Science in the fall. But in the spring of eighth grade, Ma and I ran into Mrs. Sánchez from 3B in the elevator.

"Did you hear?" she whispered loudly, her voice full of gossip. "About the Sohns' daughter in 6F? Got slashed in the face on the subway this morning! This city's going to hell. I can't wait till my husband gets his pension and we can retire in Miami in *style*."

"The Sohns' daughter . . . ," Ma said, piecing it all together. "Doesn't she go to Bronx Science?"

"Cassandra Sohn," I breathed out. Cassandra was a junior at Science. She said she'd look out for me when I started there in the fall. "Is she all right?"

"She's alive, if that's what you're asking," Mrs. Sánchez said. "But might as well be dead, with that face."

Ma let out a sharp *tsk!* Mrs. Sánchez went on, oblivious: "It's a jungle up there! Like they let all the animals out of the Bronx Zoo."

Then Mrs. Sánchez lowered her voice, ready to share the next juicy bits on her agenda. "Did you hear about the López husband in 4H and the Chaudhry wife in 5C? Julio caught them in the broom closet—"

Ma whisked us away from Mrs. Sánchez's gossipy clutches. As soon as we got home, she switched on the TV.

It was all over the news: NY 1 (back then we had cable), channels 2, 4, 5, 7, 9, and 11. Mild-mannered, studious Korean girl from Jackson Heights gets attacked on the 4 train in the Bronx. Twenty slashes to the face with a box cutter. They flashed a picture of the attacker: a homeless woman who had been discharged from Bellevue Hospital.

Ma called for a family meeting when Papi came home from work that night. In those days, he was working at a grocery in Flushing. The owner, Mr. Re, was a typical grumpy ajoshi. But he always sent Papi home with free bags of produce, so who were we to complain?

"There is no way our daughter is going to Bronx Science!" Ma said to Papi.

"It was one isolated incident," Papi pointed out. "It could have happened anywhere."

Ma gave Papi one of her withering looks. "I did *not* come all this way so our daughter could be put in danger like that! We might as well have never left Baekgu!"

When Ma and I went to visit Buenos Aires the summer before seventh grade, the cabbies refused to take us to Baekgu. "Find someone else to escort you to your funeral," they all said, in that infamous Argentine "humor negro." So I've never actually been to the villa miseria where Ma and Papi grew up.

"A whole subway full of other people, and esa loca chose the Sohn girl," Ma said to Papi. "*Don't* tell me that was just a coincidence."

"Now, Vero—"

"That could have been *our daughter.*"

This made Papi go silent.

"We should have gotten us out of this barrio a long time ago. Like your sister did."

"*Don't* compare us to them," Papi said, using his rare warning voice.

"Juan, this is not a negotiation. I already have a meeting with the admissions person. Here." She tapped her press-on-nailed finger to the Anne Austere Prep pamphlet.

I could feel Papi's shame in the face of Ma's words. I was embarrassed for him, so I left the dinner table and their fight.

THE NEXT DAY MA and I went to visit Anne Austere Prep. The building was a converted tenement in Chinatown. The "campus" was the roof, covered in Astroturf; not a single blade of grass was real. Subways rumbled across the Manhattan Bridge, muting the chaos of the city below. I could tell Ma was unimpressed. I'll admit I was a little bit, too. This wasn't the "lush green" campus I expected from the catalog.

But then we visited a classroom. Ten kids sat in a close-knit circle around the teacher. No one was self-conscious as they raised their hands to speak. In fact, no one raised their hands at all. The students called out their answers, and there wasn't a single lull in the conversation.

It was such a drastic change from my junior high, where I was tired of being the kid who was careful not to talk too much and hog all the class time, because I was the only one who raised their hand and knew the answers. I was tired of getting called "know-it-all," of being told I was trying too hard. In that classroom at Quaker Oats, no one cared about being accused of trying too hard because they *all* tried too hard.

Plus, all the desks were graffiti- and gum-free.

Quaker Oats felt like paradise. That was truly the only way I could describe it. I didn't care anymore about Bronx Science. I wanted desperately to become an Oattie. I met with an admissions counselor who looked at my transcript and Regents scores and asked me a few questions, to which I tried to come up with halfway-intelligible answers.

When Ma and I walked back to the subway, she did nod with approval at the swarming crowds. "Good," she said. "Safe," even though everyone around us were Chinos, proper. But to anyone else on the outside, they looked just like us, and we looked just like them. I know what Ma was thinking: What safer place to be Asian than in Chinatown?

RIGHT AFTER I WAS accepted at Quaker Oats, Papi started working *all the time*. Ma, too. I felt guilty because I knew they took on extra hours to pay for my school, so that's when I started working at Happy Day. But something came over Papi midway through freshperson year, and he started acting different. Okay, weird. He'd have this faraway look in his eyes, like he almost wasn't focused on the *here* when you were talking.

Then Papi lost his job at the Korean grocery, and he couldn't find another one. So Ma had to work even *more*. He never left the apartment; soon, he never left the couch. I'd come home from school to find Papi lying motionless on the cracked leather cushions, the TV blaring *Judge Judy*. He wasn't even focused on the screen; he looked out intently into space. It was like his head was playing a film reel that was entirely out of sync with our world.

"Hi, Papi," I would say, going over to give him a kiss on the cheek and a hug. He was not *not* happy to see me. "Aleja-ya, ¿veniste?" he'd say in a weak voice, like he was talking into a fan, and it took all his energy to speak but still his words came out like a warble.

For the rest of ninth grade, I tried. Tried to coax Papi off the couch. Tried to get him to play soccer in the park, to go for a Bomb Pop from the Mister Softee truck, to go for a walk. *Anything*. He would not budge. He just lay there with that awful, glazed look in his eyes that I still can't shake.

SOPHOMORE YEAR, PAPI GOT worse. But I was so focused on my own life and finally feeling like I was fitting in at Quaker Oats that Papi kind of fell to the back burner of my bigger and more immediate concerns: making friends, getting good grades, and setting my sights on Whyder. I'd deliberately come home from school late, just to avoid being alone in the house with my own father. I told no one at Quaker Oats, not even Laurel. I didn't need my not-normal dad to be one more reason for feeling like I didn't belong.

Ma and I kept Papi's problems a secret from everyone, even Tía Yoona. Though I know she suspected something was up. Tía came to our house once. It was last fall. I was coming home from the Lions—aka the library—and heard loud voices coming from inside the apartment: Papi's and Tía's. Papi hadn't said anything, let alone raised his voice, in months. I couldn't believe it. Before I could open the door, Tía Yoona stormed out. She saw me and stiffened.

"I . . . forgot this. It's for your papi." She stared down at the plastic bag in her hands. She handed me the bag—it was full of Korean food, neatly packed in Tupperware—and left.

Papi was his usual huddled self on the couch. But I could tell, by the rise and fall of his shoulders, that he had been crying.

"Papi," I called out, trying to give him his space. "Tía brought this food for you. Putting it in the fridge."

Papi didn't touch Tía Yoona's food. It lay there rotting for weeks. I never learned what Tía and Papi argued about that day.

Two months after that, Papi fell to his death at Queensboro Plaza station.

For weeks after the funeral, I'd wake up from nightmares. In one dream, Papi was lying on the couch and it was on fire. I did nothing to put it out; I was too busy trying to save myself. As I ran for the door, I glanced over my shoulder and saw Papi, caught in flames, smiling at me.

Ever since Papi's death, I find myself playing, *What if, what if.* What if Tía Yoona had never given us that pamphlet? What if Cassandra Sohn had caught the next train? What if I'd never actually gotten *into* Quaker Oats and hadn't put pressure on Papi to make more money to pay for my tuition, and then my college tuition after that?

I'll never forget the expression on his face the night before school started. He was bent over the tuition bill, and he just looked so tired, so defeated.

"Papi, I don't *have* to go," I remember saying that night. Of course I wanted to go, desperately, but I also had the nunchi to see what a burden this would be on our family.

But Papi put on a big smile. "Of course you do!" And that was when he told me to dream big. That I could be anything I want in this country.

Only after he died did I realize Papi was faking that smile.

Some days I wonder if Papi would still be alive if I'd never gone to Quaker Oats. Because 90 percent scholarship is still 10 percent too much.

PAPI USED TO TAKE me to listen to Subway Music. Maybe because we had no money, and poor people have to be resourceful in their forms of entertainment. Subway Music meant going to Queensboro Plaza and listening to the 7 and N rushing around us.

¿Escuchás, Aleja-ya? he'd say. *Hear that?*

He'd tap out their herky-jerky rhythm against my back, so I could catch a feel for it, too. The eastbound and westbound trains rumbled at each other like a call-and-response.

Some days I got into it, mimicking Papi by patting my palms to my knees, even singing out random notes to capture their melodies, which delighted him. Mostly I was bored. I'd wait until he closed his eyes and bopped his head to the beat, then I'd pull out whichever Detective Darya book I had with me (back then I was really into the series) and read until Papi was finished. Still, Papi's lessons managed to seep in—as I read, as Papi tapped, I started to feel their jarring rhythms, the music in the madness.

That's the thing about when your father passes away—you think you have a lifetime to ask all the questions, to hear all the stories.

But what really happens is that you go back to school after New Year's break, you're called out of class, and Michael Oppa is waiting in reception to take you to the hospital, where you learn that Papi is dead.

I read a ton of support and grieving websites right after Papi died, and they all urge you to "move on." I tried once, right after Papi died, to ride the 7 to Queensboro Plaza. But I started hyperventilating. I went into panic mode, I couldn't breathe.

I'm so lost in my thoughts, I don't realize I'm on the 7 train. My body just automatically got on the 6, the 4/5, then the 7 at Grand Central. Our train's now leaving Manhattan, crossing into Queens.

I start to panic. It's . . . too soon. I can't—I can't face Queensboro Plaza station. Papi's Subway Music pounds in my ears. Again, I can't breathe.

I chicken out. Jump off the train one stop before, at Court Square. Furiously wiping the stupid tears springing to my eyes, stinging worse than chopping an onion, stinging like salt to my heart.

Maybe if I were a stronger person, I could face my fears at Queensboro Plaza. Stare into the void of the train tracks to try to piece it all together: What was Papi thinking in his last moments of life? But then immediately the train rush of other thoughts would charge at me:

What if, what *if,* WHAT IF?

Papi, I miss you so much. How dare you abandon us?

How dare you abandon *me*?

Part II

CHAPTER 15

Hipster Coffee

"THEN THEY PARADED ME in front of the school like a fucking Diversity Pageant Queen," I rant to Billy. I wave my arm in the air like I'm on a float—*elbow, elbow, wrist, wrist, wrist!*

Billy studies my Distinction over Adversity Award. "White people got way too much time on their hands."

We're at Chaití, one of the new cafés that opened on Thirty-Seventh Avenue. I texted Billy when I got back to Jackson Heights after the assembly: U free? How about that coffee? And here we are. When Billy arrived, he saw my tearstained, splotchy face and knew something was up. I caught him up on everything: JBJ, the petition, the Diversity Assembly.

Billy's a great listener. He never judges or anything like that. It makes me realize how much I missed him while he was away. I used to tell him everything. Then, after Papi died and he left New York, I had no one.

"I mean, I get the school is trying to 'further the conversation,'"

I say. "But, like, they didn't even *ask* me if I wanted to be a part of that conversation. The whole thing felt so fake."

"That's kind of messed up they didn't run it by you first," Billy says. "But maybe they had a good reason. You talk to Laurel?"

"Nah, I just ran out of there."

I have approximately one thousand missed calls and texts from Laurel, but I just . . . can't. I need time to sort through my thoughts. If I were to face her right now, I'd just explode.

And Quaker Oats Ally doesn't explode.

The café is full. There's one free table, but all this stuff—blankets, diaper bags, pacifiers and milk bottles and juice packets—is strewn across the top. The next table over is a group of parents with baby strollers. The parents see us looking but don't offer to clear off their stuff.

Billy and I exchange a Look but don't say anything. We take our drinks and stand by the shelf with the milk and sugar packets and wooden stirrers.

I take a sip of my latte—I ordered "Today's Special"—and almost spit it out. It tastes like a liquefied bar of soap. Lavender and chamomile burn down my throat.

"Why can't they just make it taste normal?" I say.

"You're the one who went and ordered"—Billy squints at the menu board—"holy shit, your latte was four bucks."

I'm usually such a penny-pincher, but it's been a day. "I was just trying something new."

He holds up his cup of black coffee: $2.50. "That's why you got to stick with the basics. How many times I got to tell you, Kim?"

I finish his thought. " 'Keep it simple, stupid.' "

"Zactly." He smiles.

Billy's pretty cute when he smiles because, dimples. I wonder why he doesn't get a girlfriend. Now that he is back from the DR and "got hot," so to speak, the girls should be swarming him like bees (flies?) to honey.

"So who's your beef with, exactly?" Billy asks. "The school, your teacher, or . . . ?"

I take another hit of my latte. It actually tastes less-worse with each sip if that's saying anything.

"I don't know," I say. "I'd take JBJ any day over all this PC crap. I feel like the school only made it worse. But Laurel never would have dreamed up that award. That's just not like her."

"Is it, though?" Billy says. "Seeing as it was a 'public spectacle' and all?"

"I can't believe you still remember that."

Billy and Laurel met once—and only once—freshperson year, when we went to the Film Forum to see a French film called *Desiring*. After, Billy just sat there, drinking his red Gatorade, while Laurel and I hashed it out over lattes. The camera lingering on all the broken symbols of love: the chipped teacup, the crumpled-up napkin. The characters' elliptical dialogue. The fatalistic, Hardian tone of the film. The auteur transforming the film from private, intimate moment to "public spectacle."

Yeah, we probably sounded pretty insufferable. (To be fair, Laurel and I had to write a paper on it.) When we came up for air, Laurel asked Billy what he thought of the film.

"The guy and the girl just sat there in silence for *three*

105

hours." Billy took a gulp of his Gatorade. "I got the point after three *seconds*."

That didn't go over well.

Since then, I've never invited Billy to hang out with Laurel, and vice versa. Can you picture Laurel watching *Bikini Car Crash Parties I, II,* or *III*? Please. Some things are better left church and state.

"No, it isn't the same thing," I say to Billy. "I really think Laurel believed she was doing the right thing. So that's why I can't, like, hate her."

It takes me saying it to realize it. As infuriatingly humiliating as the assembly was, I know Laurel thought she was Doing the Right Thing.

"Then go meet up with her and hash it out, Ale," Billy says.

"No, I need to cool off some before I talk to Laurel."

"Lest you unleash the Aletude."

I shake my head. "I wouldn't wish Aletude on my worst enemy."

Aletude is when I get attitudinal and all up in people's faces. I used to be confrontational. I think it's because New York is a city of immigrants, and no one speaks the same language. You have to find the lowest common denominator. And who doesn't understand the universal language of yelling? Even if it means you're shouting at a guy on the subway to stop manspreading and make space for the rest of us.

Like the time I got into it with my old friends from growing up: Jessie Gupta, Sandy Liu, and Maggie Cisneros. It was right at the start of my first year at Quaker Oats, and I was completely overwhelmed with commuting and schoolwork. Maggie had started it. "How come you never hang out with us anymore?"

"What, I been busy!" I said. "I go to school in the *city*."

Sandy got pissed. "So now you think you're better than us?"

Which made *me* get pissed. "If you're dumb enough to think that," I said, "then maybe yeah."

I had pushed a button. Sandy was always self-conscious about being placed in the "regular" classes while Maggie and Jessie and I were in honors.

So Sandy went, "Who you calling dumb!"

It became a shouting match. The four of us were screaming in the middle of Roosevelt Avenue, but everyone kept walking by like it was just another day. I can't tell you how many screaming matches I've walked past, because New Yorkers don't passive-aggro; we just aggro.

The four of us had it out. All the gross stuff came pouring out—stuff from elementary school on. Honestly, it felt cathartic, like a pus wound had popped.

After that we could move on; I don't have to fake act like we're all friends when I run into them in the neighborhood. We're real.

But then I got to Quaker Oats and realized that screaming is not considered dignified. I learned that the hard way. Freshperson year, a girl cut in front of me on the line to the bathroom. I had to go *so* bad, and there are only five minutes between each period, and my last class was in the basement and my next class was on the third floor. The girl—her name was Violet Treacle—had her friend "saving" a spot for her.

Cronyism is real, and it trickles down even to the line for toilets.

"Hey!" I shouted. "There's a *line* over here!"

It got pin-drop quiet, real fast. The whole line of girls stared at me.

I'll never forget their faces: eyes narrowed, lips curled in disgust. They looked down at me like I was so far beneath them.

"Ohmigod, that new girl's, like, super rude," Violet Treacle whispered to her friend as she slipped in front of me on line. She didn't even acknowledge that *she* was the one in the wrong. I was so upset that day, but I didn't have the words to express my frustration.

So I've learned to quiet my voice.

And there's another reason why I don't Aletude anymore. Because the last time I got into an argument, the last time the words sprang hot and angry from my lips, I said things I could never take back again.

A TABLE FINALLY OPENS up. But another brigade of strollers enters the café and claims it before we can. More and more, Jackson Heights is starting to resemble Laurel's neighborhood. I don't know how I feel about that.

Billy's thinking the exact same thing. "It'll only be a matter of time before we're priced out of our own barrio," he says. "My mom said they've been bringing people by our building complex."

"What people?"

"Didn't your mom get the notices in the mail?"

I look away. "Ma and I don't really talk about stuff."

"Just watch," says Billy. "The developers will swoop in and kick everyone out. Then all the city people will come flooding in and buying all the fancy-ass lattes." He points to my drink.

"Like hell they will," I say.

"Not like it'll be your problem anymore, Ale," he says.

"What's that supposed to mean?"

"It means, you're leaving. You're getting out of here and going to college, so don't worry your pretty little head."

"About that," I say quickly. "I been meaning to ask you. How're your college apps going? The deadline's coming up."

Billy stalls, taking a sip of his coffee. "They're going."

I know all his tells.

"Bullshit."

"I'm sorting it out, all right, Ale?"

"Bullshit times two."

"Fine, I'll be straight with you," Billy says. "I'm not applying to college because I'm repeating junior year."

"What?" I put down my coffee. "Didn't your school in Santo Domingo count?"

"I didn't go to school while I was down there."

"Explain."

So Billy explains. The local public school was a joke—not enough chairs and books for the students, teachers who didn't show up because they were on strike—and Billy's Spanish wasn't good enough to follow along, anyway. But the American school was for the kids of diplomats and businesspeople and prohibitively expensive besides.

"So when you said you spent the year just sitting around your grandma's house—"

"I wasn't kidding."

"And there's no way they'll let you jump to senior year?"

"No, because technically I 'failed' junior year," he says. "But it got me thinking. Like, what's the point of school? Am I just going to school to go to more school?"

"Yeah," I say. "That's kind of the whole point."

"I'm not like"—Billy hesitates, and I can see his lip is wavering—"like you and your friends at Quaker Oats. How am I supposed to compete with that?"

"Why's it even a competition?" I say.

"Come on, Ale. Don't be naive."

It dawns on me. "Hey, how come you were able to meet me so early?" I was so caught up in my own drama that I didn't stop to think. "Chivi, are you cutting class right now?"

"Aren't *you*?"

Touché.

My phone buzzes. It's Laurel, again. Texting me for the 1,001st time.

> Please can we talk in person? I'm awful over text.

> Let me explain.

I just can't deal with her right now. I put my phone away.

"Look, Ale," Billy says. "I really don't want to get into school stuff now."

I can tell when Billy's approaching shut-down mode, so I spare him. For the time being.

"Fine." I hold out my latte—a peace offering. "Chivi, want a hit?"

"If I must."

Billy blanches at first, but then I see him starting to come around.

"I mean, it's definitely an acquired taste," he says.

"Which, by the look on your face, you are indeed acquiring?" I tease.

"What can I say? Champagne taste on a Gatorade budget." Billy shakes his head like he's joking/not joking. "Story of my life."

CHAPTER 16

The Aftermath

LAUREL FINDS ME BY my locker before school starts the next morning. "Ally, can we talk? You haven't been answering your phone."

Why do you think? I close my locker shut. "What's there to talk about?"

"I was afraid you'd be mad."

I'm gritting my teeth, I'm keeping the red-hot, white-cold feeling contained inside me.

Trying to, at least.

"You didn't even *tell* me the assembly was happening, Laurel."

Laurel looks down at her stack of books. "I'm sorry, Ally. I wanted to. But I was afraid you wouldn't have shown up."

"Right. Because I'm too 'passive.'"

She flinches. "I shouldn't have used that word."

I haven't felt this weird around Laurel since right after Papi's funeral. I told her I understood why she had to miss it—her mom wouldn't let her go because it was the night before the PSATs. Laurel felt awful. But then I felt like I had to comfort *her* about missing it after.

Her forehead crumples like loose-leaf paper. "Ally, for three years I've seen you struggle to find your place at Quaker Oats. And I was tired of sitting back and letting people like JBJ walk all over you. This should be as much an inclusive space for you as it is for me, or anyone else."

Laurel takes a deep breath.

"If I'm being, like, completely honest, sometimes I think . . . you're so afraid of rocking the boat that you hold yourself back."

Her words sting. But . . . Laurel's not wrong. If I had known about the assembly, I would have hidden out in the bathroom. The old Ale would have charged onstage and Shut It Down, maybe. It's hard to know anymore.

She adjusts the books in her arms. "Remember the time? When you told me some woman on the train called you a fucking . . ." Laurel trails off.

"Chink?" I provide.

"Yeah." Laurel winces at the word. "That made me *so* angry for you."

"I didn't know you remembered that."

"It still makes my blood boil, thinking about how in a train car full of people, *no one said anything.*"

"That's the way people are," I say. *See something, say* nothing.

"But that's not the way they *should* be," she says angrily. "I'm sorry I made you feel uncomfortable yesterday. That wasn't my intention. But something *had* to be said. I'm not just your best friend. I'm also your ally."

Determination floods her face. It's the same expression Laurel made when we were right here by the lockers three years ago, poring over her highlighted copy of *Huck Finn*.

My anger . . . isn't gone, exactly. But the freezing-hot pressure inside me starts to dissipate. When the woman on the train called me that ugly word, I kept looking into the crowd for an ally, someone to jump in and help. *No one stepped up.*

Laurel really was the only one in our whole school to see something and say something. And she didn't even *see* it herself! The kids who did just sat back and did nothing. It's the easier thing to do. I feel myself softening.

It's like I said to Billy yesterday: I know Laurel's coming from a good place.

Laurel opens her arms, then stops herself. I can tell she doesn't want to be presumptuous.

In that moment I decide to let it go. It's not worth it. Laurel's my best friend.

"Let's hug it out, L," I say.

And we do.

"I will always have your back," she says. "Promise."

ALL WEEK, PEOPLE COME up to me and "congratulate" me on my award. Oatties who said nothing during JBJ's actual class are now offering "allyship."

Everyone's like, "Ohmigod, that was *so* messed up what JBJ said to you!"

"Ohmigod, good thing they fired him!"

"Ohmigod, let me know if you need my help with anything!"

But they also whisper about me in the halls. I'm not a narcissist or anything, but I can sense it. As soon as I walk into the room, the other kids hush up, which only makes it súper obvious that they were talking about me.

The same thing happened right after Papi died. The whispers, the weird combo of sympathy and freak-show curiosity. Because Papi's "accident" was big and sudden, splashed all over the news.

"Unlucky Number 7 Strikes Again!"

"Wokking Dead: Asian Man Fried on Subway Tracks!" (Seriously.)

"More on this *electrifying* story at five o'clock!"

(My own cousin Jason kept sending me headlines and texting, We're famous!)

There's nothing like your father's death being so public when you're not ready to talk about it yourself.

No one actually came *up* to me and asked, "So, did your dad off himself?" but the implication, and shame, was there. Were they thinking, *Was your family so fucked up that your own father didn't want to stick around?*

TODAY, IN THE BATHROOM stall, I hear two girls talking.

"I mean, I get that she's a POC, but she's not, like, you know . . ."

I know what "you know" means.

The second girl does, too. "Totally," she laughs. "But are we even allowed to call them 'POCs' anymore?"

"Who knows? They're always changing names."

"I still can't believe she got him fired!"

"My dad says you can't say *anything* anymore. Or they'll cancel you like—" Girl One snaps her fingers.

Are these the Secret Thoughts of White People When They Think Only Other White People Are Around?

I know it's wrong to generalize. That's like saying, *All Black people think this way. All Asian people think that way.* This is just what two people in this universe who happen to be white think.

She's not, like, you know . . . I've heard this argument before, but never to my face. Because Asians are supposed to be the "model minority," so we only face *the good kind* of racism. Which is complete and utter bullshit. What the "model minority" really means is that we're invisible when it's convenient for other people—quiet, working with our heads down—and súper visible when it's not.

I hate when white people pit non-white people against each other, like we're all in a scrappy dog fight and the spoils are their leftovers. Sometimes I think kids at this school think racism only counts when it's a white-and-Black issue. It gets into an awkward game of Misery Poker—the racist edition: Who Has It Worse?

But you know what's even weirder? I also kind of get it, what the girls are saying. Laurel would say I have Stockholm syndrome—*Why would you sympathize with the enemy?* But if *I* were white, wouldn't I get sick and tired of being told to feel guilty for having pale skin? Of having my every word and action monitored and scrutinized? Of living in perpetual fear that the wrong word would get me canceled?

Cognitive dissonance *all* up inside me.

If I were still Fresh-Off-the-Boat-from-Queens Ale, I would call those girls out.

But I've gotten good at assimilating. Quaker Oats Ally does not say a word in her defense.

I make obvious sounds in my bathroom stall, like rattling the toilet paper roller and clanging the lid of the tampon disposal. I do this to give these girls time to change the subject. So that when I get out of the bathroom stall, they won't get caught flat-footed and embarrassed. They can pretend like they didn't say anything. (Hello, nunchi.)

You're a guest at this school. Don't make any trouble.

I hated Papi's advice because it made us seem *passive*—there goes Laurel's word again—more passive than people already think Asians are. But I still followed his advice.

Did Papi spend a lifetime holding it back and saying nothing? All of his anger and injustices and sorrows, wallowing up inside him like he was an Instant Pot, until he had no choice but to—

I squeeze my eyes, shutting out the 7 train flashing in my mind.

I leave the stall and smile dumbly at the two girls at the sink. I've seen them around; they're both sophomores. (They're both white.) They smile back, but I can tell by their guilty expressions that they know I heard them. I slink out of the bathroom.

* * *

LAUREL, MEANWHILE, HAS BEEN having a ball of a week. Teachers and students alike are nodding at her with newfound respect. Kids we don't even really talk to—like the sports kids—are giving her high fives in the halls. And through it all, she's smiling like she won the lottery. I've never seen her smile like that before, not even when her dad wrote her a check for $1,000 for her last birthday.

Laurel's finally getting the recognition, and the—let's be honest—popularity she's always craved.

Like a good friend, I'm happy for her.

At least, I'm trying to be.

CHAPTER 17

Cultural Studies

TWO WEEKS AFTER THE ASSEMBLY, we're sitting in the classroom waiting for Taupe period to begin. Over the weekend, Quaker Oats sent a letter to inform us of JBJ's replacement: Dr. Payal Chatterjee, a psychology professor from Hunter College who will help us "interrogate questions of culture and inclusion." We won't be doing creative writing at all. Our new elective will be called "Cultural Studies."

"That sucks they couldn't just get us another Creative Writing teacher," Chelsea Braeburn whispers to Maya Chang. "I was really hoping to work on my fantasy trilogy, you know?"

"Right?" Maya whispers back. "The only other alternative was Adventures in Quantum Mechanics."

I can feel the collective groan of disappointment from the class. And though no one comes right out and says it, I think they're kind of blaming me for this crappy elective alternative.

Josh Buck walks over to my desk. This is weird, because

he and I haven't exchanged more than three words in as many years.

Josh is the whole package. Tall swimmer from Brooklyn Heights. He's handsome, insultingly so; it's hard not to take it personally. He must move through life like he moves through water: effortlessly. I can't even look up at him for fear of burning my retinas out.

"Hey, Ally," he says. "I didn't know you wanted to be a writer."

"I don't," I admit, flattered to be singled out by his attention. I don't get into the needing an elective during Taupe period.

He runs his fingers through his flop of black hair. "So . . . let me get this straight. You got JBJ kicked out when you don't even care about writing in the first place?"

The whole class goes silent.

"Oh, by the way, Ally," he continues. "I never got to congratulate you on your *award*."

Josh Buck wasn't singling me out for any other reason than to humiliate me. I feel so stupid for the fleeting hope in my heart that, I don't know, someone like him would so much as look my way?

I abruptly get up from my desk so I can go splash cold water on my face in the bathroom and regain myself.

But a woman in an oversized blazer, ripped jeans, and Converses breezes into the classroom. She barely clears five feet. One half of her head is shaved, and the other half has long hair that runs down her back. I scuttle back to my seat.

I don't know what I was picturing of Dr. Payal Chatter-jee: a pearled, sweater-setted, pencil-skirted, Banana Republican draped in a white lab coat? Straight black hair, studious smile.

I suck at stereotypes.

"I'm Dr. Chatterjee, she/her, they/them. Welcome to Cultural Studies," she says in a deep, commanding voice. I want a voice like that—it makes people forget that you're only three apples tall. Dr. Chatterjee looks *cool*. Also, scary, like someone who doesn't take any BS.

"Now, can I please have a volunteer to write their name ten times across the whiteboard?"

"You want us to write our name on the board," Josh calls out.

"That's right. Ten times."

"Fine, I'll go." He shrugs to the rest of the class like, *This is stupid, but whatever.* He strides to the front of the room and grabs the dry-erase marker from Dr. Chatterjee.

"Students, I need your attention up here," Dr. Chatterjee says.

Joshua J. Buck Joshua J. Buck Joshua J. Buck Joshua J. Buck Joshua J. Buck Joshua J. Buck Joshua J. Buck Joshua J. Buck Joshua J. Buck Joshua J. Buck

Josh writes his name on the board with a flourish. For some reason, I'm surprised he writes in script and not print.

"Super easy, right? Well done, Joshua J. Buck." Dr. Chatter-jee's delivery is so dry, I have no idea if she's deadpanning or not. "May I ask what your best subject is at school?"

"I was going to say Creative Writing," he says. "But that's a nonstarter."

Colin Okafor calls out, "Josh Buck's in BC Calc!"

"BC?" Dr. Chatterjee whistles. "So you're quite the mathlete." Dr. Chatterjee looks pleased, but I sense a trap.

If it's a trap, Josh is totally not onto her. "Pretty much."

"Great!" She sketches the quadratic formula on the whiteboard.

$$x = \frac{-b \pm \sqrt{b^2 - 4ac}}{2a}$$

"That's the quadratic formula." Josh says it like, *Duh*.

I half expect Dr. Chatterjee to put Josh in his place, but she says an encouraging "Very good!"

"That's first-year math."

"My apologies, Joshua. I only came prepared with a very easy problem set, so please bear with me." Dr. Chatterjee writes some more on the whiteboard. "So if I tell you a=1, b=4, and c=3, then you can solve for x, no prob, right?"

"Right."

"Students, I need your attention up here, right up at this whiteboard," Dr. Chatterjee repeats.

So all our eyeballs fix on Josh as he uses the quadratic formula to solve for x.

Josh starts out with confident marker strokes. But then he falters. From where I'm sitting, I can tell Josh is beginning to sweat. Then he drops his marker. The room is *so* silent, we can even hear the plastic cap clatter to the floor.

"Uh, I can just do this much faster at my desk," Josh mumbles, then flees to his seat. He doesn't even bother to pick up the marker he dropped, leaving it for Dr. Chatterjee to stoop and pick up.

"Let's all give Joshua a big round of applause," Dr. Chatterjee says, "for taking one for the team."

We clap, sort of. We kind of feel like we're being punked.

"What Joshua J. Buck so generously demonstrated for us is the pressure we all feel to *perform,* especially in the presence of an audience. Whether it's Yo-Yo Ma at Carnegie Hall or Steffi Graf at Flushing Meadows . . ."

Dr. Chatterjee takes in our blank faces. We have no idea who she's talking about.

She starts again. "Or Drake performing at MSG—"

"Drake is *out,* Dr. C," Colin Okafor calls out. He only nicknames the teachers he likes, and everyone knows it. He's the ultimate tastemaker at Quaker Oats. What he says, everyone follows.

Which means Dr. Chatterjee—excuse me, Dr. C—is totally *in.*

"Then provide us with a better example . . . ?"

"Colin Okafor," Colin says. "He/him/his. Okay, okay. Like Michael Jackson doing the moonwalk."

"Kicking it back, old-school," Dr. Chatterjee says, nodding. "Allegations of pedophilia notwithstanding."

The whole class cracks up.

"Anyway, what our friend Joshua so generously demonstrated for us is the principle of social facilitation theory, which posits that individuals perform a task differently when they are alone versus when they're with others," Dr. C explains. "With simple tasks, like writing one's name, we actually perform *better* in the presence of an audience than when we're alone. I mean, lookit that penmanship!"

We lookit. Josh Buck does indeed have excellent penmanship. Seriously, who would have guessed?

"But for more complex tasks, like the quadratic formula, social facilitation theory posits that the reverse is actually true, and we choke up in the presence of others."

Josh raises his hand. He's been scribbling furiously in his notebook. "By the way, $x = -1$ or -3."

"Exactly!" Dr. Chatterjee says, and the whole class claps—this time for real—for Josh.

"What I want to introduce to you all is the added layer of the *cultural expectation* to perform. Think about if we didn't know Joshua was in BC Calc. How would our expectations of their performance have changed?"

Maya Chang raises her hand. She has the dreamy-eyed gaze she gets when she's in love with a teacher. "I wouldn't have been so judgy that he couldn't even do the quadratic formula on the board."

Claire says, "I feel like Josh was inflating his abilities, like a hyperbolist."

I kind of feel bad for Josh, who is glaring down at his desk, but also . . . kind of schadenfreude. He *was* kind of acting show-offy at the whiteboard.

Dr. Chatterjee goes, "There you have it. But now that we know the presence of an audience is a variable that affects performance, is it fair for us to put these expectations on a subject? These are *all* questions we need to examine in this classroom."

She pivots on her heel and starts pacing the length of the classroom in the other direction. I recognize this as one of Laurel's debate moves.

"So, Cultural Studies. It's to challenge your belief system. To make you understand where your values come from and how your environment and culture have shaped your tastes, preferences, behaviors, and actions. During the course of this class, I want us to analyze ourselves and ask, Do we want to continue these value systems? Or do we want to recognize and acknowledge our previous values and move beyond them?"

Josh raises his hand and talks at the same time. "Cultural Studies wasn't the original course offering, so Van Cortlandt gave us the option to drop the class. Is that correct?"

"Yes." Dr. C nods. "That is correct. If you feel this course isn't the right fit, you're welcome to leave."

She points to the door. "In fact, that goes for any of you."

Josh Buck grabs his bag and stalks out. Two others, Guilden and Rosen, follow.

"Any last takers?" she asks.

No one else leaves. I'm relieved for Dr. C.

Not that she needs my relief. Dr. C looks like she can hold her own.

***

TOWARD THE END OF class, Dr. C says, "Students, for homework, I want you to think about the following." Dr. Chatterjee writes on the whiteboard:

Make a list of all the things you're good at.
Make a list of all the things you're <u>expected</u> to be good at.

"Bring your lists to our next class and come prepared to discuss."

The bell rings. Then everyone spills like beans into the hallway, scattering to their next classes.

CHAPTER 18

Stereotype Threat

WHEN I GET HOME from school, I start with Dr. C's homework assignment.

THINGS I'M ACTUALLY GOOD AT:

-Telling corny jokes and making people (ok, just Laurel
    and Billy) laugh

-Navigating NYC

-Calling out BS and hypocrisy (in my head, at least)

-Being a good listener

-Being analytical, being thoughtful, trying to make sense
    of our world in non-black-and-white terms

-Understanding-or wanting to understand-how people
    think and talk and breathe, what makes them tick

THINGS I'M EXPECTED TO BE GOOD AT:

-Math

-All schoolwork

-Being hardworking

-Playing piano/violin/cello/[insert classical instrument here]

-Being polite

-Obeying authority

-Not talking back

-Being fetishized as a sexual object ("Me so horny" and that whole gross "submissive Oriental woman" trope perpetuated by pervy old white dudes)

I stare at my lists, and I realize the second list is based on all the expectations people have of someone with the last name Kim.

It's kind of making me mad. I am *none* of these things—well, except the schoolwork thing, but math is actually my worst subject. And if these are the things people expect me to be *good* at, then doesn't that mean the inverse is what they expect me to be *bad* at? People expect someone with the last name Kim to have *no* authority or assertiveness. I can't even tell you how many times people have literally *and* figuratively pushed me and my family out of their way—like we're invisible.

Because they think we don't have the guts to confront them. I remember when a Happy Day customer started screaming her head off at us, and Tía Yoona just bowed her head. The customer used a disgusting tone, like she had zero respect for us. When her friend (also white) came into the store, she immediately changed her voice, all soft and honeyed.

It happens more often than you'd think.

Once, in Mrs. McCann's class in first grade, Tracy Murray leaned over to ask me to repeat what Mrs. McCann had just said. Mrs. McCann caught us and screamed at *me* for talking in class, not at Tracy.

Last weekend I watched *Harold & Kumar Go to White Castle* with Michael Oppa. During the scene where all the white bros leave the office for happy hour and leave Harold (played by John Cho) to do all their work over the weekend, Michael Oppa started to blink back tears. Michael Oppa *never* cries. Not even when his dad told him, "You are no son of mine."

I paused the movie, and Michael Oppa kind of told me what was up. He's always putting in long nights and weekends at Goldman, and he explained he'd just been passed over for a promotion for some (white) guy who puts in half the effort but reaps double the praise.

"They said I don't 'project authority,'" he said dryly. "Meanwhile, who's the one doing all that guy's work? He talks a good game. But it's all talk and no action." Furiously, he wiped his tears. "Time to dust off the old résumé."

Before I could ask him more, Michael Oppa grabbed the remote and hit "play."

I start a new list, based on the expectations people have for me when they learn only my first name, Alejandra:

THINGS I'M EXPECTED TO BE GOOD AT (AS ALEJANDRA):

-Speaking Spanish

-Eating good food

-Dancing

. . . My list stops there. All I can think of are the things I'm expected to be *bad* at. Like not speaking English. Not doing schoolwork. Illegally crossing the border to "rape" and "deal drugs" and "spread crime." All the awful—and erroneous—stereotypes they play on the news.

When I'm talking to strangers on the phone, like customer-service people or whatever, they're often surprised to hear me speak English with no accent.

I think about Billy and how different his "Guillermo Díaz" list would look from my "Kim" list. I hate that he has to repeat junior year and that people will probably judge him for it. It doesn't feel fair.

Papi dropped out of high school when he came to America. I wonder how he dealt with what people expected him to be good (or bad) at and what he actually felt he was good at. Maybe, with the pressure coming at all sides, he felt he wasn't good at anything at all.

I find myself wondering about Ma. Papi used to nickname her "Reina." *Because all Argentine women act like they're queens,*

Papi would say, and Ma would own it, too. When she gets on the phone with people, they always put on the Spanish operator; they'd probably never guess she was ethnically Korean. She chitchats with all the bodega owners in the neighborhood in Spanish, but they still call her "China." It was the same with Papi, too.

Look, I'm not such an idiot that I'm just now waking up to the fact that people stereotype other people based on what they look like. Hello, I'm a New Yorker living in the twenty-first century, not some buttoned-up Victorian heroine in the 1800s who can't breathe because her whalebone's strapped on too tight so she can nab a husband because she lives in a society where women can't have careers or own property and marriage is her only meal ticket.

I get it.

But when this "empirical evidence" is staring at me in list form . . . it still stings.

I'm 100 percent Korean, 100 percent Latinx, and 100 percent American . . . but there's no such thing as 300 percent.

What's worse: being expected to be bad, or being invisible altogether?

Why does it even have to be a contest?

NEXT TAUPE PERIOD, DR. CHATTERJEE pairs us off to compare our lists. I'm partnered with Claire Devereaux. She still smells like overpriced shampoo. I almost think about asking her where she gets it from, but then she'll think I'm creepy for literally sniffing around.

We trade lists. I'm actually surprised that Claire has broken down her "expectations" list into categories: Girl, Cis Woman, Daughter, Granddaughter, Writer, EIC, and so on.

Claire looks up from my list. "That's funny. You and I both made ours into more than one list."

"I only did two," I say. "You did, what, like—"

"Ten," she says a little sheepishly.

"I guess it's because people expect me to act differently based on who—or what—they think I am," I say. "It makes me have to change the way I act around them."

I can't believe I'm opening up to Claire Devereaux, of all people.

"It's like we have to play to people's expectations of us," Claire says, nodding. "I'm always code-switching based on who I'm around."

"Code-switching? What do you mean by that?" I ask. I phrase it like that instead of, *What does "code-switching" mean?* because I don't want to sound like an ignoramus.

"Oh, it's, like, when you switch to a different language based on what culture you're surrounded by. With my grandmother, I know I have to put on lipstick and pearls and quote the *New Yorker*. Versus when I'm casual with people at school or the staff at *Ennui* or whatever."

I didn't realize the version of Claire we were getting at school was "casual." I didn't think it was possible for Claire Devereaux to be any more Devereauxian.

Or maybe it's the opposite, and she plays up her performance with her grandmother?

"I think I get it," I say. "I probably could have done a dozen more categories."

Quaker Oats Ally, who could be further broken down into Ally with Laurel, Ally in the classroom, Ally who overhears stupid shit in the bathroom. Queens Ale: at-home-with-Ma Ale, Ale hanging in the park with Billy, Aleja-ya with Papi. Ale with Tía Yoona. Alley-Cat with Michael Oppa. That polite little Asian girl behind the counter at Happy Day. Ah-rae with Jason (his nickname for me; we'll get to it). Jason's random Spanish cousin whose Korean sucks.

And so on.

Why can't I just be *one* Ale? Can all these different versions of yourself exist inside the same person . . . or does that make you an imposter?

Who is the "real" Alejandra Kim?

"So," Claire says, "this class isn't as bad as we all thought, right?"

"I don't think she's bad. Other people, maybe." I think of Josh Buck, Rosen, and Guilden walking out of Dr. C's classroom.

"I just mean, Dr. C has big shoes to fill coming off of the celebrity that is—was—Jonathan Brooks James. A lot of us were really looking forward to studying creative writing with him."

"Oh," I say, "because *Becoming Brooklyn* was 'perfection.'" Does Claire expect me to apologize for being responsible—or tangentially responsible—for getting him fired?

She blushes. "I *used* to think that. I just tried reading it again this weekend, and all I could see was the two-dimensionality of his woman characters."

She fidgets with her notebook. "I've been meaning to say, I owe you an apology. I should have spoken up on that first day of class. What JBJ said to you wasn't cool. It's just, I was so in awe, you know? I mean, the *New Yorker* called him 'the millennial Hemingway incarnate.'"

"Is that supposed to be a compliment?" I ask.

She pauses, then lets out a laugh. "Touché, Alejandra."

I look at Claire's last category: White-Passing.

I'm groping for a polite way to ask, What does that mean? But Dr. C is already calling all of us to rejoin as a class.

"Are any of you familiar with the concept of stereotype threat?" Dr. C asks, writing the term on the whiteboard. She is bouncing on the toes of her Converses, like she's walking across a kid's blow-up castle. She has so much energy.

Chelsea Braeburn raises her hand. "It's when we're expected to perform to certain cultural expectations. Like when an African American man is expected to play basketball well?"

She glances at Colin Okafor and quickly says, "No offense!"

He looks more offended now than if Chelsea hadn't looked at him and said, "No offense!" at all. Chelsea's about to shrivel into herself. Maya rolls her eyes. I feel bad for everybody in the class at this point, so I raise my hand and say:

"Is that like how, even though I'm bad at math, everyone expects me to be good at math because, you know, this whole situation?" I wave a hand over my face.

The joke lands with a thud. Only Dr. C laughs. The rest of the class falls silent, uncomfortable. The room is quieter than the time I accidentally farted during Mass in the fifth grade, right after homily. Pin-drop quiet.

Then Billy, sitting next to me in the pew, broke the awkward silence by letting out a fart, too.

It takes a true friend to fart in solidarity.

"I'll take it," Dr. C says. "Stereotype threat and its inverse, stereotype boost, are the pressure to conform to what people *expect* from our cultural groups. In other words, both negative and positive stereotypes. Like the Black baller or the Asian mathematician." She smiles kindly at Chelsea, then at me, as if to say, *It's okay for having taken a chance.*

"For the next few weeks, I want you all to really think about yourselves, more than you already do." Dr. C chuckles to herself, like she's enjoying her own personal joke. "Keep a journal. What's informing the things you say or don't say as you move about your world? What you do or don't do? Study yourself like you're an actor auditioning for the role of 'you.'"

I find myself saying, with a comic groan, "Like I'm not self-conscious enough already, Dr. C?"

I wait a beat, terrified by the class reaction. But I'm surprised to hear a bunch of claps in agreement.

Dr. C says, "Know thyself, young Padawan."

Colin whistles at the gratuitous *Star Wars* reference.

"I think you'll all make some pretty eye-opening discoveries about yourselves," she says. "Just as Claude Steele did. He was the psychologist who came up with the concept of stereotype threat."

Dr. C's PowerPoint flashes a picture of Claude Steele. I was expecting a shriveled-up white dude pruning in the juices of his outdated theories. Dr. Steele is Black.

***

THE BUZZ ABOUT DR. C'S class spreads. What started as a class everyone seemed to dread is now the one everyone's talking about. Three new students transfer in: Ambrose Garrison, captain of the soccer team; Colt Brenner, who was in my physics class last year; and Lacey Wade, the student body treasurer.

Even Laurel wants in.

"I mean, it's kind of a little unfair that Cultural Studies wasn't part of the initial offering," Laurel says. "If I had known, then I wouldn't have signed up for AP Comp Gov."

"Why don't you transfer in?" I say.

"Can't. Wait list." She sighs into her celery sticks. "And nobody ever gets in off the wait list."

CHAPTER 19

Weeks Go By

THE WEEKS BLUR BY, and the teachers are piling on the work, work, work. It's like they cruelly banded together and decided to assign everything at the same time—right before the holiday break. I'm busting my butt on a ten-page paper on research methodologies for Dr. C, an eleven-pager on China's air pollution, a twelve-page literary analysis on the symbolism of pickles and doughnuts in *Ethan Frome* by Edith Wharton, and cramming for all my midterms—when I could be working on my Whyder app, the one thing that will decide the future for the rest of my life.

Also, while we're at it, please can Quaker Oats ban *Ethan Frome* from the curriculum altogether? It's a snoozefest of repressed, milquetoast characters, all building up to the climax of—no joke—a *toboggan ride.* We should end on the Whartonian high of *The Age of Innocence,* which is probably the best novel set in New York City, ever. It's about rich white people planning hits and takedowns at fancy balls like it's *The God-father*. Even though *The Age of Innocence* was written a hundred years ago, you just *know* that Edith Wharton knew what was up.

When I'm not studying, I'm at Happy Day—but the days feel like anything but.

BETWEEN SCHOOLWORK AND WORK-WORK and college apps (due right after New Year's), I barely have a minute to hang out with Laurel. I'm mostly in the library while Laurel's meeting with our teachers or her debate team or working on her RD apps, now that her Whyder ED app is in. I revise and revise "Fallen Heroes, Failed Homeland" until the words are polished and crisp. But there's still something about it that doesn't feel right. *Just be yourself!* Easier said than done, Michael Oppa. I tell myself it just means I need to try harder, so I keep going at it, writing and rewriting and throwing away old drafts.

BACK AT APARTMENT 2B, Ma and I come and go, like two ships. I've decided to go ahead and apply to Whyder whether she approves or not. Ma already signed my FAFSA for all the New York schools I'm applying to, so technically I don't even need her permission. And I'll be eighteen by the time I actually start college.

Thank God for Billy. Some nights, when my schoolwork

is done and the dinner dishes are washed and put away, I meet him down at Montoya Park. We shoot the shit, we talk about dumb stuff and smart stuff or sometimes nothing at all.

And it's all good.

I don't need to be "on" for Billy. I can just, be.

CHAPTER 20

(E)D-Day

AND THEN DECEMBER 15 ROLLS around. Aka (E)D–Day, aka the day early decision notifications go out.

In Taupe period, before the bell rings, Claire Devereaux lets out a squeal. "I got in! I got in early!"

She's holding up a thick yellow envelope for all of us to see. The return address is Whyder College, 100 Pine Lane, Whyder, ME. Whyder is the only college left that still does snail-mail acceptances. They're (in)famous for that.

I congratulate Claire along with the rest of the class, but all I can think about is Laurel. I didn't see her by the lockers this morning.

Of the other earlies, Maya Chang gets into Stanford—she'll be playing D1 tennis for them. Josh Buck applied early to Yale. Maya says she asked him about it the period before—they're in BC Calc together—but he just snapped, "Mind your own fucking business, okay?" But we all know what that means: Josh was rejected. Colin Okafor is deferred at Amherst.

"Colin, that makes *no* sense!" Chelsea Braeburn says. "You're freaking class president. And you're—"

She slams the brakes on that sentence.

"Black?" Colin offers.

"No, I was going to say . . ." Chelsea trails off, flustered.

Colin brushes off the awkwardness with his usual—and literal—presidential diplomacy. "I appreciate the vote of confidence, Chelsea. But you win some, you lose some."

Dr. C strolls into the classroom, and Colin seems relieved to stop talking about college. I can imagine the devastation he must be feeling inside.

THE PERIOD WON'T END quickly enough. Nor will the one after, or the one after that. At lunch, I race to our spot on campus, but Laurel's not there. She's not in the library, not in the guidance counselor's office. I send her a text. I'm worried now—Laurel *never* misses school. She practically lives for Quaker Oats. I don't hear back. I send more texts between breaks, but still nothing.

After school, I don't have work so I head straight to Laurel's house. She answers the door still wearing her pajamas, and her red, splotchy face tells me everything.

"Oh, Laurel," I breathe out.

"Ally," she says. "I just couldn't face everyone at school—"

But it's all she can get out before her face crumples.

I fold my best friend into a hug.

In the kitchen, Laurel shows me the razor-thin white envelope. The return address is the same, but it's definitely not the thick yellow packet Claire waved during Taupe period.

Dear Ms. Greenblatt-Watkins,

Thank you for expressing strong interest in Whyder College.
We were impressed by your application and academic
excellence. However, due to the overwhelming number of
qualified applicants, we regret to inform you that you were
not selected in the Early Decision pool. But we are pleased
to inform you that your application has been deferred, and
we will reconsider your candidacy in the Regular Decision
pool . . .

"We are PLEASED to INFORM you that you've been
DEFERRED?" Laurel says. "What the eff!"

I can't believe what I'm reading. Laurel Greenblatt-Watkins,
deferred? I'm both baffled and enraged on her behalf. Laurel was
destined for Whyder!

But there's also a small part of me that thinks, *If Laurel didn't
get into Whyder ED, then there's no way I'll get accepted RD.* I feel
like a terrible friend for thinking this, so I shove that thought
deep down, where all the other thoughts I don't want to think
about live.

"At least it's not a rejection," I say weakly.

"Gee, thanks." Laurel is crying for real-real. She doesn't cry
for anything. She's one of the toughest people I know.

"I don't understand," I say, because I really don't. "How
could Whyder not accept you? Your essay on feeling at home in
Arabic and Muslim women's advocacy was *so* good!"

Laurel shreds the tissue in her hands. "I didn't end up using
that one."

"Then which one did you . . ." I trail off. I have the nunchi to tell Laurel doesn't feel like getting into it.

She reaches for another tissue and blows her nose. She wipes her eyes.

"What was the point, Ally? Why did I bust my butt for three-plus years at Quaker Oats, only to get *deferred*? I wish they had straight-up rejected me! It's like they want to keep me on their hook, just so they can reject me in the regular pool later."

"Stop. You're totally going to get in RD, you'll see," I assure her. "How can you not be the strongest candidate in the pool? I mean, Laurel Greenblatt-Watkins, look at you!"

I point to the picture of Laurel at her Lower School graduation hanging from the wall.

"This wouldn't have happened if I were a guy," Laurel says, sniffing. "Colleges are so starved for men, since their enrollments are so low, because apparently men think they're above getting an education." She scoffs. "So it's just a bunch of over-qualified women competing against each other."

Michael Oppa said the same thing about Asians—women *and* men.

"Laurel," I plead, "you cannot let this deferral define you."

"You know who's thrilled about my rejection?"

"It's not a rejection—"

"My dad. He's like"—Laurel puts on her dad voice—" 'Well, now, Laurel. Looks like you might be a Tiger after all! It's the first step to the *right* path in life. You don't want to end up a bleeding heart like your mother.' "

"He actually *said* that to you?"

"Yup. You know Dad's only offering to pay for college if I get into Princeton? Talk about emotional blackmail. I thought Mom would totally jump in and defend me. But she didn't make a peep. What the hell did she go to Yale Law School for? Speaking of hooks: she's still on his, even though he traded her in for a 'new and shinier model,' so to speak. It's such a disgusting cliché."

It's true. Mr. Greenblatt literally upgraded his Subaru Outback for a Tesla when he met Laurel's stepmom (she of Pantygate notoriety).

"Why do you have to listen to him, then?" I ask. "Why can't you just do what you want to? It's not like you're dependent on him or anything. Or . . ."

Laurel's not really answering.

"No offense," I continue, "but I thought your family was loaded."

"It's . . . complicated," Laurel says. "I mean, my mom had to buy out my dad to get the brownstone, so she's still paying that off, on a nonprofit salary. And I guess they made some kind of agreement where Dad's the one who's going to pay for my college, so."

This surprises me. I guess I was under the assumption that Laurel just had a lot of money, on both sides. It didn't really matter that her mom had less than her dad, because her mom still seemed to have a lot.

But then again, with Laurel, I'm not really sure. Because her sense of deprivation is so different from mine.

"It's annoying," Laurel goes on, "because it's *his* high salary that makes me not even remotely qualified for financial aid. Sorry!" she says, suddenly backtracking. "I hope this doesn't offend you."

She does this thing where she bites her lip and starts hemming and hawing. "I mean . . . it's because, historically, people like my parents have benefited from the system due to their privileged status as white, English-speaking Americans, and, like, I didn't mean . . ."

Laurel looks up at me with desperation.

I sit back and cross my arms over my chest. "You done over there?"

"Ally, please. Just put me out of my misery!"

"I hereby absolve you of your Guilty White Girl Tumble Act, in nomine Patris, et Filii, et Spiritus Sancti, amen," I say, making the sign of the cross. You can take the Korean Argentine American girl out of the iglesia católica, but you can't take the iglesia católica out of the girl. "Your penance shall be ten Hail Marys and a hundred monthly service hours at the Park Slope Community Garden. For *life*."

"Noooo!!!" Laurel winces, shielding her face. "Aw, Ally. I'm going to miss you so much next year." She says this in a suddenly serious tone.

"Stop it," I tell her. "We're both going to be at Whyder next year. It'll be perfect."

I stare up at the gallery wall of pictures of Laurel, Leah, and their mom. You can still see the faint outline of the family portrait—of the whole family at the beach—that was removed.

I clap my hands. "Laurel, get dressed. I'm prison-breaking you."

Laurel groans. "Please don't make me go to debate practice. I can't face any Oatties right now."

"Promise," I say. "Where we're going, I guarantee you won't see a single Oattie."

AND THEN WE'RE ON the A train, leaving Brooklyn for Queens. Some of the passengers in our car have suitcases and duffel bags. "Are you taking me to JFK?" Laurel asks eagerly. "I forgot my passport, so domestic flights only."

"Patience, L. You'll ruin the surprise."

But we don't get off at Howard Beach to catch the AirTrain, like the other travelers with their baggage. We keep going, crossing Jamaica Bay before it feeds into the Atlantic Ocean.

Laurel and I ride the A almost to the bitter end. The smell of sea salt hits us as we exit the station.

She slaps my arm. "Shut up. You are *not* taking me to Rockaway Beach, Alejandra Kim!"

"Too late, L. We're already here."

She lets out a squeal. "Holy bleep! I haven't been here since . . . since . . ."

She's memory groping.

"The picture of your family that used to be in your kitchen," I say.

"I can't believe you remember that," she says. "We used to come here all the time. Back when we were one big happy."

"We used to come here, too," I say. "Before my dad, you know . . ."

I think of the last time Papi and I were at the Rockaways. I pulled out the old picture the other day, and I didn't feel the same intensity of sadness that usually overwhelms me. Maybe I shouldn't keep it tucked in my bottom desk drawer anymore.

"I didn't know you guys used to come here," she says. "You never really say anything about your dad. . . ."

Her words are snatched away by the wind. On the board-walk, the ocean is roaring, and our hair keeps whipping around our faces.

The Atlantic Ocean is blue green from far away and green brown up close, stretching across with no beginning and seemingly no end.

I'm flashing back to the last time we were here. The time we left Ma behind in the car after their fight about the umbrella. Papi stretched his arms wide, like he was Jay Gatsby trying to give the ocean a hug. "Always I imagine Tierra del Fuego looks like this. Like I'm at the end of my world."

I corrected his English. "Papi, you mean 'edge,' not 'end.'"

He smiled that strange smile he had when he didn't agree with what you said but was too polite to argue.

We dove in. The shock of freezing-cold, murky water contrasted the two hours of hot and sticky traffic inside the Olds-mobile with the broken AC. It's funny, though, how in life things are always one extreme or the other—too hot or too cold, and never firmly in the Goldilocks middle.

"I can't believe Mami is missing all this," I said. The guilt of leaving her behind in the car, even though it had been her choice, was hanging heavy in the air.

Suddenly there was a commotion by the water's edge. A

crowd hovered around something lying on the sand. What was it? A drowned child? Papi rushed over in a panic; I followed.

But no—it was just a jellyfish. It was lifeless, dead. The crowd dispersed.

"Let's head back, Aleja-ya," Papi said abruptly, and he began to pack up our things.

It took some time to find where we were parked. Now the late beachgoers were tailing us like slow-moving sharks, following us back to our parking spot.

When we found our Oldsmobile, the engine was off, and all the windows were, strangely, rolled up. Mami lay reclined on the passenger seat side. Something was odd. Her eyes were closed, and instead of her usual scowl lines, her expression was blank. My old copy of *Detective Darya* was facedown on her chest. But the book did not move up-down with her breathing.

The stillness of her face scared me. Scared Papi.

Papi began banging on the window with his fists. "¡Vero! Vero-ya, ¡wake up!" Under his breath he began to chant. "Santa María, Madre de Dios. Santa María, Madre de Dios . . ." He was praying the Hail Mary, banging and pounding away. I slapped the windows, too, the glass sizzling against my palms.

Papi gave one last yank on the locked door handle.

Suddenly Mami jolted awake. "What the . . . !"

My heart, which had stopped beating, was now pounding rapidly. Mami unlocked the car, and Papi threw open the door and clutched her to his chest.

Once Mami was released and her eyes blinked open, she looked from my father to me, her frown deepening. "Juan, I told you not to let Ale get too morenita," she snapped.

She was *definitely* still alive.

That day on Rockaway Beach was the hot, searing peak of summer. Now it's off-season and freezing, and the sun is starting to set. Many of the boardwalk stores are closed, but we find a pizza shop.

"Hallelujah, capitalism!" Laurel cries. "I can't believe this place is still open. We always used to get their zeppole. Oh my God, Ally, it's so good."

We pop the fried dough into our mouths, and it's sizzling and sweet, and soon our faces are coated in sugary white powder.

"You look like you just did a line," Laurel laughs, pointing at my face.

"I'm so coked up, man," I say, squinting my eyes like I'm high. "I just spent my entire trust fund scoring this fine-ass powder, but whatevs."

Laurel straightens her face. "Actually, it's not nice to make fun of drug addicts," she says. "Addiction is a serious affliction, and not just for those on the extreme echelons of the socio-economic ladder."

"Laurel's gonna Laurel."

"Damn it, Ally Kim!"

She's furiously blinking back tears. At first I thought it was the salt breeze; now I feel really bad. Maybe this trip to the beach was too triggering?

"I'm sorry, Laurel. Maybe we shouldn't have come—"

She interrupts me. "You're the bestest friend a girl could ever have!"

Laurel hugs me, with her everything. I hug her back, with my everything. With that hug, I let go of our fight, my residual anger. She's my best friend, and I love her. Sometimes Laurel's gonna Laurel.

Our phones buzz. All the ED kids are posting their announcements: yes, no, and deferred.

"Oh my God," Laurel says, clutching her phone. "Claire Devereaux got into Whyder. What the hell!"

"Forget her. You do you," I say. "Positive thoughts only today, okay? Promise?"

I hold out my pinky; Laurel hesitates before hooking it.

"Promise," she says.

THERE ARE FEW PLACES in New York City where you feel like you're on your own island. But the Rockaways in December feels hauntingly, devastatingly empty. They feel like the "shell chords" Papi used to play on the piano, the ones I always thought of as "ghost chords."

On that last trip to the Rockaways, Mami berated Papi for letting me fry in the sun. But he was so relieved to find her alive, he'd have taken her quejas any day. We sat in traffic and passed back and forth the now-cold bucket of Kentucky Fried Chicken. Salt and sand and crispy chicken skin crunched under my teeth until I washed it out with a flood of sweet but warm and flat soda. The fried chicken and Coke churned in my stomach as we sat in the sticky heat through traffic crossing Jamaica Bay, then the Belt Parkway to the Van Wyck, then the Grand Central to the BQE, until we finally reached home.

CHAPTER 21

Boston Market

"**WHEN I WAS IN** the DR, know what I missed the most?" Billy says, blowing on his bare hands in Montoya Park. The white vapor curls around his mouth, it's so cold. "It was this. New York at Christmastime."

"But you left *after* Christmas," I remind him.

"You know what I mean. It's winter, the seasons, Ma's lasagna, your pa's empanadas—"

"It's too cold out here," I interrupt. "Can we, like, move this indoors?"

"You want to go spend another four bucks on a coffee?"

"Point taken."

Christmas was Papi's favorite holiday. Last Christmas he went all out. It was the first and only time Papi had gotten up from the couch—let alone left the *apartment*—in a long time. It was weird, eerie almost. At the dinner table, filled with candles and pine and holly, Papi told stories of his past. We sat as a family, talking, laughing. The way normal families do. The way our family hadn't in years. At the time I remember thinking it was kind of weird, and random, that Papi had come to the literal table, but I quickly forgot it because I was having too much of a good time. Turned out, it was too good to be true.

I shake my head free of the thought.

"What are you and your parents"—Billy quickly catches himself—"you and your mom doing for Christmas?"

"Nothing, probably."

I have a feeling I have an anti-Christmas to look forward to with Ma. Just her and me, sitting awkwardly across from each other at the kitchen counter, picking at our plates of warmed-up leftovers.

"Bah humbug," Billy says. "You guys should do something. Especially *this* year."

You guys should do something. Especially this *year.* I know what Billy meant. That this is the first year without Papi.

So I broach it with Ma over breakfast.

"Ma, Christmas is next week. Are we doing anything?"

Ma is surprised. Her pink-frosted mouth goes round as a wreath.

"Already?" she says. "Honestly, I completely forgot, Aleja."

I've been going back and forth. Part of me wants to do something that would celebrate Papi. But the other part of me feels like it'd be too soon, too painful.

Maybe it's about baby steps?

"I was thinking . . ." I pause. "Maybe we could make empanadas together."

Ma makes a *plewwww* sound from her mouth, like farting. "Oh, Ale. That's too much work. It's a very busy time for me."

"It's a very busy time for me, too," I say.

I say that to mean *That's no excuse,* but Ma takes it to mean the other thing.

"Then neither of us has the time," she says briskly. She takes her uneaten bowl of Raisin Bran and my not-quite-finished bowl and drops them in the kitchen sink.

"Or what about a parrilla?" I call out to her as she rinses the bowls. When she says nothing, I go to her in the kitchen and say, "On the fire escape?"

"Don't be ridiculous, Aleja. You want to get in trouble with the super?"

Funny how she never put up a stink about it in the past. But I don't mention that.

I get the sense that if Ma had her way, we'd just sit around and do nothing and wait for the day to be over. But she sees me not giving up on this.

"Okay, okay," Ma says after she finishes in the kitchen and gets ready for work. She zips her coat over her uniform. "I'll think of something special for the two of us."

PAPI AND I USED to make empanadas the week before Christmas, the way some families make holiday cookies. We'd distribute some to the neighbors and friends and family and save the rest for Christmas Day.

Then, come Christmas, Papi would grill asado on a charcoal hibachi on the fire escape (it was the holidays; our building management must have looked the other way). Mami would make the chimichurri sauce to go with the barbecued meat. I can still see Papi huddled in the cold, cupping his hands to his mouth and blowing over them with his warm breath. "Why don't you just cook it in the oven?" I once asked.

Papi and Mami exchanged a knowing smile. "¡Ojo!" Mami had said. "Never tell an Argentine man how to grill his meat."

We'd sit down to our Christmas dinner, in the glow of our miniature plastic tree, and dig into our steaks and empanadas.

It was, corny as it sounds, the Most Wonderful Time of the Year.

WHILE MA'S AT WORK on Christmas Day, I get the apartment ready. (Ma works on Christmas because we can't *not* afford her overtime pay.) I drag out the artificial tree from the back of the closet and set it up in the living room. I hang all our old ornaments we accumulated through the years: Snoopy and his red doghouse, Yoda with a lightsaber, My Little Pony mid-neigh. I drape the silver tinsel around the plastic branches, then wind the string of multicolored Christmas lights with the big fat bulbs around them.

Then I stand back and admire my handiwork. Not too shabby.

I plug in the lights. They twitch on. Then one bulb goes out—and the whole line goes down.

Ma and Papi got into a fight buying these lights at Target

in an after-Christmas sale. Papi wanted colorful and ginormous bulbs, and Ma wanted tasteful, tiny white ones that cost double. "The cheap ones are no good," Ma argued. "When one light goes, all the lights go dead. It's better to pay once instead of buying new ones every year."

"Your lights are boring," Papi said. "These"—he shook the box of rainbow lights—"look like joy."

I tipped the vote in Papi's favor, so we bought the cheap colorful ones.

And now the lights don't even work.

If I had to write an English class essay about my family, the metaphor of those Christmas lights would be a little *too* on point.

But my life isn't an English class essay. My life is just, life.

I hear Ma's key in the lock.

"Merry Christmas, Ma!" I say. I make an exaggerated sweep of my arms, just like those infomercial sales ladies, at the fake plastic tree with the dead Christmas lights.

Ma's eyes don't even flicker in that direction.

"Feliz navi." She says it all tired, like she's just going through the motions.

She's got plastic food bags, which she dumps on the table with little ceremony. She looks tired, annoyed, bedraggled.

Ma's *I'll think of something special* means two turkey platters she picked up from Boston Market on her way home. I know I should be grateful. Dinner probably cost her more than an hour's wages. I think of all the starving children in Syria *and* Ethiopia *and* North Korea. I think of the blatant Hallmarkification of Christmas, with its sickly saccharine promise of cheery tidings.

But still, but still—I want a proper Christmas. A home-cooked meal prepared together. A sliver of light through this whole mess of a year.

"Don't bother with plates," Ma calls out. "Less dishes to deal with later—" She stops midsentence. She's staring at the dining table, which I've set with three place settings. One for Ma, one for me, and one for—

"Alejandra, what's that?" Ma says sharply.

"I just thought . . ."

There's nothing to think. Ma's already briskly clearing off the third place setting.

She sinks into a chair and slides over a Boston Market platter to me. She's still wearing her scrubs.

"Aren't you going to change?" I ask her. I dressed up, wearing a red sweater and a green skirt I dug out of the closet.

"Alejandra, I'm tired."

I can't help but think how the molecules of her patients, their debris and the dust of their decaying junk, are sitting right there at the table with us, coating an invisible layer over the Boston Market and filling in the air we breathe. But whatever.

Ma splurged on the holiday platter: white meat turkey plus three sides. So I try to make an effort.

"So how was . . . your day?" I ask.

After a long pause, Ma finally answers me. "Horrible," she says. "My day was horrible."

"What happened?"

"I don't want to talk about it."

Ma doesn't touch her food. Instead she reaches for her cigarettes. She fixes her large eyes on me. They once shined black—with anger, with passion; they mirrored whatever it was she was feeling. Now they're mostly dull and flat, like she's seeing but not seeing.

Ma used to be so beautiful, so sophisticated. I'd look at old pictures of her with envy, wondering when I would start to grow into her features. But I take after Papi, with a round face and chubby cheeks, more cute than pretty.

Now Ma's face is lined with age and unhappiness and too much smoking. Her once-alabaster skin is stretched thin over the bones of her face. Maybe it's the bad lighting from the fluorescent bulbs, but I have never seen her so ashen.

I stab my turkey. "You never want to talk about anything."

"Let's just try to have a nice day, okay?" Ma flicks ash over her uneaten turkey.

"Why'd you buy the Boston Market"—I point my plastic spork at her plate—"if you're not going to bother to eat it?"

Instead of answering, Ma lets out a long and exasperated cigarette exhale. I cough exaggeratedly.

"You should quit that. Smoking's disgusting."

"¡Por favor, Ale!" Ma cries. "Dejame en paz."

So for the rest of the meal, I leave her in peace, just like she requested. I eat my dry turkey and she just picks at hers.

For dessert, Ma brings out a chocolate cupcake in a bakery box.

"Papi hated chocolate," I blurt out. It's true—he had a raging sweet tooth, but it was always for stuff like caramelly dulce de leche and fruity desserts. For whatever reason, he hated chocolate.

Ma sinks her fork into the cupcake and takes a bite. Which is weird, because she ate none of her actual dinner.

I don't eat the cupcake. I say, "How could you forget that?"

Ma's mouth is full of chocolate. "Ale, don't start."

I start.

"First you don't want to celebrate Christmas. Then you clear his place setting from the table, and now with the chocolate. It's like you're trying to erase him from memory!"

She grits her teeth. "Stop this nonsense *right now*."

"You know how much Papi loved this holiday. Why do you have to pretend like he's not even here?" I say. "I feel him, right here at this table, sitting down to dinner with us. I feel him out there on the fire escape, cooking asado." I point to the black leather couch. "And I feel him lying there, depressed, before he decided to—"

"STOP!" Ma shoves her hands to her ears. "Stop it, stop it, stop it! Your father had an *accident*."

The neighbors in 1B are banging broomsticks on their ceiling, the universal sign for *Keep it down*. I ignore them.

"STOP LYING, MA!" I shout back. "Papi died by—by *suicide*." I can barely get the word out; it dribbles out like a whisper.

I'm too mad to tell her I don't actually have any empirical proof of this. But deep down, I just *know*.

Ma looks like the word punched her in the mouth. She swallows hard. "Don't you dare use that word in this house," she warns.

"Come on, Ma! You and I both know it. Stop being in denial!"

"IT'S CHRISTMAS, FOR CHRISSAKES!" screams 1B. "SHUT THE FUCK UP!"

Now Ma ignores them. "I swear, Alejandra Verónica Kim, if you say that word one more time—"

The words, heavy in my chest, can't stop themselves from bubbling up:

"Face the truth, Ma. Papi was unhappy and depressed and he killed himself!"

BOOM. Then, quiet. It's like the aftermath of an explosion, the silence post-storm. The dust settles, and Ma is staring back at me with a strange, wild look I've never seen before.

She gets up and sweeps the chocolate cupcake into the garbage. Then she grabs her keys and coat.

"So you're going to walk out on me, too?" I retort as she goes to the door.

Ma musters a calm voice. "I'm going to leave before *I* say something I regret."

That's the way I hear it, anyway. Which only drives a knife of guilt through me.

The door slams shut behind her.

I feel like crap, because I know I've ruined Christmas for the both of us. But I just can't take Ma's denials any longer. I throw out the remains of dinner. I brush my teeth and climb into bed. I didn't even get to give Ma the gift I made her: a playlist of Argentine pop hits from the 1980s she can listen to on her phone on her commute to work.

After Papi died, I found his old flannel work shirt in the

back of the hallway closet. Ma threw out all his things immediately after the funeral, so this was all that was left. Every night, I clutched the work shirt in bed like a security blanket. It smelled like parsley and Irish Spring soap and WD-40. As the days passed, Papi's smell receded, and my smell, my fruity shampoos and whatever junior-year junk I was dousing myself with, overwhelmed the shirt, until all traces of Papi disappeared from the cloth entirely and I felt like I had nothing left of him.

Then Ma found the flannel shirt in my closet and threw it in the trash.

Of course, I have my memories. But I fear they will grow patchy and worn, just like Papi's shirt. My memories of him are already starting to fade—the way all vivid colors do when exposed to the light.

CAN'T SLEEP, SO I open Michael Oppa's laptop. I stare again at the revised draft of my Whyder essay. It's polished, the writing's clear, the topic is relevant—trendy, even. I could hit "send" and be done with it. *It just doesn't sound like the Alley-Cat I know. Just be yourself!*

I delete the essay file and start from scratch. I write and write, until the light starts filtering in through the windows and I hear Ma coming home from wherever she was. I don't ask, and I know she won't tell.

***

THE NEXT MORNING I can smell Ma's lavender shampoo and lotion scent, but there's no sign of her or her coat and bag and keys. She's already left for work.

I spot a present under the tree. It's from Ma, and it's wrapped in plain brown paper. I open it.

It's a book of Borges poems called *Fervor de Buenos Aires*. I open it. There's an inscription in faded blue ink:

JUAN KIM, ESCUELA Nº 5 GENERAL ROCA

It's Papi's school copy from when he was a kid. I press the book close to my heart.

CHAPTER 22

Melty's

ON BOXING DAY, per annual tradition, Billy and I go ice-skating. We don't go to amateur hour at the ice rink in Rockefeller Center, with all the Christmas-tree gawkers. We go to Bryant Park, where you can skate for free if you bring your own. Billy borrows skates for us from his cousin and his cousin's girlfriend. They're a size too big, but nothing that an extra pair of socks doesn't fix.

The line to get in is still half a million people long, all cheapskates like us. Because when you're a New York City kid with no money, time becomes your bargaining chip. You do things like wait on line for free stuff or schlep all the way to the Bronx for half-priced movies. Once, Billy and I even stood on line in Central Park all day because some Wall Streeter on Craigslist offered to pay us a hundred bucks each to score him free tickets to Shakespeare in the Park.

Everything's a hustle in New York.

Finally we get to the front of the line. We hit the ice. Billy and I are both terrible at skating, but that's part of the fun: first one to fall has to buy the other one hot chocolate.

Billy goes down first. "Damn!" he says, skidding across the ice, nearly knocking over two kids and their parents like a bowling ball picking up a spare.

"That hot chocolate is going to taste *so* good," I say, rubbing my hands together like a TV supervillain.

This makes me lose my balance, and I fall down, too.

Billy laughs at my sorry ass. There go his dimples again.

We skate a few laps, which is taking all the core strength I don't have. Yeah, I'm clumsy on ice, but at least I'm trying. Unlike those people over there hugging the guard rail the whole way around the rink. I put myself out there, even if it means falling down and getting bruised all over ad nauseam.

"So? How was Christmas?" Billy asks as we try to weave around a family spread five-across. Even on ice, there's traffic.

"You go first."

"We went to Tito's. His girlfriend made pernil, tía made rice and beans, and Ma made her famous lasagna."

"And what'd the menfolk make?" I ask.

That's something our cultures have in common: traditionally the women do all the cooking, cleaning, and serving, and the men sit back and watch TV and eat the platters of food placed on their laps. Gary Gomobu is exactly the same way, and so are all our extended relatives. I guess it makes me lucky that Papi never was that way—he loved to cook.

"You know how it is." Billy shrugs. Not like he's going to change the system single-handedly. "Meanwhile, Ma made me her sous-chef. I had to chop up everything, and she swooped in and got all the Lasagna Glory." Billy smiles.

Unfair division of labor notwithstanding, Billy's Christmas sounds magical compared to mine. When it's my turn to talk, I briefly sketch our Christmas Day. Billy infers more from the silences than the actual words I'm saying.

"Lots of negative energy coming off you," he says.

"Well, I didn't sleep," I tell him. "I kept worrying about where Ma was in the middle of the night."

Billy gives it to me straight. "I don't know, Ale. To me, it kind of sounds like you were a dick to your mom."

"Excuse me. *She* was being a 'dick' to me."

I put it in quotes because Laurel *hates* that word—*I mean, would you call someone a "vagina"?* Then I tell Billy how much *I* hate that word and how I shouldn't have used it.

"Chill, Ale. I don't police your language," Billy says, "unlike everyone at your school."

"Still."

Billy moves on to make his bigger point. "I totally get that you want to do things like your papi's— Like things are the way they used to be. Like the tree, or the place setting, whatever. But sounds like your ma's not there yet."

As Billy talks, I start to see things his way: That Ma tried to make an effort. That she is coping in her own way.

"Why you got to be the voice of reason all of a sudden?" I say to Billy. But it's not the first time I've thought it. He always shows both sides of the story.

***

AFTER A WHILE, THE ice rink starts to feel as crowded as the 7 express at rush hour, and we've worked up an appetite. We leave Bryant Park and head to my favorite deli in the city, Melty's. I like it because it's a lone mom-and-pop, run by an older Korean couple, smack in the middle of Corporate America. We get our hot chocolates and wait for our sandwich orders.

A distinctly Korean-looking girl is working the grill. She's just a kid. Yet she's cracking eggs with one hand and tossing bacon and potatoes with the other. She whirls—catches potatoes in midair with a spatula, flips the eggs, plates up an order, then the next and the next and the next. It's like watching a prodigy circus performer on a tightrope, juggling a dozen plates.

I nudge Billy to watch. He whistles. "Damn, she's good."

We grab two stools that face the street and dig into our lunches. Melty's sandwiches are the best. Billy got a roast beef hero with house-made horseradish mayo, and I got an egg-and-cheese on a roll, because I'm classic like that.

"You done with your Whyder app yet?" Billy asks, already halfway through his sandwich.

I take a bite of mine. Nom. I don't know how they get the egg filling so fluffy yet creamy. My eggs always turn out sad and overcooked.

"Just about," I say, trying not to think of the mess of a computer file waiting for me back home. I have one week before the deadline. "Then I hear back sometime in April. Whyder's always the last to send out notifications."

"Right," Billy says, remembering. "Because they send them by carrier pigeon."

"Ha ha."

"So this is really happening," Billy says. "You, leaving New York."

"Only *if* I get into Whyder," I point out. "And if Ma lets me go. Both of which are huge ifs."

"Leaving's not all it's cracked up to be," Billy says. "Sometimes it's good to be home."

I brush sandwich crumbs off the counter. Then reach for my pen in my purse and a fresh napkin. "So. What's your list of colleges, Chivi? Let's hash it out: dreams, reaches, and safeties."

"Ale—"

"If we start now, you can use the summer to work on your—"

"Ale!" Billy swipes the napkin from under me. It crumples in his hand.

"Some recruiters stopped by the body shop today. Tito tried to chase them off, but . . . I don't know, it actually sounded not bad. There's a good signing bonus. And maybe my mom won't have to keep working like a dog."

I'm confused at first; since when do college recruiters show up at auto body shops and offer signing bonuses? But Billy's not talking about college. He's talking about—

"The Marines," he continues, "offer some pretty good benefits, too. I mean, I'm practically eighteen. I play my cards right, maybe I could retire at forty."

"If you *live* to see forty!" I cry. "What the hell, Billy! You're too smart for that. Did we or did we not watch that special on channel 13 about the Vietnam vets? What, you want to sign up so you can become cannon fodder?"

"It's just an idea," Billy says. "Chill out, Ale."

My silence lets Billy know I think his military idea is bullshit.

"Does your mom know about this?" I finally ask.

"Not yet." Billy flexes his fingers and starts cracking his knuckles, which he does whenever he's anxious.

"Good," I say, relieved. Because I know, and he knows, that Mrs. D would *never* approve.

"But she could really use the signing bonus," he adds. "Now that the building's going co-op."

I remember seeing the envelopes from Jackson Heights Residential Services on the counter. Like most of Ma's mail, they're in an unopened heap. "Give it to me straight, Billy. What's going on? Ma won't tell me a thing."

"The building's going co-op," Billy explains. "And they're offering us renters first dibs to buy our apartments."

"That's . . . a good thing?" I say tentatively.

"Yeah, if you have the plata"—Billy rubs his fingers together—"to make it work."

"Otherwise?"

"Otherwise . . ." Billy shrugs. "I guess they let you stick around for a while. Before they find someone else to take your place."

"Chivi. Promise me you won't go running off and doing something stupid. Look me dead in the eyes—" I stop, start again. "Just swear to me you won't."

I hold out my pinky finger. Billy laughs.

"What are we, back in junior high?"

Billy grabs my hand with his hand. Is it just me, or is that . . . tingles? This feels súper weird. My nostrils are filled with Billy's peppery-mapley cologne. I should make a joke—*Billy, stop dousing yourself in Tito's Axe! You're single-handedly burning through the ozone layer!*—but I don't. My cheeks are burning a little. Maybe it's from being out in the freezing cold and suddenly coming indoors? Or maybe—

Billy's eyes catch mine. They look questioningly at me.

"Excuse me," a voice interrupts.

We turn around. Someone's reaching for the napkin dispenser between us.

"Sorry," we mumble, and break apart.

Whatever I thought this was, I was definitely imagining it. Billy and I are *so* friend zone. Always have been and always will be.

"Yo, Kim," Billy says when the customer is gone. He's putting on his extra bro-ey voice, like he thinks I'm one of the dudes. "Let me get a bite of that."

We switch sandwiches. "Damn, that's good," he says.

"Yours, too," I say, wiping the horseradish mayo from my mouth.

"They do something different here," he says. "It's just an egg-and-cheese, but it's also *not* just an egg-and-cheese."

And whatever moment that was—or was not—is gone.

AFTER MELTY'S, NEITHER OF us feels like heading home yet, so we walk around. We head north, and the sidewalks grow denser with people. I wouldn't mind the tourists if only they didn't walk like clueless zombies down the street. They stop dead in their tracks to gawk at the Empire State Building/30 Rock/

Chrysler Building, leaving you to crash into them from behind. They're practically wearing signs around their Panasonicked necks saying, MUG ME! I will *not* be that chump caught between them. I swivel my pocketbook so it's flat against my stomach instead of draped unattended down my back.

We step out to cross Fifth Avenue when the M4 comes barreling down the street. "Watch out!" Billy yells, pulling us back. Just in time—or the bus would have sideswiped us.

"Fuck you, asshole!" we shout in unison at the driver as the bus speeds away.

"Are you all right?" I ask.

"Are *you* all right?"

"I'm fine," we both say at the same time.

We keep walking. We're practically at the Park. We pass an abandoned building with a high, arched doorway. There's something familiar about it, and I realize I've been here before, with Papi.

I stop dead in my tracks. Which causes the person behind me to crash into *me*. A suit with a briefcase glares at me.

"My bad," I say sheepishly, but I'm already in the suit's rear-view mirror.

It's FAO Schwarz. Papi used to take me to this toy store as a kid. But it's no longer what it once was. It's closed down now.

When I was really little, Papi would take me to FAO. We'd wait our turn to stomp on the gigantic piano keyboard. Together we would play the simple tunes he taught me on the Casio back home: "Chopsticks," "Hot Cross Buns." The last time we went, though, things felt different. Papi told me to hop on B, while he struck C at the same time. I hesitated. You weren't supposed to play two keys right next to each other, I told Papi.

It's jazz, Papi said. No such thing as "supposed to."

We jammed down on the notes. They sounded haunting, hollow—like an eerie mistake.

I stare into the abandoned building, a shell of the former FAO. It looks like how Papi's chords feel. I pull Billy away.

CHAPTER 23

Deathiversary

NEW YEAR, NEW YOU! says just about every subway and bus ad. But it feels more like New Year, Same Old Me.

January 2. One year ago today is the day that Papi died. Ma and I take the LIRR to Great Neck, where we'll get a car service to Tía Yoona's house. Tía Yoona would have picked us up at the station, but Ma wants to save her the trouble. From there, we'll drive out to the cemetery where Papi is buried.

I mentioned the memorial to Billy after we left Melty's. Told him I wished he could come, but it was kind of Tía Yoona's thing. He waved off the not-offer. "Why would I want to celebrate your dad's death?" Billy scoffed. "That's so dumb. I'd rather remember all the ways he was alive."

Billy texts me while I'm on the LIRR. You hangin in?

Trying to.

Stay strong, avoid the bullshit.

Laurel texts, too: Thinking of you today. Sending all the hugs.

It warms my heart that my two best friends remembered today.

MA GLARES UP AT Tía Yoona's house as our taxi pulls into the circular driveway. The house is—no joke—straight out of Gatsby, if Gatsby were a Korean immigrant who ran a dry cleaners instead of a white Midwestern bootlegger from the roaring twenties. It's the whole obscene, nouveau riche West Egg thing, right down to the Greco-Roman columns and rose-bushes. I mean—columns! If only the Happy Day customers knew. Maybe they'd treat us with a little more dignity.

Then again, prob not.

Ma and I crunch up to the door. On second thought, I doubt Gatsby would be okay with anchovies and ginger slices drying out on newspapers in the front yard. Tía Yoona is so funny like that. She drives a white Mercedes—it's parked right out front—but in some ways she's as frugal as a Great Depression granny. She saves Ziploc baggies and yells at Michael Oppa and Jason for wasting paper towels.

People are full of contradictions.

Tía Yoona greets us at the door. She and Ma have a chilly hello. Ma hands her our salad bowl. It's a wilted, pathetic-looking salad, straight out of a bag with premade dressing. I think it died on us by the time we passed Flushing.

Tía Yoona accepts the salad like it's the awesomest thing in the world.

"Thank you, Ale-Umma. Not necessary." Tía calls Ma

172

"Ale's-Mom." It's this Korean thing where parents refer to each other by the name of their firstborn. It's like you're literally defined by your role as a mother.

"Thank you to have us, Michael-Umma."

They're doing fake-nice speak. I can tell because Tía Yoona switches over to Korean, and Ma speaks in English.

Their move reminds me of a study we talked about in Dr. C's class, where a trauma victim refused to tell her story in any other language but English, even though it wasn't her first language. She was a Chinese immigrant. She said it would be "impossible" to do it in Chinese because the language was too close to her emotions. English gave her a safe and sterile distance.

I can't help but wonder if that's what Ma and Tía Yoona are doing now by not speaking in Spanish. They're each using their weaker tongue to try to keep the peace.

Unlike last year when shit went down—todo transmitido en español—between them after the funeral. Hundreds of people I had never met, and doubt Papi had ever met, showed up at Joongang Funeral Home in Flushing. They were Gary Gomobu and Tía Yoona's friends from church. Ma and Tía had been simmering all day—from the funeral Mass to the limo ride to the cemetery, then to Tía Yoona's house for a funeral banquet. After all the guests left, we were cleaning up in the kitchen. Ma, drying dishes, stopped to dab her eyes and blow her nose. Tía Yoona, scrubbing a pot, threw down her sponge and said:

"So *now* you pretend like you care about my brother?"

"What's that supposed to mean?"

"Dale, Vero. You made him miserable since the day you two got married."

Ma let out a *chuh!* of disbelief. "¡Mirá a vos! It's disgusting, how you and your husband keep showing off your money! You think that didn't start to eat away at Juan? You think—"

Tía Yoona let out a short laugh. "Like you didn't chew him up and spit him out every single day? You Chu women are all the same. Waving your pretty noses in the air, treating everyone like servants. You've always thought you're too good for Juan!"

Ma glared at Tía Yoona, ice-hot. "Says the woman who bossed Juan around his whole life. ¡Vos tenés la culpa igual!"

"Damn! Our moms are going at it," Jason said, smacking my arm.

"Shut up, Jason," I say, wishing for a pithier comeback.

"You shut up, Ah-rae."

That's Jason's nickname for me: Ah-rae. It's the Korean word for "below" or "beneath." It's also a stupid play on "Ale"—native Korean speakers have trouble pronouncing the "l" sound, and it comes out kind of like an "r"—and Jason took that and ran with it. So he's also kind of doing yellow-face.

I wished so badly that Michael Oppa had come back to the house after the funeral. But he and Gary Gomobu don't talk, period.

Tía Yoona went quiet. It was eerie. Tía Yoona never *doesn't* have something to say. She and Papi were like that—always anxious to fill dead silences.

Finally Tía spoke. "Lo amabas, ¿Verónica?"

Ma was hunched over the sink, shaking.

"You never loved him, did you."

Ma made no answer.

"Lamento el día en que se conocieron," Tía Yoona said, and turned her back on Ma.

They haven't spoken since. Until now.

TÍA YOONA PLACES MA'S sorry salad bowl on a table already swimming with other dishes.

"That's so much food, Tía," I say.

"Really? I'm afraid is not enough." Tía Yoona frowns. "Is late, vamos. Jason, ¡Apurate!" Then, in a softer tone, she calls out to Gary Gomobu in Korean, "Yobo! Naeryeo-o-saeyo!"

I don't know what we're going to be late for—it's not like Papi's waiting for us six feet under. I think about making that joke, because that's what I sometimes do in uncomfortable situations. But it's in poor taste, and I know better than that.

My cousin Jason comes bounding down the stairs. His long bangs fall in front of his pimply forehead.

"What up, Ah-rae," he says.

Jason has the IQ of an Idaho potato but somehow got into Brooklyn Tech. With all due respect to the people of Idaho and their signature crop. He started flunking out of Tech—it's what happens when you cut class every day to play *StarCraft* at PC bangs on Bell Boulevard—and Tía Yoona packed up the family and moved from Bayside to Long Island so Jason could start over at Great Neck South.

"You still applying to Whyder?" he says. "I hear those girls never shave their legs. Don't go turning into Sasquatch."

"I'm ninety-nine-point-five-percent sure you're being sexist,"

I retort. "Where are *you* applying? Nassau Community, or are your grades not good enough?"

Jason laughs it off. "For your information, I applied to Princeton. 1510 on the SATs, baby."

Like I said: Idaho potato.

"Your mom told me you got a seventy-eight on your last history test."

He turns red in the face and says something in Korean I can't catch. He does this on purpose because he knows I can't really speak it. At home, Ma and Papi mostly spoke Spanish with some English. Korean was only for when they were reaching for words untranslatable in the other two languages. Ma and Papi are second-generation Argentines. But Tía Yoona, who was born in Korea, is 1.5-generation—Korean's technically her first language, even though she did all her schooling in Spanish. And Gary Gomobu was born and raised in Korea and came to America as an adult. In Jason's house, they mostly speak Korean with some English, and only a tiny bit of Spanish when Tía Yoona is in a hurry or her tongue gets confused.

"You didn't understand that, right?" Jason sneers. "What kind of Korean are you, Ah-rae?"

His words wouldn't sting so much if he were a complete loser. But the thing is, Jason is considered a "cool Korean." He and all his Korean American friends dress and style their hair like they're in a K-pop band. I am considered—at least by Jason and his friends—to be a "bad" Korean because I don't know the first thing about what it means to be one.

"Whatever, Jason," I say, and when Gary Gomobu finally

comes down the stairs, we all pile into the car and head to the cemetery.

JUAN KIM

EXPECTAMUS DOMINUM
REST IN PEACE

I stare at Papi's gravestone. I can't believe he's buried just beneath us—so close physically, and yet he's never been farther away. We do three rounds of the rosary, everyone saying the Hail Mary in different languages: Tía Yoona and Gary Gomobu in Korean, Ma in Spanish, Jason and me in English. It's freezing cold at the cemetery. I slip on a patch of ice; I'm about to fall, but Jason of all people catches me.

"Dork," he says as he helps me right myself.

CARS ARE LINED UP in Tía Yoona's driveway. Tía mutters, "We're late, we're late."

More and more cars pull up to the house. Dozens of people spill out. It's like all the Koreans of New York have arrived. I don't know any of these people. Tía Yoona goes into full-on host mode, rushing out to greet everyone.

I turn to Ma. "I thought it was just supposed to be the family. Did you know all these people would be here?"

"Church people, I don't know." Ma shrugs. "I don't control your tía and gomobu."

Now I understand the feast Tía's prepared: galbi, japchae

noodles, pajeon, boiled pork slices, hwe (raw fish), at least five different kinds of kimchi. Tía had this meal catered, like it's a freaking party instead of the memorial for Papi's death. Even a priest walks in, like the opening line of a bad joke.

The cura blesses the meal. Then the church people are shoving to get closer to the food. I wonder if any of them said so much as a kind word to Papi when he was alive. If these people even knew who he was.

On the banquet table, pushed nearly to the edge, is a platter of deep-fried dumplings. They look rough-and-not-so-ready: the crimp is imperfect, and they're all uneven—some burnt, some pale and underdone. Some are overstuffed, others deflated with too little filling. They stand out in sharp contrast to all the picture-perfect catered Korean food. Empanadas. I realize this is the only dish Tía Yoona made by hand. Tears spring to my eyes.

An ahjumma with a bad perm elbows me out of the way and points at the platter of empanadas. "Michael-Umma," she calls out noisily to my aunt, "i-mandu-ga wae-i-rae?" She's staring at them with lips curled.

What's wrong with these mandu? This much Korean I do understand.

"They're not mandu," I say in English. "They're *empanadas*."

My tone is frosty. Tía Yoona flashes me a warning look: *Be nice.*

The ahjumma's frown deepens. "Mandu-deun, mwuh-deun," she says, which I think means *Mandu, schmandu.*

Then the ahjumma *pokes* the empanadas—my father's

empanadas, at *his* memorial—with her chopsticks, causing the thin skin to tear. Filling comes pouring out. I lose it.

I snatch the platter from the woman's prying chopsticks. "Get your HANDS OFF Papi's empanadas!"

Ma, who's been standing beside me, suddenly claws my arm. The universal signal for *Shut. It. Down.*

The ahjumma blinks and blinks and blinks, like my words are unseemly drops of spittle I've just spewed in her face. "Yae-neun wae-i-rae?" she says to Tía Yoona, not even bothering to address me. *What's wrong with this one?*

And then, like a knife twist to the heart, Tía Yoona does not swoop to my defense. She does not say, "Stop disrespecting my family! Get the *hell* out of my house. And take your bad ahjumma perm with you!"

Instead, Tía offers the ahjumma an embarrassed smile. "Please forgive my niece." She goes on about my disrespectfulness in way-too-complicated Korean.

Before I can say another word, Ma pulls me away.

MA GETS US A call-taxi home. The whole ride, I expect her to flip her shit at my outburst. *How dare you act like a child? You humiliated the whole family!* My cheeks are already burning with embarrassment at my little tantrum. I don't know where all that emotion was coming from. But all day, I've been feeling run-down. From standing over Papi's grave, knowing that he was buried just six feet below me—so close and yet not there at all. And he's never coming back. I was feeling *everything* in that moment—that stupid ahjumma who insulted the empanadas, the assembly at school, my quasi fight and makeup with Laurel, everything I talked about with Billy—

And that's what made me burst.

How's it going? Michael Oppa texts me while we're in the taxi. He's minding the fort at Happy Day. Thinking of you today. Sending biceps.

You don't want to know. I'll tell him all about what went down at Tía Yoona's later. Also no one spells out emojis.

"Your papi would have hated that," Ma says.

"I know, Ma. I already said I'm sorry—"

"No, I mean, the memorial," Ma interrupts. "The whole showiness of it. It wasn't his style."

"I hated it, too, Ma. All those people who probably never knew him. It was . . . demasiado."

Ma says, "Your little outburst there—it reminded me just of your father." She lets out a chuckle. "When he used to play piano, that is. In those clubs, back when we were dating. He played with so much genuine emotion, like he couldn't contain himself."

"Really?" I like this picture of Papi. Because he was always so gentle and mild mannered. I never got to see this other side of him.

"He played jazz with—how do you say? Fervor. I don't know how you say in English. He played with his whole body and energy. It was like the whole world went away, and the music was the only thing that mattered."

I stare out the windshield of our taxi. Far off, I can see the elevated subway lines in the distance. The 7 and N/W trains crisscross ahead, and deeper in the distance is the jagged edge of the Midtown skyline. I think of Papi's Subway Music.

"Ma," I say. "I'm sorry. For our fight on Christmas. I just . . . I wanted him there—"

Ma stops me. "*I'm* sorry. I didn't want to fight with you, either. But the Irish viejita I worked for, Mrs. O'Gall, she died." I'm struck by the baldness of Mom's words. "I was hoping for a half day, and this is God's sense of irony."

"She passed away on *Christmas?*"

I feel like the biggest jerk, the world's worst daughter. I had no idea Ma's patient died that day. She must have felt awful. "Horrible" was Ma's word for the day, but she didn't elaborate.

Based on the few stories Ma's shared about Mrs. O'Gall, the old lady seemed to take a special pleasure in tormenting my mother. In her encroaching senility, she called Ma "the Chinawoman" and would ask her if she was there to pick up the laundry. She'd hold back the last of her excrement until just after my mother swaddled her into a new diaper before defecating again, and she'd laugh as my mother had to clean up yet another shitty mess.

"The worst of it," Ma goes on, surprising me with her talkative mood, "was the family. You couldn't drag her son from his Westchester mansion. His poor mother passes, and all he thinks about is his Christmas turkey." Her eyes flash, briefly, with anger before they resume their dull luster.

Usually Ma speaks about her patients with a cool, sterile tone. But she cannot shake the emotion from her voice.

"I couldn't help but think: *Did she hold out until today? Just to spite them?*" she says. "We carried so many years together."

For a moment I think she is talking about Papi, but I realize she's talking about Mrs. O'Gall.

"I felt—a feel—jung for the viejita."

"What's 'jung'?" I ask. It must be a Spanish word I don't know.

"'Jung' is . . ." She pauses to think. "It's like love, but not as apasionado. It's like affection, but something deeper. It's when you carry so many years together, when you endure not just the ups but the downs—it brings you closer. I learned the word from my own mother."

"Jung" is not Spanish at all, but Korean.

"Aleja, querida." She hasn't called me "sweetie" since I was little. "I know you're going through a lot of pain right now. I am, too. But . . . can't you just let me hurt in my own way? You're all I have left, Alejandra. ¿Entendés? And if I lose you, too—"

She blinks rapidly.

"And Tía is hurting in her own way," Ma says, composing herself. "Who knows? Maybe she felt she owed it to Papi to give him a big banquet, ¡qué sé yo! To honor him in ways she couldn't when he was still alive."

I never thought of it that way. And what Ma says now makes sense.

"Do you know how much Tía Yoona sacrificed for your father?" Ma goes on. "She immigrated here when she was very young and married Gary Gomobu. Don't tell your cousins this, but Tía did it so she could bring Papi to America."

"I had no idea," I say to Ma. I always thought it was weird how in their wedding portrait, Gary Gomobu looks like a full-on ajoshi, and Tía Yoona looks like a teen bride. "Is that really true?"

Ma nods. "Please, querida. Give Tía more time. Time to heal." She blinks hard. "And . . . Mami needs time to heal, too."

I stopped calling Ma "Mami" when Papi died. And she hasn't referred to herself that way since.

I feel a surge of tenderness. I feel like Ma and I haven't been right since Papi died, but even long before. And now we're taking steps to get closer.

I decide to tell Ma. Even though I know it will hurt her more. But sometimes you just have to Band-Aid it. She deserves to know.

"Ma, I have to tell you something. I'm applying to Whyder College. I know you don't want me to, but—"

Her mouth makes a tight line. It's like whatever steps we took forward together, I've undone them all now.

"It's a long shot," I add hastily. "I'm probably not getting in anyway. But it's something I need to do."

"Who am I to tell you what to do?" Ma says flatly. She turns away from me, staring out the window.

As soon as I start to think we're coming together, as soon as I think Ma and I are overcoming our differences and starting to make a breakthrough . . .

The moment is lost.

We ride the rest of the way home in silence.

CHAPTER 24

Korean Empanadas

THE NEXT MORNING AT Happy Day, I tell Tía Yoona I'm sorry. "No pasa nada," she says, waving off my apology. *No biggie.*

"But I ruined the memorial. I'm so sorry, Tía. I don't know what came over me."

"I confess to you something?" Tía says.

"What?"

"That ahjumma with the empanadas . . . ! She makes me so angry."

"Right?" I say, surprised.

"No respect," Tía tuts.

"Tía, why did you make those empanadas?" I ask.

But now there's a line of customers. After we process them, Tía says, "In Argentina, your papi used to beg your halmoni to make him empanadas. He wants to be like all the other boys at school. But Halmoni has no idea how to make empanadas!" So my grandmother improvised the recipe using the food vocabulary she knew.

"So that's why there's japchae noodles in the filling," I say. "And soy sauce marinade for the beef."

"Eso," Tía Yoona says, nodding. "Your papi used to *hate* those empanadas. So embarrassing!" She lets out a laugh.

"Your papi has a hard time," she continues. "At school, they tease him, che, Chino! En Argentina, no les importa si somos coreanos o japoneses o lo que sea; somos todos 'chinos' iguales."

"That's so racist," I say.

"Maybe you not understand, Ale-ya. You are born here. But in Argentina, they think is 'okay.' No such thing as, what you call? 'PC.' You have tan, they nickname you 'Negra.' You gain weight, they call you 'Gorda.' Jewish, you are 'Rusa.' Big nose"—I wonder if Tía Yoona realizes this rather offensive free association she's just made—"you're 'Narigón.' You have wheelchair, you're 'Rueda.' They not care, just think is funny and irónico."

"Then why didn't Papi just start making the empanadas the 'normal' way?" I ask. Baked, not fried. No cellophane noodles or soy sauce marinade.

"When we immigrate to Mi-Guk," Tía explains, "your papi was homesick for Nam-Mi. *That's* when he started to miss them."

"Why would he be homesick for Argentina if everyone was racist to him?"

"Because your papi had jung for Nam-Mi."

There's Ma's word again, from yesterday. It starts to take shape and meaning inside me.

Tía Yoona lets out another laugh. "Sabías, your halmoni forced me to help make those empanadas? I hate so much! I always burn myself with oil and smell greasy. Your papi never has to lift one finger, because he was boy. After we immigrate here, your papi start to make them."

"But Tía Yoona, you forgot to add the parsley. Papi always made them with parsley." Hastily I add, "No offense."

"I *knew* I forget something!" Tía laughs. "Even though he never make not even once in Argentina, why his empanadas always better than mine? No tiene sentido."

But it makes perfect sense. Because for Papi, those neither-this-nor-that empanadas were what started to taste like home.

WHEN I GET HOME from Happy Day, I open my Whyder application file. I know what I need to write.

Korean Empanadas

By Alejandra Kim
Whyder College Supplemental Essay, Final Draft
Word Count: 566

Most people are confused by my family's empanadas, but that's kind of been the story of my life: my normal is everyone else's weird.

Papi and I used to make empanadas every Christmas. While Ma wrestled with lighting the hibachi on our fire escape so we could grill steaks for dinner, Papi and I got to work chopping and seasoning and crimping and frying. Our empanadas are Goya wrappers filled with soy-sauce-marinated ground beef, hard-boiled eggs, japchae noodles, Spanish olives, and parsley. Deep-fried to a perfect golden crust.

To be honest, empanadas are kind of a pain to cook. You have to prep each ingredient individually. Then you mix the cooked filling together and wait for it to cool down, before stuffing and crimping them just right with a perfectly tight seal. Otherwise, the thin empanada skins will tear, and everything inside will come spilling out, like a bad secret.

When we'd bring them to Lunar New Year, my extended family was all, "What's up with these demented* mandu?"

When we'd bring them to Mrs. González down the hall before she went to the nursing home, she was all, "Estas no son empanadas."

I think Papi used to like making them because he was homesick. The traditional Argentine empanada is baked, but when Papi was growing up in Buenos Aires, his family didn't have an oven. All they had was a hot plate, so they had to make do.

I never brought our family's empanadas to school on International Day. All the other kids brought "normal" foods like pastelitos and pork bao and samosas. I was too ashamed, because our empanadas were neither this nor that.

Most days at school, I feel like those empanadas: not at all fitting neatly into what people expect me to be. Doing all I can not to let the confused mess of my insides come

---

* Please note this is a direct quote and the author does not condone the usage of such ableist language.

spilling out. Maybe if I had a name like Ji-Sun Kim, which is what I look like. Maybe if I had a name like Alejandra Ramírez, which is what I don't look like. My classmates and teachers don't really understand, even though they'd all call themselves "woke."

Instead I'm Alejandra Kim, which just confuses everybody.

I tried to make empanadas by myself once, right after Papi died, but they turned out gummy and sad and lacking all "sabor."

And at the same time tasting, weirdly, too American instead of Latin or Korean.

I never tried making them again.

When I leave for college, I long to meet people who don't do a double take each time they see my face and hear my name, demanding to know my Origin Story.

I long to leave behind our apartment in Jackson Heights that still smells like fry grease no matter how much you scrub and scrub and scrub.

I long to finally feel at home.

Our apartment has an oven, unlike Papi's when he was growing up. Which I guess in almost every way means we've achieved the "American dream." But strangely, Papi never once used the oven to make his empanadas. I guess after you get used to doing things in your own weird, lopsided way, it's what starts to feel "normal" to you—even though it's far from it.

It's what starts to feel like home.

CHAPTER 25

First-Gen American Testimony

AFTER WINTER BREAK DR. C tells us about a research project she's working on called First-Generation American Testimony. She's conducting interviews with first-generation Americans in New York, asking them about their experiences with immigration, migration, and loss of homeland. And she's hiring an intern to come work with her one day a week.

Now that my college apps are in—I sent off my Whyder app one day before the deadline—I'm definitely interested in this internship.

"It won't pay much," Dr. C admits. "Minimum wage. But if you stick it out till the end of the semester, you'll *also* get—"

"A yacht!" says Colin Okafor.

"A Subaru Outback!" adds Colt Brenner.

"Wow." Dr. C shakes her head. "You all are going to be *sorely* disappointed."

"A . . . new computer?" Chelsea Braeburn tries, a beat too late.

Dr. C lets her down gently. "No, sorry." She wiggles her jazz hands. "It's . . . a hundred-dollar stipend!"

Everyone groans—loudly. They're meant to be comic groans, I get it. But I'm still the only one jotting down the application information Dr. C writes on the board.

AFTER SCHOOL, LAUREL AND I meet up with Maya and her girl-friend, Drae Woodward. We head over to Glüt, a "casual comfort food eatery" owned by a TV celebrity chef.

Laurel gets gluten-free chocolate-chip pancakes ($16) and a blueberry kombucha on draft ($8).

Maya gets a kale-spirulina juice ($13) and nutritional yeast–dusted kale chips ($9).

Drae gets a cauliflower-crust pizza with buffalo mozzarella and San Marzano tomatoes ($18) and a ginger beer ($7).

And I get a hot tea with lemon, which still costs an outrageous $6.

Glüt wasn't my first choice. But I felt too self-conscious to offer up a different (read: cheaper) suggestion. Sometimes I get awkward at the kinds of places Oatties prefer to go, which are usually not the places I can afford. Blue Bottle versus Dunkin' Donuts. Vintage boutiques versus H&M. Whole Foods versus the corner grocery store. Bareburger versus McDonald's. I feel like every place I would choose is worsening the planet and/or humanity, which makes me a Horrible Person. So I just go along with the expensive place and buy the cheapest thing.

Plus the tuition check for next semester is due at the end of the week, so I'm in penny-scrounging mode.

"So, Ally," Maya says, "are you going to apply for Dr. C's internship at Hunter?" She explains the details of First-Generation American Testimony to the table.

Laurel turns to me. "An internship? You didn't mention that."

It kind of annoys me how Laurel just *assumes* I'd tell her everything.

So I ignore her comment. "Thinking about it," I tell Maya. "You?"

"No way! I'm done with all that." Maya shakes her head. "It's not like I need a rec letter from Dr. C."

"If only we could *all* get in early to Stanford," Drae says teasingly.

"Plus, it only pays minimum wage." Maya drains her green juice. "Who even works for that little anymore?"

Ma, I think but don't say. I busy myself with my overpriced tea, pretending it's the most delicious thing in the universe. Even though I'm dying for a grilled cheese and fries ($16).

I can feel Laurel studying my face.

"You should apply, Ally," she says. "That sounds pretty sweet."

"Are you saying I need the money?" I say. There's a cut to my tone.

Maya and Drae exchange a glance, but they don't say anything.

Laurel puts down her fork. She seems hurt. "That's not what I meant at all."

I catch myself before I say more. "Never mind."

Maya sips kale spirulina. Drae picks at her cauliflower pizza crust.

"Oh my God. Can we talk about Claire Devereaux?" Maya says, breaking the awkward silence. "You won't believe what she said to me in class today."

"She is such a snob," Laurel says. "Just because her family built Devereaux Theatre doesn't mean the rest of us are her handservants."

"You know, she's not so bad," I say to Laurel.

Laurel is shocked. "What? We hate Claire Devereaux."

"What is this, the buddy system?" I say. "You don't need me to hold your hand. You can hate her all by yourself."

"Okaaaay," says Maya.

"You're acting kind of weird, Ally," Laurel says.

I poke my lemon with a sustainable bamboo stirrer. I'm already done with my tea, but I don't want to flag the waiter for more hot water just yet. I'll look cheap.

"I didn't mean—sorry, I have a lot on my mind." Maybe Laurel's right. I am a little on edge, being at this restaurant, doing the mathematical gymnastics of computing tax and tip for my one drink.

On top of everything else.

"Anyway, you guys are so lucky to get Dr. C," Drae says to Maya and me. "She sounds amazing."

Maya says, "I heard she's an Oattie."

"I heard that, too." Laurel nods. "Probably why she gets it, you know? Like, she's so woke."

"You don't need to keep saying 'woke' all the time," I say to Laurel, my tone sharper than I meant. "I think we get it by now."

Maya and Drae are exchanging Looks, big-time. They're not even trying to hide it.

"Ally, I don't know what just happened there," Laurel says. "I didn't mean anything by, you know. Earlier. About the internship. Or anything else."

She talks súper staccato when she's broaching awkward territory. "Anyway, I'm, uh . . . I'm sorry."

Now I feel like a jerk for jumping down Laurel's throat. I shouldn't have gotten so defensive. "No, *I'm* sorry. That was my bad."

We're doing that Apology Dance of the Girl Friends—*I'm sorry!; No, I'm sorry!*—so neither of us feels like the bad guy. Girl. Person. I wonder where we learn this stuff.

Laurel says, "You should totally apply for that internship, Ally. The research sounds really great, that's all I meant. And everything I hear about Dr. C—she sounds mad cool."

Laurel looks at me for confirmation. People stopped saying "mad" as an adjective, like, yesterday, but I don't tell Laurel that. I nod anyway.

"You're good," I say. "And yeah, I think I will apply."

WHEN THE CHECK ARRIVES, Maya says, "Let's just split the bill. It'll be easier."

My throat catches. I'm the only one who ordered something

under ten bucks. And now I'm going to have to foot their over-priced "comfort" food bill when all I drank was watered-down tea with a soggy lemon wedge?

None of them blinked before ordering exactly what they wanted. A lot of Oatties are like that. They probably think they're "slumming" it at a diner. And they all think they're above a minimum wage internship with a hundred-dollar stipend. Which, to my ears, sounds pretty damn good.

Before I can think of a counterprotest to splitting the bill, let alone carry through with actually voicing it, Laurel jumps in.

"That's not fair, Maya. My pancakes came out to way more than everyone else's. Let's just put in for what we ordered."

Laurel's pancakes were actually cheaper than Drae's pizza (or "pizza"), but I know what she's doing. Laurel has the nunchi to speak up for me to save me the embarrassment. Now I feel bad for being prickly with her the whole time.

I shoot Laurel a grateful glance. She's my best friend, and like she said, she always has my back.

SO I GO AHEAD and apply for Dr. C's internship. And I actually get it. Once a week after school, I work in her lab at Hunter. It turns out I was the only Oattie to apply. The internship started after college apps were due, so I think a lot of Oatties thought there was no point.

First-Gen Testimony takes a qualitative research approach, which means Dr. C is conducting interviews and collecting and analyzing this "unfiltered data" to look for any patterns in the testimonies. She warns me the work is not glamorous. On my first day, I photocopy and scan and fix typos in transcribed interviews. But to me, the work I'm adjacent-working on is fascinating. The interviews tell the stories of the first-gen American subjects: their dreams, their fears, their day-to-day.

I move on to transcribing the interviews myself. And listening to the subjects makes me think about Papi's life.

Would New York Papi have been the same person as the Papi who never left Argentina? Or if his parents had never left Korea and he'd been born and raised there instead? Would he still have fallen in love with jazz? Or would he have chosen the oboe, oil painting, quantum physics?

Would he have fallen for Ma, married her, had me?

Would he still have taken to the couch in the last year of his life?

AND THAT'S PRETTY MUCH how the rest of winter goes. I work in Dr. C's lab and at Happy Day. Laurel and I do our thing at school. Billy and I catch up over Gatorades in the park or overpriced coffees at Chaití, depending on the vagaries of global warming.

But we're all pretty much biting nails until the spring, when regular decision notifications will be made.

Part III

CHAPTER 26

The Nasties

IN SPRING, AS THE college acceptance—and rejection—letters start pouring in, the Nasties come out in all of us Oatties. It's like we're all competing against each other in a zero-sum game. One Oattie's acceptance means another's rejection. Bettina Abrams and Colt Brenner, who've been dating since freshperson year, break up immediately after she gets into Brown and he is wait-listed. Chelsea Braeburn and Fiona McIntosh, who've been best friends since in utero, become sworn enemies when they find out Chelsea got into Wellesley when Fiona didn't and Fiona got into Smith when Chelsea didn't.

Every day in the halls, I hear the whispered and not-so-whispered tidbits:

"With only a 3.5 GPA?"

"And a 1400 on the SATs."

"They're legacy, that's why."

It's all pretty ugly. I can't wait for spring to be over.

I get into my safeties: SUNY Purchase, Queens College, Brooklyn College, and Hunter. I also get acceptances from Barnard and NYU, but—surprise, surprise—the financial aid packages are crap. It doesn't make sense for me to pay a premium for a private college in the city I'm trying to leave in the first place.

It always amazes me how people not from New York glamorize our city from afar. Like everyone stepping off the Greyhound in dingy Port Authority thinks they're going to "make it big" on Broadway or Wall Street. Even Jay Gatsby, né James Gatz, made *bank* in New York and still ended up shot and had only two people show up for his funeral.

When you're from New York, your "Dodge" is everyone else's final destination.

So where do you go to get out?

For me, the answer to that is a leafy campus set in a forest in the middle of Nowhere, New England.

But my Whyder letter has yet to arrive, even though I check the mail compulsively every single day.

Laurel's college acceptances roll in, too. She gets into her safeties (only for Laurel would they be considered "safeties"): Kenyon, Macalester, Mount Holyoke. But Laurel won't let herself enjoy any of it.

When she gets into Princeton, she gets a call from her father.

"Dad doesn't even call me on my *birthday*," she says. "And now he wants to take me out for dinner to celebrate?"

"Did you tell him no?" I ask.

But Laurel has a complicated relationship with her father. She both resents him and vies for his attention. Of course she'd say yes.

"Of course I said yes," Laurel says, and she goes to meet her dad for dinner.

"SO WHERE'D HE TAKE you?" I ask Laurel at lunch the day after.

"Another steakhouse near Grand Central." Laurel rolls her eyes. "So he could catch the 8:01 back to Darien."

Laurel always (and only) eats steak with her dad. I guess it's, like, their thing.

"He's already trying to Machiavelli my future! Like which eating club to join—he wants me to bicker Ivy, even though they rejected him for, oh, I don't know, *being Jewish?*—which profs to take classes with—"

"You're speaking English," I interrupt, "but I literally have no idea what you're talking about."

"That's the point!" Laurel says. "Everything about Princeton is snooty and exclusive! To add insult to injury, Dad offered up Jocelyn to take me shopping for new clothes. Right, because that kind of 'invisible labor' is women's work. Also, Jocelyn's only like five years older than Leah. Ugh! Why are old white men so gross? And so . . . predictable?"

Laurel seethes. "I hate that I got into Princeton. I do *not* want to end up like one of them."

Princeton was Jason's first choice, but they rejected his ass so hard. He also got rejected from Columbia and NYU. I could see it all over his face last week at Happy Day, but he was too proud to say. Michael Oppa told me Jason only just got into Stony Brook.

I tell Laurel, "This is kind of a good problem to have." *You get to go to an Ivy League, debt-free. Poor you.* I should be more sympathetic to Laurel's plight. Princeton's not her dream; it's her dad's.

But Laurel's so lost in her own thoughts, in her own problems.

"You just don't understand," she says, her teeth setting in a tight line.

And she's probably right. I don't really understand her situation at all.

CHAPTER 27

Racial Melancholia

I IGNORE THE NASTIES by burying myself in Dr. C's First-Gen American Testimony project.

Dr. C has me reading about a psych theory called "racial melancholia." The academic journal articles are a little hard for me to understand, but Dr. C helps me unpack them. And once I do, it's like—whoa. I can't unsee what I've just learned.

Racial melancholia is this idea that immigration is its own form of trauma. Losing your language, culture, and homeland in one fell swoop—along with facing all the racism in your new country—is a huge shock to your mind *and* body. You feel neither here nor there; you're melancholy all the time.

As I transcribe interviews with the test subjects, I think about Dr. C's advice warning me not to get too emotional. In her lab, I'm supposed to be an impartial scribe.

I type up three reports easily—they just document eating

and sleep patterns. One more report to type up before I'm done for the day. I'm having a hard time making out the voice through the static, but then it comes out piercingly clear:

Boss yell me. Everybody yell me. Say I stupid. My English ugly. Ten years, make no money. One day I stop.

Two month I sleep. So tired. No go outside.

Why I come America? I no belong here. Better I suffer my country. But dictator say, "Do my way or I kill you."

Where I belong?

It's like I'm hearing Papi's life.

But . . . I'm hearing the *other* side of his life. When all I could see was the depressed figure lying on the couch.

Where I belong?

Is this how Papi felt the whole time, too?

I couldn't understand why he didn't go find another job. I couldn't understand why he was sleeping all day. I used to think it was because he got lazy. I was busting my butt at Quaker Oats, and he was just lying around all the time. I was mad at him for not working hard like the other parents at school, like Laurel's private-equity dad, who rakes in bonuses in the six figures.

Junior fall, I asked my parents for money for a college trip during spring break. The school was organizing a visit to a bunch of schools—including Whyder—up and down the East Coast. And all the other kids at school had no problems getting their parents to fork over the $500. They cut those checks like it was NBD. But Ma said we didn't have that kind of money to spare. And I was so pissed, because everyone at Quaker Oats was going, and if I didn't, then they'd all know the reason why: pobrecita Alejandra Kim couldn't afford to go.

I was so mad, I couldn't contain it. I shouted at Papi, "Maybe if you had a *real* job like a normal dad, then I could actually afford to go on the trip!"

Papi just lay there, stunned. Then he sat up and said, "Tenés razón, Aleja-ya."

He didn't even yell at me for talking back or anything. He said I was *right*. How fucked up is that?

I stormed out of the house, feeling pissed off and sorry for myself, and at the same time guilty for what I'd said to Papi but not really admitting it. When I came home, he was back to his usual lethargic state, face buried in the couch cushions with his back to the rest of us.

A few months later, Papi threw himself onto the 7 train tracks.

I never got to say I'm sorry. Let alone goodbye.

Deep down I *knew* Papi was depressed, even if we never talked about it at home. Because that's not what immigrant families do. Mental health is a luxury. At best it is an afterthought; more often than not, it's a never-thought. In Jackson Heights, all our problems always boil down to money: the pursuit of its never-enough-ness.

The interview goes on, but I can't listen anymore because I'm crying. I can't help it. Big, fat, hot, stupid tears sear down my face.

It's unprofessional to cry at work. I know this, and I *know* Dr. C knows this. I haven't cried like this since Ma threw out Papi's old flannel shirt that she found in my closet.

"Alejandra?" Dr. C calls out. I know she can see my reflection on her computer monitor. "Alejandra, are you all right?"

"Muh-huh . . ."

I can't answer because, sniffles. I'm trying to snort back my tears, but now I just sound like a noisy vacuum. At least I have the sense to hold the recording device *away* from me, so I don't ruin it by splashing juicy tears all over it.

Dr. C swivels around and faces me. She looks at me expectantly.

"It's just . . . my father."

And it all comes spilling out.

I hate that I am TMI, because if there's one thing Ma taught me—Papi, too—it's not to waste More Important People's time.

"I'm so stupid, I'm sorry," I manage to get out.

"No," says Dr. C sternly. I look up, alarmed. But she says, "You should not apologize. And you should *never* call yourself 'stupid.'"

"I'm sorry," I say again. Seriously, it's like a reflex.

"Thank you for sharing that about your father, Alejandra," she says. "I'm sure it was difficult, and the pain is still raw."

"Do you think Papi suffered from . . . racial melancholia?" I ask.

"Having not evaluated him, I have no way of knowing," she says.

"Oh," I say, feeling like I was out of line for asking.

"But I will say that other test subjects who *do* suffer from racial melancholia seem to have similar backgrounds and experiences as your father," she adds. "Your dad had to navigate and negotiate not one, not two, but three cultures at any given moment?"

I nod, confirming. "That's the thing. Papi never looked like what he *was*. Like, we'd walk into a store speaking perfect Spanish, and still people would be like, 'What's up with that Chino?' "

And the Koreans at my cousins' church, they always looked down at us like we were dirty Nam-Mi people. But white people looked at Papi and Ma and thought they were fresh off the boat from the Orient. How could Papi *not* have felt like an imposter?

And maybe Ma feels like one, too.

"I cannot imagine that cognitive load," Dr. C says. The way she's shaking her head and squeezing her eyes shut makes me think this hits close to home for her.

"Dr. C," I ask suddenly. "How did you decide to get into this work?"

Dr. C spreads her hands. It's almost like she's laying her cards bare. But then she curls them back into fists.

"I won't get too into it, because it's my policy to not blur lines between students and teachers. But the short answer is: like many of our First-Gen subjects, I felt like I did not belong. And I wanted to unpack that.

"Some people go along to get along. That's a survival tactic.

Others subsume the pain and trauma that come with cultural displacement. But we have no idea the extent of the psychological repercussions of absorbing that trauma, particularly for first-genners in the Asian community. We're grossly underfunded."

Dr. C lets out a wry laugh. "There are twenty-two million Asians in America, yet we're allotted only *0.17 of a percentage point* of the National Institutes of Health budget. We're the quote-unquote model minority, yet we remain 'understudied.' Forgive the pun."

The statistic makes me mad. I read about it in one of Dr. C's articles. I'm not great at math, but that means you could multiply the existing budget for Asian American health by five and you'd *still* be under 1 percent.

"But back to your dad," Dr. C says. "Alejandra, if I can offer some off-the-record, nonclinical advice: from my experience, it helps to talk to your family. Other people who knew your father, to share your memories of him. Happy memories, sad. It will be hard at first, and you'll be met with a lot of resistance. But try. In this small way, you can honor his spirit together."

My cheeks are flushed—from the painful memories of Papi, from crying, from the embarrassment of crying, from Dr. C's words.

It's bullshit when people like Josh Buck say Dr. C is a "stone-faced B." Or maybe it's true that she seems tough, but she's got a heart under all that toughness, too.

CHAPTER 28

Coney Island

EVERY DAY I RACE to the mailbox at home. Every day it's the same: bills, bills, and more bills.

At lunch one day, we learn MK Hausen got into Whyder. I'm worried, because my Whyder letter hasn't arrived one way or the other. Laurel's worried, too. She starts dissecting their credentials.

"President of the Trans-Oatties. 1450 and 3.8, I heard. That's, like, lower than mine."

"Good!" I say. "Then it probably means you'll get your acceptance letter next."

"How am I supposed to—" Laurel bites her lip.

"To what?"

"Never mind." She breathes in deep. "I still can't believe Claire Devereaux got into Whyder," she says, regaining herself. "I thought at best she'd get into Vassar."

"She's editor in chief of *Ennui*," I point out.

"Big deal," Laurel says. "*Ennui*'s not even a top-ranking lit journal."

"We're in high school, Laurel. This isn't the freaking *New Yorker*."

The edge in my tone seems to put Laurel in her place.

"It's probably because her fancy editor grandma got, like, Jonathan Franzen to write her a rec," Laurel grumbles.

"He's the one who wrote those creepy, flirty emails with Natalie Portman?" I ask.

"Different Jonathan," Laurel says. I leave it at that.

THE NEXT DAY, I reach for the stack of envelopes in our mail slot. Con Ed. National Grid. Jackson Heights Residential Services. "Corporal Life Insurance"—probably spam. I flip those aside, and that's when I see it: a yellow packet, thicker than all the rest. Shivers run through me. No, it can't be.

I let out a yelp, and Julio, mopping the floors, glances my way. "You okay, little miss?" Julio's been calling me that my whole life. I don't think he knows my actual name.

I nod, still jittery. "Yeah. College stuff."

"Good, good," he says. "You're a smart kid." He goes back to mopping the mail room.

I tear open the letter. I stare at the words. I can't believe it:

Dear Alejandra Kim,

After reviewing your application, we are pleased to inform you of your acceptance to Whyder College! In an especially

competitive pool, your candidacy stood out among the
thousands of qualified applicants . . .

I GOT IN I GOT IN I GOT IN!!!

There's even a handwritten postscript from the dean of
admissions:

*PS: Alejandra, I was so moved by the double narrative of your
family's recipe and migration story. We'd be honored for you to
join our community this fall.*

Out of all the thousands of applicants, the dean found time
to write me a personal note. Which only confirms, with every
fiber in my body, that Whyder is the perfect school for me.

You'll *have no trouble getting into college.* Well, eff you, too, JBJ.

I feel two things: happiness, like a bottle of ginger ale just
exploded inside me; and dread, because I have to find a way to
tell both Laurel and Ma.

THE ADMISSIONS PACKET IS chunky and daunting. The financial
aid package stares back at me. "We are pleased to inform you
that we can meet 25% of your need . . ."

This doesn't make any sense. Twenty-five percent? I thought
Whyder met full need. They have a two-billion-dollar endow-
ment. That's a big part of why I applied.

This doesn't make sense.

This doesn't make sense at *all.*

I END UP JUST Band-Aiding it. I text Laurel: Have you heard back from Whyder?

> Not yet. You?

I text back a snapshot of my acceptance letter.

> OMG!!!! CONGRATS, ALLY!!!!

Laurel sends all the virtual balloons.

> It is IMPERATIVE that we celebrate. Drop what you're doing and jump on the F.
> Meet at my stop, but stay on the train.
> 3rd car, 1st door.

AT 7TH AVENUE, LAUREL jumps onto my train car. Our timing is perfect.

"Ally!! I'm so, so happy for you!" she cries, bounding up to me and folding me into the biggest hug. She gives great hugs—warm and feely, without invading *too* much personal space.

I'm *so* relieved. "Really? Thanks, Laurel."

"Yeah," she says as we break apart. "Why wouldn't I be?"

"No, yeah. Sorry." I wave off my stupid thought.

But actually, no, it's not a stupid thought. Of course it feels a little weird that I got into Whyder and Laurel's still waiting for her letter.

So I call it out.

"No, actually," I start again, "let's just state the obvious. It's a little awkward, right? I mean, you're still waiting to hear back—"

"Ally," she interrupts. "This is *huge*! Everything you've worked so hard for has finally paid off. Let's enjoy the moment, shall we?"

Laurel's being real. It means so much to me that Laurel's not only cool with this, but that she's genuinely happy for me. That's the mark of a good friend.

And anyway, her acceptance letter's going to arrive any day now. I just know it.

And we'll go off to Whyder together in the fall.

Never mind that 25 percent, which I'm trying to put out of my mind.

"So," I say. "What's this mysterious place you're taking me to?"

"It's a surprise."

"*This* sounds familiar."

Laurel leans back in her seat, arms crossed. She is pleased as punch. "Well, Ally, payback's a B."

"Touché."

WE ARE HEADING DEEP into the heart of Brooklyn. We've left the hipsters and stroller parents and all vestiges of Laurel's world behind. Our fellow passengers are old ladies speaking what I think is Russian. They're dressed in heavy black skirts and thick, woolen black stockings. Men with black hats and beards and sidelocks speak in brisk Yiddish. Elderly couples with carts filled with empty recycled cans whisper in hushed Cantonese.

On the way down, Laurel asks me about my internship with Dr. C. I tell her about the work, the articles Dr. C is having me read. But I don't tell her about my breakdown in the lab, or about Papi.

As I'm talking, I become very aware of the other passengers in our train car. Maybe they are first-gen Americans, too. I think about how important the work Dr. C is doing in gathering these testimonies is. I wonder how many of these passengers live with racial melancholia, too.

We ride the F to the bitter end. I catch a whiff of salty ocean breeze laced with hot dogs and sauerkraut.

"Shut up. You did not just take me to Coney Island, Laurel Greenblatt-Watkins!" I say.

"You said you've never been," she says, suddenly shy. "And I just thought, before you leave New York for good . . ."

I told Laurel freshperson year that I'd never been to Coney Island. I've always wanted to, but never got around to it. I can't believe her flytrap memory.

"L, you're the best friend ever!" I hug her tightly. "This is so cool! Do you think Luna Park is open yet for the season?"

"It is, I checked," Laurel says. "Hallelujah, global warming."

We head to the boardwalk. Indeed, global warming—it's only April and we're practically in T-shirts. We pass another set of old ladies in heavy black talking loudly over each other.

"What do you think they're going on about?" I ask.

"Kvetching about their kids." Laurel clears her throat and goes:

"Yevgeny, I tell him, playtime over! Find girl, have babies, die.

"But girl must make good borscht! Then babies, then die."

My mouth drops. Did Laurel . . . just stereotype?

"Laurel, did you just—"

"Yeah." Laurel looks chagrined, but also . . . tickled. "I don't have a Ukrainian grandma for nothing."

I have never seen this side of Laurel. She's offensive. She's funny. She's—both?

We start cracking up. The old ladies stare at us like we've lost it, which only makes us laugh harder.

"Who even *are* you?" I say to Laurel.

She sighs. "I've been asking myself that a lot lately, to be honest."

WE REACH THE ENTRANCE to Luna Park and join the line for the Cyclone. Laurel's sniffling. At first I think it's from our earlier giggle fest, or maybe the salted air stinging her eyes. But as we reach the front of the line, there are full-out tears dribbling down her face.

"I'm sorry, Ally," she says. "I'm trying to put on a brave face, but . . . I can't."

"Laurel, what's going on?"

"I didn't get in, okay? Whyder rejected me. They said thanks, but no thanks."

"But you said your letter didn't arrive—"

"Of *course* it arrived, Ally. I just said that so you wouldn't feel bad."

I feel all the feels: Horrible for my friend. Guilty for me. Frustrated that she lied to me.

"Laurel—"

We're interrupted by the Cyclone guy: "Ladies, you're up."

I look expectantly at Laurel. I get that she was trying to do something nice for me, to celebrate my big win. But dragging me all the way to Coney Island just to prove that she was cool with me getting into Whyder when she never actually was?

What am I going to do? Force her to ride on roller coasters with me when it's clear she's miserable?

"Let's just go."

"But . . . we're here to celebrate you."

"Then you go, Laurel. I'll be fine."

"And leave you here alone?"

"You girls are holding up the line."

"Just go, Laurel. *Seriously,* I'll be okay."

"You sure, Ally? I'm sorry—"

"Ticket for one."

AT FIRST I'M A little embarrassed to be riding the Cyclone alone. I feel like everyone's thinking, *Look at that girl with no friends.*

But then I realize: NO ONE CARES. They're all here in their little pods, doing their own thing. Just like I'm doing mine.

The wood tracks of the roller coaster feel rickety and precarious, which adds to the thrill of potentially getting smashed to smithereens on the way down. Climbing up, I forget about Laurel. I forget the dread I feel about having to talk with Ma. And I try to forget about Whyder's crappy financial aid, which I'm going to clear up in the college counselor's office tomorrow. I can see the Atlantic Ocean stretching endlessly in either direction. I breathe in deep, then let it all out. Raise my hands in the air—

Wheeeeee.

CHAPTER 29

Expected Family Contribution

WHEN I GET HOME from Coney Island, Laurel texts: I'm so sorry, Ally. I'm SUCH a shitty friend to you. You deserve better.

I text back: You're not. You're just human.

> Also: Coney Island
> is da bomb.

I thought you said no one says "da bomb" anymore. Also: appropriation?

> I was using it ironically.

...

> ...

> But it IS awk, let's be real.

YESSS. Glad we're being real.

Btw debate team's hectic bc Nationals. So won't be around lunch for the next couple.

Ok. I'll survive.

Thank you for understanding, friend. I'm still SO happy for you.

THE NEXT MORNING I'M sitting in Mr. Landibadeau's office, staring up at the motivational posters:

SHOOT FOR THE STARS!

STEP ON DOWN TO SMILETOWN!

I'M GOOD ENOUGH, I'M SMART ENOUGH, AND DOGGONE IT, PEOPLE LIKE ME!

My Whyder acceptance package is spread before us on the table.

"Mr. Landibadeau, there must be some mistake," I say. "I should have qualified for full financial aid."

"I see no reason why you wouldn't qualify for a full ride from any institution that meets full need, Alley-JOHN-druh," he says, peering at my file.

He bends over my college file. Dandruff from his comb-over sprinkles down, like salt from a shaker.

"Your EFC must have changed between last year and now," he says, tapping his no. 2 pencil to his chin. "The amount you put down on the form and the amount they found your family has in assets don't add up."

"Assets?" I scoff. "My family doesn't have any assets. My mom makes nothing. And my dad, he"—I rush through this part of the sentence—"passed away."

"My condolences." Mr. Landibadeau bows his head and folds his hands in prayer.

"Sorry if my question sounds insensitive, Alley-JOHN-druh," he continues, "but did you perhaps come into money recently? An inheritance, maybe?"

The question is so ridiculous. I shake my head.

"I'll call the dean of admissions over there to see if we can get some clarity on this. But, in the words of a very wise man, Stanley Landibadeau, my late and great father, I say, 'Talk to your mother.'" Mr. L kisses his thumb and taps it to his chest. "I think you should have an honest conversation about your family's financial picture."

I am dreading this so hard. But I say, "Yes, Mr. Landibadeau." Because he's probably right.

"Nothing wrong with CUNY, Alley-JOHN-druh," he says. "As a proud product of one, I think they're worth a shot."

His assistant, Ms. Jess, comes in with a stack of folders. As she places them on Mr. L's desk, she offers me a smile.

"You should still go to the Prospective Students Festival at Whyder," she says. "It might help with your decision-making, one way or the other."

Right, Spec Fest. The one Laurel and I dreamed about going to together.

"Just let me know. Whyder will take care of the arrangements, transportation and all."

"Thanks, Ms. Jess," I say. I mean it.

"It'll all work out in the end," she continues. "These things always do, Alejandra."

Ms. Jess gets my name exactly right.

* * *

"ASSETS? THAT'S RIDICULOUS. We have no assets," Ma says when she gets home from work. She is bleary-eyed from a double shift—she had an overnight, then the morning aide called out so she had to cover. The last thing she wants to hear about is my Whyder acceptance, the financial aid package, and what Mr. Landibadeau said.

Still, there's no *Congratulations!* No *Everything you've worked so hard for has finally paid off!*

"It doesn't make sense," I say, showing her the Whyder financial aid stuff.

Ma pushes aside the stacks of unopened mail on the dining table and spreads the Whyder folder before her. But she's not actually reading any of it. She closes her eyes and massages her temples.

"I thought you chose this college because they have good scholarships."

"They're supposed to. But for some reason, this is all they're offering."

She says nothing.

"Ma, do you have any idea how hard it is to get into Whyder? It has an eight-percent acceptance rate."

Technically 8.5, but with Ma, I round down.

"I know this college is your dream," she says finally. "But it's impossible. You need to set your heart somewhere else."

"Ma, we're talking about my future!" What I don't say, but what I'm thinking, is how much she's checked out of this whole college process, leaving me all on my own. "Do you have any idea what it means to put Whyder College on your résumé? Do you know how many doors will open for me with this degree?"

"I can only think of how many will slam shut."

"Ma." I'm starting to lose it. "Would it kill you to be happy for me? For once?"

"Don't you *dare* talk to your mother like that," she hisses.

That shuts me up.

Ma starts again, softer this time. "No mother would be happy to see their child making a big mistake."

Then she pushes the Whyder folder in with the rest of the neglected mail and gets up from the table to start on dinner.

THIS IS SUCH BS, I text Billy later that night. Everyone else's parents would be throwing them a freakin PARADE if they found out their kid got into Whyder.

Billy writes: #1: CONGRATS!! Ale, this is UGE!!!

That's an inside joke between us. Our fifth-grade teacher, Mr. O'Claren, would always drop his "h"s.

> #2: Cool it w the hyperbole. Pretty sure not a parade. Steak dinner, maybe.

> #3: Give your ma time to process. She might surprise you.

> F this! I don't need her blessing. I'm going to find a way to pay for it myself.

> #4: You and me, let's celebrate. Fri after next ok? I'm working the next bunch of wknds so it's my only night free for a while.

> Cool, yeah. That's the Fri bf spring break.
> Was maybe supposed to hang out w
> Laurel, but she's being flaky (SIGH)
> so . . . OK!

I'll take it.

FOR THE REST OF the night, I research college loans. I continue my research all week. I meant what I texted Billy.

After Papi died, I realized I couldn't rely on Ma, or the rest of my family, or anyone else.

It's all on me.

CHAPTER 30

Happy Day, or Is It?

MICHAEL OPPA'S ALREADY THERE when I get to Happy Day on Saturday. On warm days like today, the dry cleaner, which already feels like a sauna (minus the soothing spa setting and cucumber face masks), roasts like a broiler.

"Congrats on Whyder!" Michael Oppa says, giving me a hug.

"Thanks, Michael Oppa," I say.

"But . . . ?"

"What?"

"I hear a 'but' in your voice." Michael Oppa is all-knowing like that.

I shrug. "There are, like, a million 'but's."

"Such as?"

We have customers, so we can't talk. Two women walk in together: an older white woman with a smart gray bob and even smarter linen suit, and a middle-aged Latinx woman wearing a MARTHA'S VINEYARD sweatshirt with a Clorox stain over the black dog. They're dropping off two Canada Goose jackets, two black peacoats, two cream-colored peacoats, ten wool skirt suits, and twenty cashmere sweaters in beiges and creams.

"Looks like winter's finally over!" the bobbed woman says as the other woman heaves the clothes onto the counter.

"And then some," Michael Oppa says in his kissing-up-to-the-customers voice. "It's barely spring, and it feels like practically summer."

"That's global warming for you," I add, tagging the clothes. "We can have this delivered to you," I offer.

The Latinx woman gives us an exasperated look like, *Please, God, help!*

The bobbed woman goes, "Heavens, no! We don't need that extravagance."

Customers are funny like that. Drop-off service is only a dollar extra. But I guess they pick and choose what they feel guilty about spending their money on. Based on these clothes alone, this woman's probably loaded. Seriously, *twenty* cashmere sweaters? If you've never worn a cashmere sweater before, then do yourself a favor and don't. Yeah, they're súper soft and make you feel like you're being hugged by a cuddly teddy bear, but they're a pain in the ass to clean, which keeps dry cleaners like Happy Day in business.

But people in this neighborhood treat their dry cleaners like their washing machines, which also keeps Happy Day in the ka-ching.

Although people nowadays are renting their clothes by mail, which is *not* so good for business.

Just before they turn to leave, the bobbed woman says, "I'm sure you kids have bright futures ahead."

225

The pity on her face is unmistakable.

Customer pity used to bother me, a lot. Work is hard enough without having people look down on what you do. It still kind of does, but Michael Oppa's taught me to laugh it off. "They don't know your story," he said to me once. "So you can spend all day worrying about what they think of you. Or you can be out there hashtag living your best life. Or whatever you Gen Z-ers say."

"Uh, hashtags are *so* millennial," I teased back.

Maybe Michael Oppa can afford to say that because the customers might regard him with pity, but meanwhile he's better educated than most of them.

"Back to Whyder," Michael Oppa says after we get through the next batch of customers. "It's your dream school. So what's the holdup?"

"For one, it got kind of weird with Laurel. Whyder's her dream school, too, but she got deferred, then rejected."

"Ouch."

"For two, Whyder's financial aid package is *phbbbt*." I make a thumbs-down.

Michael Oppa looks thoughtful. He knows there's nothing he can do to help, and I don't want to make him feel like he has to ask his parents to help me. They've done more than enough for me my whole life.

"Well, if you want to go badly enough, you can just take out college loans."

"But then I'd come out of school with all this debt, and it's not like I'd be guaranteed a job on graduation." I hear Billy's words in mine.

"There's that," Michael Oppa concedes. "By the way, how's your *other* job going? The one with the prof at Hunter?"

"Well, things in the lab got a little . . . I don't know. It was kind of . . . triggering."

There's a line of customers now, so we help them. After, I tell Michael Oppa what happened in Dr. C's office. He listens patiently. He's not like his dad, who only wants to talk and never listen. He's not like Jason, who's about as attuned to his emotions as a tapeworm.

Michael Oppa is like Papi in that way.

"I'm really going to miss working with Dr. C when I go to college," I tell him. "I've learned so much in her lab already."

"You know you don't have to," Michael Oppa says slowly.

"Have to what?"

"Miss working with her. You still could. You got into Hunter, right?"

"Yeah, but . . . I can't *not* go to Whyder."

"Remind me again why you want to go to Whyder so badly." I give him a Look; I've only told him thousands of times since freshperson year. "Indulge me," he adds.

"Fine. One: It's prestigious and has prestigious profs. Two: It's the dream of *everyone* at Quaker Oats. But they only accepted three of us in my whole graduating class. I can't *not* take the spot. Three: I need to get the hell out of New York. If I have to spend one more night living under Ma's roof . . ."

"Don't get me wrong," Michael Oppa goes on. "Whyder is a great school, and you deserve to go to your dream school. If it's *your* dream school. But in my infinite wisdom as your older cousin—"

"Cue the eyeroll," I say.

"Sometimes the thing we really want—the thing we *think* we really want—is just a cover for the thing we're trying to avoid. Take it from someone who knows."

Michael Oppa does know.

"I really miss Juan Samchon," he says. "Your dad was the first person I felt comfortable coming out to."

We don't have time to really get into it, because customers and cleaning and, you know, work. But I'm smiling the whole time, thinking of Michael Oppa still carrying Papi in his heart.

And I realize something funny but also wonderful: This is the first time I'm thinking of Papi without the obligatory stabs of guilt. And anger.

Maybe it's like Dr. C said: *Share your memories of him. In this small way, you can honor his spirit together.*

"I have to say, Alley-Cat," Michael Oppa says, breaking my thoughts. "Hearing you talk about working with Dr. C . . . I haven't seen you this excited about, well, anything in a while. It's inspiring, actually."

"Does that mean you're getting out of Goldman?" I ask. "It sounds way toxic."

"I'm meeting with a headhunter, so we'll see." Even as he says it, Michael Oppa's face relaxes. I realize how much tension he's been carrying since he started working there, which feels like forever ago.

"I'll keep my fingers crossed for you, Michael Oppa."

"You, too," he says. "I don't think enough people know

about—what's it called again?" I tell him. "Racial melancholia. There aren't enough immigrant stories out there for the public. I mean, besides the obligatory trauma porn."

"The work is really meaningful," I say. "It feels like we're making a difference." And I mean it.

CHAPTER 31

In Vino Veritas

IT'S THE FRIDAY BEFORE spring break, and Claire Devereaux is having a "Hey, we got into college!" party. Billy is my plus-one. No, not my "date."

I wouldn't have invited Billy to an Oattie thing. But this is his last free weekend for the next couple of months, and we made plans to hang and celebrate my Whyder acceptance. Then Claire announced her party. In true Quaker fashion, the whole senior class is invited. Plus-ones, too.

It seemed bad friend-ish to cancel plans with Billy, so I invited him along. But it's one of those complicated things—negotiating the politics of hanging out with your friends.

Of course I'm anxious. Because worlds potentially clashing.

I also don't want to show up at Claire's party alone.

"I finally get to meet your fancy friends," Billy says on the train ride up to Claire's on the Upper West Side. "What if I mix up the salad fork and dessert fork? Should I have rented a tux?" He looks down at his T-shirt in mock horror.

"You're fine, Chivi."

"Your friend Laurel going to be there?" he asks.

I shrug. Laurel mentioned she might stop by if she was up for it. She didn't offer to go together, so neither did I.

Things are and aren't the same between Laurel and me ever since I found out I got into Whyder. We haven't hung out since Coney Island. We picked up where we left off, kind of. It's not that the air isn't clear between us, but it's also not *not* that, either.

Papi used to play these funky harmonies on the piano. The music sounds like it's *about* to resolve, but it doesn't. The notes are just a little too flat or a little too sharp. That's how things feel with Laurel—a little off-key.

Or maybe I'm just being paranoid, and everything's fine.

I can feel Billy reading me, reading between my unspoken lines. He clears his throat.

"You look very cute, by the way," he says.

I'm wearing a new dress from an "evil fast fashion" store, but it was $19.99.

"Thanks," I say. But complimenting each other on our looks isn't our dynamic. Billy and I are usually too busy telling fart jokes or whatever. "You look arright, too, Chivi."

He looks more than "arright." Billy's actually wearing clothes that are his size, instead of three sizes too big. His fitted light blue T-shirt hugs his shoulders, which have been looking quite defined of late. And his black jeans make his legs look súper long. He's doused in cologne again—which I'm actually coming around on, because it smells like his smell.

"Hey, you didn't make a joke about the Axe this time," Billy says.

"It's growing on me," I say.

"Wow, a rare compliment from Miss Ale."

"Two," I correct him.

"What'd I do to get so lucky?" He's smiling deep, setting off his dimples.

Now *I* clear my throat. "Hey, so." I'm trying to sound súper casual. "Just, like, try not to say certain things in front of my school friends."

"Like what? Fracking is good! Abortion is murder! Build the wall!"

"Ha ha, very funny. But seriously, Billy. For one, *don't* say the N-word. Not even playing around."

Billy looks scandalized. "When was the last time I said—"

"Stop, don't even joke like that! You shouldn't ever use that word, period."

"I get it," Billy mutters. "Don't commit crimes of political incorrectness."

"It's just . . . my school friends do things different from how we do back home."

"What am I, a Neanderthal from the Pleistocene?"

"Actually, I read in *Smithsonian* that the Neanderthals were very intelligent. They were just misunderstood in their time."

"Okay, Oattie," Billy says, doing the pushing-up-his-imaginary-glasses thing. But he's struggling to hold back a laugh, and now I'm laughing, and now we're both full-out laughing as our train crosses from Queens into Manhattan.

***

CLAIRE DEVEREAUX LIVES IN a prewar high-rise on Central Park West. The building has actual gargoyles and pointy spires and lots of fancy architectural features I don't know the names of.

The doorman gives us side-eye. "Can I help you?"

"We're here for Claire Devereaux's party," I tell him.

"And your names are?"

Here's the problem: my name is on the list, but Billy's is not.

"I'll just have to confirm with Miss Devereaux," the doorman says.

Billy and I move toward the overstuffed couches in the lobby. The doorman shakes his head. "Outside, please."

"That's so fucked up," I say after the doorman shoos us out. "I'm sorry, Billy."

"It is what it is," Billy says, shrugging. "So. Any other no-no's I should be aware of?"

I lightly slap his arm. "Stop, Chivi."

Billy grabs my hand. I swat him with my other hand. He grabs that one, too. Then Billy's spreading my arms wide, like I'm a doofy Superman.

"Damn, Billy. You been working out?" I act fake impressed, but I'm actually real impressed. "When'd you get so strong—"

"Hey!" It's the doorman.

Billy and I drop hands.

The doorman waves us back in, like it's nothing that he tried to bounce us a moment ago. I tense up. But Billy grips my arm, shakes his head. *It's not worth it.*

* * *

THE ELEVATOR DINGS OPEN, straight into the penthouse. "Welcome, welcome!" Claire swoops air-kisses on both my cheeks. "Congrats again on Whyder, Ally! That's huge!"

"You, too!" It's kind of crazy to think Claire and I will be going to school together. "Thanks for having us," I say, and introduce her to Billy.

"Billy, I'm *so* sorry about . . . downstairs," she says. "Mickey, the doorman, he gets protective. . . ." She shakes her head. "That came out all wrong."

Billy shrugs like it's no big deal. It isn't, but he tells Claire, "It's all good."

CLAIRE'S APARTMENT IS NICE: high ceilings with crown molding that I'm sure is a literal pain in the neck to dust. But I'm also surprised her house is not *as* nice as I thought it would be. It's a little old and musty. And the kitchen looks dated, like it's stuck in the 1900s. The sticky brown cabinets are the same as the ones we have in our kitchen.

"Please. Help yourself." Claire waves her arm at the spread of bottles in the kitchen. All of them are champagne. She starts filling paper cups.

"Do you have any Coke?" Billy asks.

"No, sorry," Claire says. "Grandmama has a 'no brown beverages' rule."

"A what?" I ask.

"I know, it's silly." Claire sounds genuinely apologetic. "It's to protect her furniture and rugs."

"It kind of sounds—"

"Racist, I know," she interrupts.

"I was going to say 'fussy,'" I say. I really was.

Claire laughs awkwardly. "That, too. Sorry. But whatever. Her rules, not mine."

"You live with your grandmother?" I ask.

The door buzzes. "Excuse me," she says, and heads to answer it.

Fiona McIntosh is perched on a stool in the kitchen. I only vaguely know her; I think she does *Ennui* with Claire.

After I introduce her to Billy—she holds out the back of her hand to him, but he just takes it and shakes it sideways—I ask, "So, Fiona. You want to be a writer, like Claire?"

I'm just trying to make small talk, but Fiona scoffs. "I'm a *poet*.

> *"Eternity bores me,*
> *"I never wanted it."*

She hops off her stool and stalks out of the room.

"People here are weird," Billy says. I don't correct him.

The paper cup of champagne is disintegrating in my hand, and the champagne is starting to spill, and I remember "Grandmama's" rule about the liquids, and then I remember all the uppity ladies who come into Happy Day complaining about the imaginary spots on their clothing, and even though we're on the West Side, those ladies probably live in buildings like this, and I think of Mrs. D, who didn't *want trouble* with her jefa, and even the rugs in the kitchen (yes, there are rugs in the kitchen) look súper expensive, so I say, "Toast?"

Billy and I "clink" our "glasses" and drink.

Champagne is kind of tasty—like unsweet ginger ale. Spicy bubbles tingle my tongue.

More Oatties arrive. First Maya Chang and Drae Woodward, then MK Hausen, then Chelsea Braeburn. Now Ambrose Garrison and Colt Brenner stride into the kitchen.

"Everyone, this is my friend Billy," I say.

"What's up, everyone," Billy says, and they all slap hands hello.

"Hey, where are you going next year, man?" Colt asks Billy.

I jump in with "So technically Billy's credits from his old school didn't transfer over, so he didn't, like, apply to college at the same time as us."

Billy gives me a funny look but doesn't say anything.

"You mean, he got left back?" Maya asks, oblivious to Billy's growing discomfort.

"No!" I say. "Billy's, like, super smart. Back in junior high, he was ranked second in our whole grade."

"Yeah, *thanks,* Ale. I can speak for myself." Billy sets down his paper cup. "Actually, I probably won't apply to college."

The room goes nails-to-the-chalkboard quiet.

Billy goes on. "It's not like I'll be guaranteed a job even with a college degree."

"College isn't just about finding a job," MK says. "It's about finding yourself."

Billy laughs; it's short, dry, rough. "I can 'find myself' for a lot cheaper."

Billy is *not* coming off well. What was I thinking, bringing him to an Oattie party? I have to break the growing judginess in the room.

"What Billy means is—"

"Colleges offer scholarships," Chelsea Braeburn interrupts. She says it tentatively, like it's some theoretical thing she has heard of but doesn't know firsthand.

Maya pulls me aside. "What is up with your boyfriend?"

"Billy's not my boyfriend," I say. "He's just my friend from growing up."

"Okaaay," she says. She reaches for the bottle of champagne. "Hey, come talk with me a sec? Drae is being *so* annoying."

Then Maya drags me out of the kitchen, leaving Billy to fend for himself.

OVER THE NEXT TWO paper cups of champagne, Maya goes from "Ohmigod, Drae's getting on my nerves" to "Ohmigod, I miss Drae so much," and ditches me to go find Drae again.

On my way back to the kitchen and to Billy, I bump into Colin Okafor.

"Ally! What up," he says. We slap hands hi.

"Congrats on Swarthmore!" I say. I heard Colin ended up getting in RD at Amherst after he'd been deferred, but by then he'd decided on Swat.

"Thanks. And you on Whyder! That's big."

I think about making a joke, riffing back to JBJ's remark. But I can't bring myself to do it.

"Hey, I'm so jealous you got that internship with Dr. C," Colin says.

"Surprised your ass didn't apply," I blurt out. "You're, like, practically in love with her."

"Damn, Ally." Colin whistles. "You're no bullshit."

"I'm *so* done with bullshit."

Colin fiddles with his champagne cup. "Look, Ally. I've been wanting to say. About that Diversity Assembly stuff. I feel you."

"If you 'feel me,' Colin, then why didn't you say anything?" My voice comes out with some Aletude, which I do and don't mean. The most popular boy in the senior class could have thrown his weight behind this.

Colin says, "You think they like it when someone who looks like me starts TALKING LOUD?"

As if to prove his point, two girls standing by the kitchen door look up with fraidy-cat eyes. They scuttle out.

"See what I mean?" Colin says.

"I get you."

We head into the kitchen. No Billy.

"Remember February of our first year?"

"Vaguely," I say.

"We had an assembly for Black History Month," Colin says. "Van Cortlandt called me up to the stage and handed me a Student of Distinction Award. For *being Black*."

"Shit," I say, the details of that assembly now rushing back to me. I remember sitting in the auditorium, thinking, *Okay, that's weird,* but also thinking, *I guess that's how they do things here?* Me being the "foreigner" at Quaker Oats, I felt like the onus was on *me* to adapt to the native culture, and not the other way around.

So I clapped along like everyone else.

"Colin, I'm really sorry." I truly am. I feel like a hypocrite. "I was too all up in my own insecure crap to speak out."

"We all were. We all *are*." Colin drains his cup. "You know how this system works. We are what we are to them."

"So, then what?" I say. "We're just . . . supposed to say nothing?"

"You do you," Colin says. "Me? This shit's all going in my book someday."

Suddenly I feel a heavy arm around my neck.

"Greetings, cultural classmates!" It's Josh Buck. He head-locks me with one arm and Colin with the other. It's awkward and uncomfortable, like we're trapped in a medieval pillory.

Colin breaks free from Josh, which sets me free, too.

"How dreary—to be—Somebody!" calls out Fiona McIntosh, appearing out of nowhere. She's holding out the bottle of champagne.

"Fill 'er up," Josh tells Fiona. "Cheers, you fuckheads. I'm going to miss you."

We clink and drink.

Champers is probably meant to be sipped, but I am not a classy upper-crust lady. Down the hatch it goes. And again.

Now all the scenes in *The Great Gatsby* make sense to me.

It's not that I've never been to a party. I don't live in a cave— I've been socialized and housebroken and all that crap. It's just that parties weren't ever Laurel's and my thing. Laurel doesn't really go to parties, and I just kind of do whatever Laurel does.

Do, or *did*?

"I was just telling Ally," Colin says, "how Dr. C is such a badass."

"More like ass*hole*," says Josh Buck. "If I'd stayed in that class, she would've failed me just for being a *white man*." He throws up his arms in frustration. "I get it, we're the devil incarnate."

"Aw, you're just mad Dr. C punked you on the first day," I say.

Colin whistles. "Damn, Ally Kim!"

Josh stares back at me—with some combination of vitriol and . . . admiration? Then—it's kind of weird—he starts to open up:

Josh was really banking on JBJ's class because it was the last chance his dad was giving him to pursue creative writing. "You know what my parents told me? They said, 'Don't bother majoring in English.' Because people like *me* never get hired in the humanities."

"What's that mean?" Colin asks, but we all know it's a rhetorical question. Josh doesn't answer it.

"Which means I'm going to have to major in finance and join a bro-ey frat," Josh says. "Welcome to the next fifty years of my life."

And I thought I was the one dropping truths all over the party.

"Whoa, dude," Colin says. "You're getting dark."

"That's why I got so mad they canceled JBJ's class," he continues. "But I do kind of regret transferring out of Cultural Studies." Josh fixes his eyes on me. They're *so* blue. Bluer than JBJ's. "I could have stayed in class with you."

"I'm . . . gonna go." Colin grabs his cup and busts out of the kitchen.

Josh moves in closer. "So, Ally. You want to hang out sometime?"

First-year Ally would be *so* flattered that Josh Buck is paying attention to me. He's the whole package, right down to the Superman hair and patrician jawline. Josh Buck is a modern-day aristocrat if there ever was one.

But that's the thing: I'm not freshperson Ally anymore. I'm not even the Ally from senior-year fall.

Just because Josh Buck is being nice to me now doesn't mean he's a nice person.

So I go:

"No, thanks. I don't do jerks. But cheers."

I clink my cup to a speechless Josh and leave the kitchen to find Billy.

SUDDENLY CLAIRE'S HOUSE IS a maze. I take a lap, but there's no sign of Billy. In the living room, which is filled with antique furniture that belongs in a museum, a gold-framed portrait of the Devereaux family hangs on the wall: Claire, her father, and her grandmother. The genteel older woman with a sweep of silver hair is seated in a velvet chair in the foreground of the portrait. She's wearing both a beige bouclé skirt suit with gold buttons and a condescending hint of a smile. Claire's dad stands tall and handsome, like a blond Kennedy. Claire's wearing a pink taffeta dress. They're all so stylized, they look like one of the aristocratic families in the telenovelas Ma likes to watch, only whiter.

But Claire looks different in her family portrait. Awkward. Gawky. Her hair is dark and frizzy, so unlike her usual sleek blond tresses.

She seems *so* uncomfortable, standing there with her family. She looks . . . like she doesn't belong.

"Notice how there are zero pictures of my mom," Claire calls out from the doorway, catching me staring at her family portrait. "Again, Grandmama's rules."

"I'm sorry," I say. "Is your mother . . ."

"Dead? Yeah. Car accident," she says. "My dad was behind the wheel. He survived. He's still around, somewhere." She flicks her wrist like he's far, far away.

In four years of going to school with Claire, I can't believe I didn't know anything about her mother, her family.

"I'm so sorry," I say, with feeling.

"It is what it is." Claire pulls out her phone. "Want to see my mom?" The lock screen is a picture of a young brown-skinned woman standing in front of a spewing fountain.

Wait, what?

I thought Claire was straight-up WASP. Which I hope isn't offensive to say. I had no idea she was—

"My mom's parents were from Colombia," Claire says.

Latinx.

White-passing. I remember Claire's list from Cultural Studies.

Now I feel shitty, with all the assumptions I've made of her over the years.

Is this the same guilt white people feel when they bungle up what we are?

At any rate, stereotype threat is real.

I look again at Claire's screen, seeing now the resemblance between Claire and her late mother. I also recognize that fountain—

"Hey, wait, that's Montoya Park!"

"Yup." Claire nods. "Mom was born and raised in Jackson Heights."

"For real?" I say. "I live right around the corner from there." I point to the background of the picture. "Also, I'm sad to report that Montoya Fountain hasn't worked for years."

"Maybe . . . sometime you could show it to me? I mean, no pressure. . . ." She's faltering. But Claire Devereaux never falters.

"Sure, of course," I say, and I mean it.

"I'd like that." Claire smiles, but the sadness is still there. I know because that same sadness echoes back at me in the mirror each morning.

"My dad died, too. A year ago." I don't mean to spill, but the words just bubble up like the champagne in my now-empty cup. "I thought things are supposed to get better. That I'd be able to forget. 'Time heals all wounds.' That's what they say, right? But . . . it still hurts. Here." I touch my hand to my heart.

"What they say is bullshit," Claire says. "Hallmark® drivel. You never forget. But you know what? I don't *want* to forget. I want to keep Mom alive."

"What do you mean?" I ask.

"Well, like this." Claire points to her phone. "Or going to her favorite ice cream shop and ordering her usual maple swirl. Or visiting all the places she used to take me, and sharing stories with family members, at least the ones who still acknowledge she ever existed. I try to keep the memory of her"—Claire touches her heart, mirroring me—"alive."

It's just like Dr. C said, how it helps to talk about them.

"Wow," I say, blinking back tears. "That's . . . deep."

"Sorry, sorry. I'm totally bringing down the mood of the party. It's supposed to be *fun!*" She throws up her arms like a *rah-rah!* cheerleader. "But, like, seriously. If you ever want to talk about stuff, I'm here."

Who *is* this Claire Devereaux? She's actually being nice. Why did Laurel and I talk so much shit about her?

"Thanks, I guess," Claire says, and I suddenly realize I've shared these thoughts *out loud.*

"Oh, fuck! I'm so sorry, Claire, I didn't mean—"

Claire interrupts me. "No, it's cool. I know people talk shit about me all the time."

"You know why, right?" I say. "I mean, look at you. You're, like, perfect. I thought you'd never want to be friends with me."

"Shut up, Ally Kim," Claire says. "I thought *you* never wanted to be friends with *me.* You're so cool and Queens. But you were always kind of standoffish with me."

Cool? Queens? An oxymoron if there ever was one.

"I'm shy," I say shyly.

"I'm shy, too. But everyone thinks it's just snobbiness."

Claire laughs. "We should probably stop before this girl-crush fest gets out of hand."

Which makes *me* laugh. I'm glad Claire and I are breaking bread, or making peace, or whatever it is we're doing. It will be nice to have a friendly face at Whyder in the fall.

"But seriously, I think you're the first person who's had the guts to say that to my face. About the people-hating-me thing. Are you always this—"

"Blunt? Not really. Sometimes. Yeah. Sorry." I trip over all my words.

"I was going to say 'honest.' It's actually refreshing," Claire says. She holds up a bottle of champagne. "Speaking of which, more bubbly?"

"Please."

She refills our cups, and we clink.

"You know that"—Claire glances around the room to make sure no one is there—"Laurel talks shit about everyone, right?"

My guard goes up. "That's my best friend," I warn.

"Do you know what she wrote her Whyder essay on?"

"She wrote about Muslim women's rights and feeling 'at home' in Arabic. . . ."

But then I remember what Laurel said on (E)D-Day. *I didn't end up using that one. . . .*

I trail off.

"Not according to what she's telling people in the kitchen," Claire says.

"Laurel's here?"

"She doesn't deserve you." The doorbell rings. "I should go host." And with that, Claire leaves me in the literal dark.

I NEED TO FIND Laurel. So she can tell me everything Claire said is not true. Because right now my mind is reaching for the worst. I feel the heat of the stage lights from the Diversity Assembly all over again. Back in the kitchen, the party has suddenly multiplied. But still no sign of Laurel. Or Billy.

I weave through the party, bumping into Chelsea Braeburn. "Hey, have you seen Laurel?"

"Sorry, Ally." Chelsea shakes her head.

Fiona McIntosh floats by. I grab her arm before she disappears on me again. "Fiona, do you know what Laurel wrote her Whyder essay on?"

"The art of losing isn't hard to master."

And Fiona turns down a hallway and is gone.

I also start down the hallway, when I hear Laurel's voice. It comes in like a whisper, yet it echoes against the walls. I follow it through the apartment, where it comes into louder focus.

And that's when I spot Laurel, with *Billy*. They're standing close. *Too* close.

Laurel doesn't even hide the fact that she's kind of, sort of . . . checking him out all over.

And what's even stranger is that Billy is now staring back at Laurel. She's wearing a tight-fitting camisole tucked into tight jeans. Gone is her usual uniform of flowy top and culottes. He seems like he's enjoying Laurel's attention. Which makes no sense, because right after they met freshperson year, Billy was like, "Uh, does that girl not shave her pits?"

The look between them lasts for seconds, minutes, I don't know. I want to step in and block it with my body.

Now Laurel puts her hands on Billy's chest.

What the hell?

She leans in closer and says something *almost* too faint to catch:

"You're Latinx, Billy. You'll get in everywhere."

I can't help myself—I start cracking up.

They break free.

"Ally!" Laurel's face is all guilt.

"What the fuck is going on?"

I hear my Queens accent slipping in. My tone is coarse, like rusty flakes of iron. It scares me. It scares Laurel.

"That's not what—it wasn't," Laurel sputters. "It's not what it sounded like."

"Ale, where were you? We were looking all over for you." Billy touches my arm. "You okay? Because you seem a little—"

I ignore him. "You hear yourself, Laurel? You're a fucking hypocrite!"

There's no mistaking my voice now; I am *all* Queens. I've never used that voice at Quaker Oats.

"Ally, just calm down." Laurel is putting on her *Let's all be reasonable* voice. Her fake-ass, *You don't know what you're talking about, I'm right and you're wrong, but let's be civilized about it* voice.

"What'd you really write your Whyder essay about?"

Laurel's tearing up the edges of her paper cup.

Her silence tells me everything.

Sometimes you just got to do whatever it takes. Laurel said that, back in the fall when we sat down to write our Whyder essays in the first place.

"You wrote about the Diversity Assembly, didn't you."

"You weren't . . . supposed to find out like this," Laurel says slowly.

"First you humiliate me with that assembly in front of the whole school. And I gave you a free pass—"

" *'Free pass'?*" Laurel spits back. "That's rich. I spoke up for *you*. When no one else here did!" She points an accusatory finger around the room.

"Then you turn around and use it, all for your fucking essay? You *used* me, Laurel!"

"That's not how it went down!" Laurel argues. "Let me explain—"

Laurel tries to put her hands on my shoulders, but I'm not having it.

"Bullshit. You did it so you could get into Whyder."

"Is that what you really think of me? Of our friendship?" Laurel shouts. "I have stood by your side for four years, Ally. That fucking hurts."

"You know what else 'fucking hurts'? That my own best friend didn't come to my dad's wake!"

The words come pouring out. I told her it was no big deal at the time—I told *myself* it was no big deal—but deep down, it really hurt that she wasn't there for me on that big day.

"It was the night before the PSATs!" Laurel shouts back. "I offered to come the day after!"

"Ale, c'mon." Billy grabs my arm, but I throw him off.

"Damn!" I hear Colin in the background.

"Girl fight!" Josh shouts, punching a fist in the air.

"Fuck you, Josh Buck!" all the girls in the room shout in unison.

When did we get an audience? We are now two boxers in the ring. Everyone standing and gawking. Whatever, this is about Laurel and me. And the truth is out—pus and all.

"You know what, Laurel? I can't afford to go to Whyder, anyway. Just take my spot."

"How *charitable* of you, Ally," she scoffs.

Charity. It suddenly clicks. From loaned Post-its and highlighters to all those study sessions at her house—has this been the whole basis of our friendship?

"Speaking of charity, you only liked it when I was worse off than you," I say.

"What?" Laurel says. "That is *such* a leap!"

"Do you even *see* me, Laurel?" I spit out. "Or am I just 'multi-culti' to you, too?"

Laurel stares at me, her mouth hanging open.

"That was low," she says slowly. "Who even *are* you, Ally?"

Billy and Claire are at us now. Claire puts both hands between us like a traffic cop. Billy is holding me back.

"Laurel, Ally," Claire cries, "just *stop*!"

I shake off Billy, push past Claire. "I'm out of here," I say, glaring at Laurel, who can't even meet my eye.

Whatever.

"Adiós, jerkos."

I flash "peace" to the other Oatties at the periphery who see everything but say nothing at all.

I TUMBLE OFF THE elevator, Billy following right behind me. We ignore the evil eye of the doorman. I trip in the lobby; Billy catches me; I spill into his arms. Everything feels out of context.

"Billy." My voice is hoarse from all the yelling. "Take me home."

And that's pretty much where the film fades out—my memory cuts to black.

CHAPTER 32

Morning After

HEAD POUNDING. STOMACH TWISTING. Bile rising in my throat. The sun streaming through the window feels like murder. I am lying on the bathroom floor, tiles as pillow. I'm still wearing my dress from last night.

What the fuck happened?

The night comes back to me in disjointed shards.

Fighting with Laurel.

You're a fucking hypocrite!

How charitable *of you.*

You weren't . . . supposed to find out like this.

Crowds of Oatties watching, staring, smirking.

Crossing over the East River, rushing into Queensboro Plaza.

The lights from the bridge striking all the hard lines of Billy's face.

Pressing my lips to his—

Oh God.

I put my hands over my face.

WTF have I just done?

Billy and I were in the friend zone. And yeah, he suddenly got hot—that has not escaped my notice. But I ruined that. The last part of the night comes into crisper focus, like a photograph developing in a darkroom. Tiny pixels rearrange themselves, reconstructing the whole scene from the train ride home. I remember:

Billy cracking his knuckles, like he always does when he's nervous. The veins in his arms taut, like he's been hauling furniture all day. Billy catches me staring at him.

"You okay, Kim?"

He only calls me by my last name when he's trying to be bro-ey. It forces distance between us like a shot of compressed air.

Billy's so close I can smell him: breath mints and way too much cologne. Billy's lips look so soft, and there's stubble on his face.

"What was up with you and Laurel? You were flirting, big-time."

Wow, words are hard; they slooze out of my mouth like it's a Slip 'N Slide.

"Surprised you even noticed," Billy says. "You were so busy flirting with all the guys there."

"Was not!" I slur. "You like Laurel or something? J'accuse!" My finger is all up in Billy's face. "Why don't you go ask her to be your girlfriend?"

His jaw clenches. "Come on, Ale."

"I'm *serious*. Answer the damn question."

"You *know* why."

"But you said . . ."

Don't worry. I don't feel like that anymore.

"I only said that so it wouldn't be awkward around us anymore." Billy's looking down at his hands. They're trembling. "It's . . . always been you, Ale."

Right after Papi's funeral, when Billy confessed, I shut him down; I pushed him away. But I've known pretty much all my life.

Billy's always been there for me. Not my alleged "best friend," who couldn't bother to show up to Papi's wake. He's been the only one who gives a shit about me. Why *not* Billy?

I reach out, my fingers tracing the veins of his forearms.

"Knock it off, Kim," he says, but his tone is soft.

"You want me to stop?"

"No."

And that's when I start kissing Billy.

"Whoa, Ale," he says. But he doesn't stop me. He kisses me back.

We're kissing for a while. It feels right. It feels wrong. I don't know *what* I feel, and all that champagne is gurgling inside me. The white lights of our empty subway car are blinding; I close my eyes.

Suddenly Billy stops, pushing me off. "This isn't right. You're drunk."

"I'm not drunk!" I say drunkenly.

"Kim, do you even like me?"

"Shut up, Chivi." I reach for him again, but with one hand, he holds me back.

"Because I really like you. I always have," Billy says. "And I was fine with you not liking me back. I accepted it for what it was. But now—"

"I'm practically *throwing* myself at you, Billy. And now you're *rejecting* me?"

I feel humiliated.

"Why did you bring me to this stupid party, Ale?"

I don't answer.

"You're just trying to kiss me because you feel sorry for yourself. And I . . . I just can't go along with your act anymore, Ale. I'm tired of your games."

Billy's words are a sucker punch to the gut. A knife to my heart. All the clichés because I'm too drunk to think of something more original.

"What the fuck, Billy?" I say, crumpling into my seat. "*'Games'?* Where are you pulling this shit from?"

"All night you kept making excuses for me. Like . . . like you're ashamed of me." He lets out a stiff laugh. "You don't have to be, Ale. I'm *perfectly* comfortable with who I am."

"It's not that I'm ashamed of *you*," I protest. The words bubble up inside me: *It's that I'm ashamed of myself.*

I can't bring myself to say them aloud.

"Yeah, well." Billy doesn't buy it. "And then you go picking a fight with Laurel? What the fuck was that?"

"Oh, I don't know." I am all sarcasm. "Staging the Diversity Assembly so she could *write about it* for her Whyder app? Then all that shit she said to you about getting into college, which was the same exact thing JBJ said!"

"I mean, the college counselor at school basically told me as much," Billy starts.

"That's not the fucking point! What kind of friend *does* that to another friend? To her *best* friend?"

"Wouldn't you have done that, too? If you wanted it badly enough?"

"No!" I say. "That's the difference between me and Laurel."

"Is it?"

"Oh, so now suddenly you two are so tight?" I snap. "Why don't you go back to staring at her boobs all night?"

Billy lets out a chuff. "You are *so* blind."

"That's ableist."

"God!" Billy runs his fingers through his hair. "For four years I've heard you ragging on everyone at your school, how they're just a bunch of fakes. And that was fun for a while. But . . ."

"But what?"

He doesn't answer.

"What are you trying to say, Billy?"

Our faces are reflected in the train car window.

"Take a long, hard look at yourself, Alejandra Kim." Billy says it slow and steady, like he wants me to take it in. "Because you're just like them."

Billy's words hit cold as ice.

We're rushing toward Queensboro Plaza. How did we get here? Too drunk to remember boarding the 7. Or maybe there's weekend track work that forced us to take it.

"You've changed, Ale. I wonder if your pa would even recognize you now."

The 7 screeches into the station. *Rat-tat-tat, rat-tat-tat.* Subway Music pounding in my ears.

I'm frozen in place.

"Take it back," I whisper.

I squeeze my eyes, shutting out my reflection.

"Take it back, take it back, take it back."

I'm rocking, repeating the words like a lullaby.

But Billy doesn't take it back.

THE SICK RISES UP again. It takes all the strength I don't have to hoist my head up to the toilet. I dry heave. Some eau de toilet splashes back at me. My mouth tastes like HCl-coated vomit. As much as I'd like to stay home and feel the cold tiles on my hot skin, I have to go to Happy Day. Thank God Ma is working an overnight shift; I'll leave before she gets home. She'd kill me if she found me like this. Or would she? Who knows—maybe she'd be glad I finally got a life.

I pick myself up off the floor. I take a long, hard look at myself. But all I can see are the lines of tile grout crisscrossing my face like the tracks of a train.

"DON'T YOU LOOK LIKE Little Miss Sunshine," Michael Oppa says brightly when I get to Happy Day. He waves his hand over his nose. "And you smell like it, too."

"Coffee. Now," I say. "And I don't want to talk about it."

"Touché," says Michael Oppa, handing me a mug of the

insta-stuff. I down it all, and the foggy swamp of my brain is starting to clear. Last night was the first time I've gotten drunk. And I am never, ever drinking again.

ON MY WAY HOME from Happy Day, I get a text from a number I don't recognize.

> We didn't get to say goodbye. I'm really glad you spoke your truth at my party.

It's from Claire Devereaux. I'll write her back when I get home, when I'm in a better headspace.

There's still nothing from either Billy or Laurel.

Maybe I imagined it all. Maybe there was no fight with Laurel, no kiss with Billy.

I shoot Billy a text: We need to talk.

Billy writes: . . .

. . .

Nothing at all.

CHAPTER 33

Spec Fest

THANK GOD FOR SPRING break. I don't have to see or talk to anyone after Claire's party. Not that Laurel's gone out of her way to reach out to me. She sent one dinky text: We need to talk. Which was the cheapest cop-out ever. It puts the onus on the recipient of said text to do the work of interpreting. Besides, Laurel and I already "talked." There's nothing left to say.

So I'm on a Greyhound heading north. I always thought Laurel and I would be making this trip together, as prospective (aka "spec") students. But here I am, heading to Spec Fest alone.

Whyder costs $75,000 a year for tuition, room, and board—not counting books, travel, and everything else. Ever since my acceptance letter came in the mail, I've been researching options for federal and private loans, which I won't have to start paying back until *after* I graduate. The interest rates swirled in my head, but I already sat down and did the math. Plenty of people go to college even if they can't afford it.

I'll have to find a good, high-paying job after I graduate, just for the first year or three or ten. A sell-out, corporate, just-get-the-bills-paid kind of job. Once I pay off my college loans, then I can do what I *really* want.

Ma doesn't know what's best for my life. It isn't her decision to make. It's mine.

I ran into Mrs. D on my way to Port Authority. It was too late to avoid her; you can't hide from anyone in our barrio.

"¡Ale!" she called out. "M'hija, ¡ya vente!"

So I vení. "Hi, Mrs. D. I'm actually on my way to catch a bus—"

"Why this face? ¿Qué te pasa?"

"Nothing, Mrs. D."

Mrs. D doesn't take bullshit. She put a finger under my chin, holding my face to the light. "Have you been fighting with my son?"

". . ." I shrugged. What was said was said.

Mrs. D said, "Go talk to him."

I kicked free a pebble embedded in a crack in the sidewalk. "We're not really talking."

"Tsk! There's no such thing as 'not really talking.'" She wagged her finger in the air. "You're hurting! And Billy's hurting, too."

I shook my head, but Mrs. D started shaking her head over *my* head, like she was trying to cancel it out.

"If you care about each other, you'll talk it out. If not, pues, *ya.*"

She brushed her hands together, all Pontius Pilate, like the matter was done.

I STARE OUT THE window. I-95 is pretty ugly. Funny how to get out of the place you're in to the place you want to be, you literally have to pass through the most dreadful highway, riddled with potholes and ROAD WORK and CAUTION signs.

I get a text from Claire. Grandmama has a "work thing" she's dragging Claire to this weekend, so she can't make Spec Fest. I text back a picture of the standstill of cars on I-95: Not missing much. Traffic must be backed up all the way to Boston.

But it will be so worth it once I get to Whyder's campus. My old life will just fall away.

"OUR WHOLE CAMPUS IS set on a national park. Every tree, plant, and flower is labeled by its genus and species," Lexa, our tour guide, says, waving her arm across the wide expanse of the campus green.

"And this is our rose garden." She gestures to the greenhouse, where three gardeners meticulously prune flower buds that have yet to bloom.

My life has been all the shades of gray up to this point, from concrete to pavement to asphalt. I'm Dorothy from *The Wizard of Oz;* I click my heels and suddenly my world floods into

Technicolor. Whyder is gorgeous, lush and vibrant as far as the eye can see. The catalog was not lying.

Actually, it *was* lying: Whyder looks even better in real life.

I see MK Hausen passing by on another tour. I'm glad we're in different tour groups. I do *not* want to rehash what went down at Claire's party over the weekend.

A circle of students sits on the lawn with their professor. The prof is wearing jeans and a fleece.

"You can have class outside?" asks a kid on our tour. "That's so cool!"

Lexa nods. "It's pretty common here," she says, then waves to the professor. "Hey, Cam!"

"Hi, Lexa." He waves back.

"We're on a first-name basis with our profs here," Lexa says (okay, boasts).

I'd be boasting, too, if I were on a first-name basis with my professors. Our tour group murmurs with approval.

I'm smitten. I feel a rush through me—*Holy bleep, I got into this place!* The rush is immediately replaced by a nagging *Do I deserve to be here?*

The feelings go up-down throughout the tour.

"Whyder now has one of the most competitive diversity rates of any SLAC," Lexa announces.

She looks at me pointedly. "For example, our Asian American Coalition meets every Monday."

"That's cool," I say, since it's obvious she's directing her comments to me. "But what about the German student group? Or the Swedish one?"

Lexa lets out an uncomfortable laugh, like she thinks she's being punked but doesn't know what the joke is.

I swear I'm not trying to be an asshole. But it bothers me that Lexa looked at me and immediately felt she needed to make a comment about the Asian coalition. We've talked about this in Dr. C's class. When you look at someone's face and decide to make a comment or assumption about their ethnicity, *is that not* the literal textbook definition of racism? You're priming their race or perceived race. It makes me feel like that's *all* Lexa can see, and not the human behind my face/race/peoples.

"I don't know about those groups, but I can definitely check!" Lexa says. "But there *is* a Latinx group that meets Tuesdays, the African American Student Association on Wednesdays, and the Muslim Student Alliance on Thursdays . . ."

And Lexa counts off her fingers, ticking off a different "minority" group for each day of the week.

WHYDER'S CAFETERIA HAS, in addition to the main entrée stations and the grill, a pasta bar, a salad bar, and a dedicated vegan bar. I reach for a helping of vegan lasagna (because why not), made with cashew cream "cheese." This sounds exactly up Laurel's alley. I think about texting her a pic—but even if we were on speaking terms, texting her would feel like I was rubbing it in.

I grab my tray and head into the dining room. Gemma, the first-year who's been assigned as my "chaperone" for Spec Fest, waves me over to her table.

"Ohmigod," she says, embarrassed. "There are *so* many white people here, right?"

I mean, there are, but Gemma is also white.

"Can I ask you a question?" I ask her.

"Sure!"

"Would you have said the same thing to me if *I* were white?"

Gemma's mouth hangs open, but no words actually come out.

An awkward silence spreads across the table. Everyone picks at their vegan bean salads.

I *so* want to text Billy right now. It'd be the kind of thing we'd laugh about in Montoya Park.

But Billy and I aren't like that anymore.

Finally, a fourth-year named Brynne says, "Thank you for sharing that, Alexandra. I want you to know that *we* are *listening*."

Then she puts her hands together, in prayer, and bows at me like we're Buddhist monks.

Oh *no* she didn't.

"Why did you just do that?" I ask.

Brynne blinks. "Do what?"

"The bowing thing."

"Oh!" She tries to brush it off. "Because . . ."

Kayle, a sophomore, steps in. "We should listen to Alexandra if they feel like we're appropriating from their culture."

Oh my God. This is turning into Diversity Assembly 2.0.

I can feel the Aletude rising. I know I should stop myself. These are my future classmates! But I can't stop, I won't stop; I let loose:

"You don't even know *what* my culture is! And for the record, my name is *Alejandra*."

263

I crossed a line. This isn't how someone like me is "supposed" to behave. I can feel it. Everyone glances around like they're embarrassed *for* me.

But I'm not embarrassed. No more. *They* should be the ones who are embarrassed.

Quaker freshperson Ally would never have behaved like this. She would have said zip, zero, nada. She would have listened to Papi when he said, *You're a guest at this school. Don't make any trouble.*

I made it to Whyder, despite or maybe because of what JBJ said. I'm here; I arrived. But I'm here without the person I thought was my best friend. And the person who was my actual best friend, my only true friend, told me I'm no better than the rest of them—that I'm a fake.

For four years, I went to Quaker Oats with a tightness all over my body. A tightness I'd carry through eight periods a day, five days a week. Maybe this is how some people carry themselves all day, every day, for the rest of their lives. I think of Ma, trudging through life now that Papi's gone.

I think of the interviews I transcribe for the First-Generation American Testimony. I think of Papi's words to me. Is this how he "behaved" when he was alive? Always suppressing his thoughts for the sake of getting along?

Some people go along to get along. That's a survival tactic.

I no belong.

At what point does the "imposter" you start to become the "real" you?

At what point do you no longer care?

***

AFTER AN AWKWARDLY SILENT lunch, I join the Specs filing up the hill to the white clapboard Meeting House. There, we'll be breaking into small groups to discuss our definitions of "culture" and "community." All over campus, groundskeepers are hard at work, trimming hedges and pushing wheelbarrows uphill.

I'm surrounded by so much beauty here.

None of it comes for free.

CHAPTER 34

Bathroom Confidential

AFTER SPRING BREAK, I'M no longer afraid to face everyone at school. Because now I just don't give a bleep. At lunch I'm fine sitting by myself. Sometimes Claire or MK stop by to say hi. The old Ally would have felt self-conscious about being alone; now I don't care.

On Friday, right before lunch, I stop at the bathroom. I hear crunching in the stall next to me, then sniffling. They alternate: *sniff, crunch; sniff, crunch.* The sniffles turn to a straight-up sob.

The bathroom air, which smells like bleach, is now filled with the distinct odor of celery.

"Laurel?" I call out.

"Yeah." Sniffle. "It's me."

"What are you doing in the girls' bathroom?"

"You mean the gender nonconforming bathroom?" she corrects me. *Sniffle, sniffle.* "Trying to avoid you."

"So you're eating your lunch in *here*?"

"Yeah, I know. It's kind of gross," she says.

"Kinda, yeah."

"Ally, after Claire's party, I kept searching for the right words, but . . . I can't even begin to say how sorry I am."

"You used me, Laurel. And you expect me to just forget that? Let alone forgive?"

"I know that. I wouldn't forgive me, either," she says. "But could I just . . . try to explain?"

I don't say yes *or* no, so Laurel goes:

"Right after I learned what JBJ said to you, I was at my dad's. He went off on this whole spiel about his firm's new 'diversity' initiatives and how he thinks it's total BS. Dad has no sympathy for people of color. He thinks, because he picked himself up by his bootstraps and got himself out of Borough Park, *as a white man,* anyone else can do it. Meanwhile, Dad needs to get over his whole Philip Roth self-hatred complex, but I'm pinning that discussion for my therapist.

"In a fucked-up way, I think he was trying to empathize with me, like we were two poor white people in a sea of 'coloreds' [*sic*]! I swear that was *his* word. All that was running through my head was *I cannot end up like my dad.* Which was why I was willing to do whatever it took to get into Whyder. And I started writing a rant about allyship, and proposing the assembly, and one thing led to another. . . ."

She trails off. "In trying not to end up like my asshole dad, I ended up being a much bigger asshole. I hurt you, Ally. I hurt my best friend."

"I felt bamboozled, Laurel. You didn't even *ask* me about the assembly," I say, heat in my voice. "I'm not saying I would have said, 'Hells yeah!' but—"

"Instead I went behind your back. I know."

"I gave you the benefit of the doubt," I say. "I let it go. But then, what you said to Billy—"

"I'm sorry. I know," Laurel says. "I don't know, I was trying to cite a statistic, and the words came out all wrong. I never meant to make you, or Billy, feel unseen."

"And then writing about me for Whyder? Laurel, that's so fucking low!"

"You're right. I'm sorry."

I can hear Laurel tearing up toilet paper. Tearing paper is a bad habit of hers when she's anxious. The shreds fall like ribbons to the floor of the bathroom.

"Ally, have you just been holding it in this whole time? How pissed off you were about the assembly? Because, when we talked after, you seemed fine. If I'd had any idea . . ." Laurel trails off again.

I think back to our not-quite fight. How I vented my head off to Billy, but I muted my feelings when it came to actually confronting Laurel.

"Honestly, Laurel? I can't always be real with you." I swallow hard. Admitting the truth is not easy. "Like, if I tell you what I'm really thinking and feeling, then you'll just tell me it's not the *right* way. The Oattie way. And it makes me not trust what I think and feel."

I'm finding my words now. I can feel a lightness inside me, instead of the usual tightness I feel all day at Quaker Oats.

"So, yeah. I should have dropped the Aletude and cursed you out after." I shrug, even though she can't see me. We're still in our separate stalls. "But for four years, Laurel, I was afraid.

Afraid of getting called out as an imposter. So that's why I didn't say anything. That's why I often *don't* say anything."

"I had no idea you felt like that, Ally. I wish I had. Instead of making you feel like I was judging you so you couldn't say what you were really feeling." Laurel's sniffling again. "I've been a really shitty friend."

I remember lunch at Glüt, and how Laurel stood up to Maya about the check. I remember the time by the lockers when she shyly showed me her approach to studying. I remember the indignation that flared across her face when she found out about JBJ.

But then I remember Laurel on the podium. Oblivious to my feelings. Lying by omission about her Whyder essay. *Exploiting* me.

I remember her stabbing her steak across from her dad—

Laurel, easy there on the potatoes. . . .

Laurel, that frizz is out of control. . . .

The Koreans keep their heads down and put in the output!

Does it all boil down to a "shitty" friendship?

"While we're being real"—Laurel takes a deep breath—"can I be completely honest, Ally? Like, unfiltered?"

"Yeah."

"Sometimes I feel like, as a white person, I'm always apologizing for everything in the system. Like, you're always being told you're a bad person for being white. And some days . . . I don't know. It all kind of gets to you. Like, I'm trying to be a good ally. But most days it feels like I'm damned if I do, damned if I don't."

She reaches for more toilet paper, but all I can hear is the *clink-clink* of the empty roll.

"I know that's hard for you to hear," she goes on. "Even I hate my guts for what I just said. But I need to get that nuclear truth bomb off my chest."

Laurel has *never* expressed these feelings to me, ever. Not in the four years I've known her. She's the first at school to initiate conversations about how white people need to "step up" and be "active allies to POCs." I know Laurel's always trying to Do the Right Thing.

But you can't just front like you're a good person. You have to *be* one first.

"How come you never told me how you felt?" I ask.

"How could I?" Laurel says. "It would have just sounded like I was complaining about my privilege. Hashtag: white girl problems. Hashtag: world's tiniest violin."

"No one speaks in hashtags anymore, Laurel."

"Damn it," she says, "always the last one to the party."

I can't help but laugh. She laughs, too.

"Remember that time you invited me up to your family's house in Vermont?" I say.

"Yeah."

"We stopped at that grocery store in the middle of nowhere, and they had those celery sticks that were blatantly labeled 'gluten-free'?"

"It's so dumb," Laurel says, "how people in this country don't understand that veggies are by default gluten-free. Talk about redundant. Duh."

"Exactly," I say. "I feel like those celery sticks."

"Lost you there."

"The Diversity Assembly felt like that loud, blaring, redundant packaging on the celery, announcing its gluten-freeness," I say. "Like, if I really belonged, then why would we need a whole assembly just to prove it? I could just . . . be. Like how *normal* celery in *normal* grocery stores doesn't need the GF label. Because everyone already knows."

I take a deep breath. "So instead of priming its 'sameness,' all you're doing is pointing out its 'differentness' in people's minds."

I'm peddling the new language we learned in Dr. C's class. For the first time in a long time, the words feel right.

I can hear Laurel thinking. "I never thought of it like that. I always hate being the same as everyone else. I've always wanted to be different."

"That's because you get to take being 'normal' for granted," I say. "I don't have that privilege."

This makes Laurel go quiet.

"I'm so tired, Laurel," I say. "Tired of having to teach people that celery is gluten-free. Obviously I'm not talking about literal celery."

"Ally," Laurel continues, "I don't expect you to forgive me. But I want to say, from the bottom of my heart, I'm truly sorry. I'm sorry for all the hurt I caused you. Because of my selfishness."

I say, "It isn't fair."

"You're right," Laurel says. "It was fucked up of me—"

"That's not what I mean," I interrupt. "Yeah, it isn't fair what I've had to put up with. But I also think it's not fair that you have to feel what you're feeling. Like you're always walking on eggshells, worried about getting canceled. *None* of it is fair. And I wish I had the solution. But . . . I don't."

I fold up a piece of toilet paper like origami. The folds stare back at me in a delicate, intricate pattern.

"You shouldn't have to be the one proselytizing about celery's gluten-freedom," Laurel says slowly. "That's not your job. But . . . I still think people out there need to be taught that. Because they're out there, Ally. And they'll start lumping celery into the same 'evil' carby category as bread and cake. . . ."

She pauses. "This analogy is *way* not holding up."

"I think I get what you mean," I say. "Kind of sort of."

Laurel starts again. "I feel like it's *my* job to educate those people. In fact, I've never felt that more deeply. I think that's what I want to do with my life."

"You're right. I don't want that job," I say. "But you do you."

"This is stupid." I hear Laurel getting out of her stall. She knocks on mine. "We should have been talking this whole time face to face," she says when I open my door.

"It kind of feels like we're in the confession box," I say.

Laurel laughs. "Bless me, Father, for I have sinned. The last time I went to confession was never."

"My inner Catholic feels scandalized," I say.

"My inner half WASP feels dead inside," she quips back. "Don't get me started on the Jewish half."

"Whatcha got for lunch today?" I ask.

Laurel shows me. "Same old. Quinoa with roasted-black-garlic hummus and celery. You?"

"Same old. Kraft on Wonder." I add, hotly, "And if you,

272

Laurel Greenblatt-Watkins, call my lunch 'über-Americana provisions' one more time, I'm going to—"

"And if you call *my* lunch 'bougie' one more time, I'm going to—"

We interrupt each other, laughing.

She slides her lunch box over to me. "Trade you?"

I hesitate before sliding my brown baggie over to her. "Sure."

I know this will be one of our last lunches together. Not just because senior year is ending and Laurel and I are going to different schools.

We won't be walking together to the same train station anymore. We're bound for separate tracks.

I take a bite of Laurel's lunch, just as she takes a bite out of my Kraft-Wonder sandwich.

Laurel's food is not something I'd want to eat every day. But I needed to try it for myself. I look over at Laurel chewing *my* food. I can tell she's thinking similar.

"Not bad," we say at exactly the same time.

CHAPTER 35

Imposter Syndrome

AT THE END OF our "bathroom confessional," Laurel asks me about Billy. "Do you know if he's okay?"

Then, reading the room, "I swear I'm not asking for me. It's just, he was going on, about the not applying to college—"

"He hasn't been answering my calls," I tell her.

"Yeah, but . . ." Then Laurel gives me her no-nonsense, tough-love tone: "Have you been eating lunch in the bathroom?"

"Literally or metaphorically?"

"Obviously metaphorically," she tuts. "Maybe you're hiding out instead of confronting what you don't want to confront."

"What's there to say?" I shrug. "Billy basically told me to fuck off."

Because you're just like them.

"Maybe he just said that because he was mad," Laurel says, switching now to her "concluding remarks" voice. "Ale, it's so obvious he's in love with you. You need to go to him."

***

I'M NOT "YA" WITH Billy. Or am I? Is this the end of . . . whatever we are?

As much as it stings to think about what Billy said to me that night after I kissed him, the way I treated him stings more.

I wish we could go back to the old days of sitting together at the fountain, laughing about all kinds of dumb crap. But like Ms. Zinn always used to say in junior-year English, *"You can't go home again."*

But just because Billy makes me feel less alone in the world, just because when I'm around him, I feel like I'm at home . . .

Billy's my best friend. He also has feelings for me—feelings he made *very clear* the other night, but also the night I played dumb and shut him down before he left for the Dominican Republic. And honestly, I'm flattered by the attention. And even more honestly, I'm lonely. I've been lonely for a long time.

Kissing someone is nice and makes you feel wanted.

But feeling wanted isn't the same as wanting that person you're kissing.

Or is it?

AFTER SCHOOL I PULL out Michael Oppa's laptop and open a fresh document. The blank white page looks intimidating.

Can I explain to Billy?

Maybe he'll understand. So I sit down to write him a letter.

Dear Billy,

We said some pretty hurtful things to each other. I said
some pretty hurtful things to you. You don't know
how sorry I am—in more ways than I can count. I'm
sorry I took advantage of your feelings when I tried to
kiss you.

I tell Billy he was right to call me out on my Oattie shit.
Because the truth is, I *was* ashamed. Of who I was and where
I came from. For four years, I've been comparing myself to
people whose parents and grandparents and great-grandparents
are doctors and lawyers and editors at the *New York* freaking
Times. They live in million-dollar houses and still feel "middle
class," aka "normal."

That kind of thing gets to you after a while. Seeing how
their lunches are all organic and local and made by their maids,
and mine are down-market bread and processed meat and
cheese. Even our *pens* are different. I use cheap Bic disposables
from the 99-cent store, and they all have refillable-ink pens that
were handcrafted in Japan.

And don't even get me started on college.

Those are small, stupid, little things, but they add up.
For four years, I felt self-conscious of who I was and what
I didn't have. For four years, I had Imposter Syndrome, always feeling like I didn't deserve to be here. Always fear-
ing some Oattie would call me out on how much I didn't
belong.

Because WE ALL BELONG is bullshit. It's what the higher-ups

at Quaker Oats say to make themselves feel better about the inequality all around us.

I tell him about Spec Fest, and how Whyder both is and isn't everything I thought it would be.

Then I start to tell Billy about something I have never, *ever* told anyone before because I was too ashamed. My fingers tremble as I type.

I tell him about what I said to Papi, about the junior-year college trip. I tell him Papi's death wasn't just "some accident." I tell him about the fights Ma and I have about that, how we're at odds. The words hurt as I type them, as I relive the pain I caused to my own father. Part of me is afraid Billy will judge me. But I'm also not afraid.

Because I'm telling him my truth. The truth I was too ashamed to admit.

The other truth I tell Billy is that I am legit confused about my feelings for him. Ever since we were kids, we were like brother and sister. And when he confessed his feelings for me, it made things even *more* confusing.

And now I realize my confusion, and my mixed signals, have only hurt Billy more than if I'd just said flat-out yes or no in the first place.

So I tell Billy all of it. Even though it hurts to be so in-your-face honest, and I'm not proud of the things I've said and done. Because what I'm realizing is this: if you're afraid of saying your truth, then that's worse than supposedly "belonging." That's the true definition of "imposter."

* * *

AND . . . I'M DONE. Four single-spaced pages stare back at me. I'm looking for my flash drive to take to KopyKatz, but when I open my desk drawer, it knocks the power cord from Michael Oppa's laptop and—

The computer goes dead.

Oh no, oh no, oh no.

Quickly I jam the cord back into the laptop, but—the computer won't boot up. I hold down the power button, do the whole Ctrl + Alt + Del thing, blow air into the socket, pop out the battery and blow on that, too, before popping it back in; I do an Our Father and a round of the rosary; I send a prayer to Saint Anthony because Sor Juana at our old church said he was the patron saint of lost things. . . .

Nothing. Still dead. And because the operating system is too old to sync with new updates, *nothing is backed up.*

Michael Oppa's laptop has officially given up the ghost. It was only a matter of time. The red eyes of his Transformers decal glower at me.

Everything I wrote to Billy is lost.

Just like all the work I've done for the last four years at Quaker Oats is—*poof*—gone.

At least I don't have any papers due this week.

Small mercies.

I HAVE NO OTHER choice but to start again. I take out a fresh sheet of loose-leaf paper. But . . . somehow it doesn't feel right. Like the magic of my words to Billy is now lost.

So I just text him:

I said and did some pretty shitty things after that party. Even bf the party. I'm so sorry, Billy. You're my best friend. You deserve better than the way I've been treating you.

Meet me tonight, 7pm, at our usual spot. So much I want to say to you. Stuff it's better to say in person than over text. I promise I'll be REAL.

AT TEN TO, I head down to Montoya Fountain. Billy gets off work by then, so he should be around. I wait, and I wait. But Billy never shows.

CHAPTER 36

Sobremesa

I DON'T EVEN HAVE a minute to process Billy not showing up. Because when I get home, Ma's sitting at the dining table. The piles and piles of ignored bills, bills, bills have been opened and sorted. She's holding an envelope in her hands.

"There's something important I have to tell you, Aleja-ya," Ma says.

She never calls me Aleja-ya. Only Papi did.

"I know you already made your decision about Whyder."

"Ma, I—"

"Let me finish. You won't have to work with the loan sharks for college. Here!"

She thrusts the envelope at me. I open it: a check for $300,000 from Corporal Life Insurance. Made out to *me*.

I stare down at the check in disbelief. "I don't understand."

"Your father took out a life insurance plan," she explains. "Papi did everything in secret. Yo no tenía *ni idea*." She flicks the back of her hand under her chin for emphasis.

I had no idea, either. I think about all the unanswered mail—now, apparently, answered—that had taken over the dining table. Mounds became hills, hills became mountains, like a never-ending range of grief.

Just like how Ma and I never actually *dealt* with what was going on, deep down, under all of it.

No more.

"Take this check, Ale," Ma is saying now. "Use it for where you want to go to college. And in every action you take, do it in your father's kind spirit. He would be so proud of you, mi querida. You worked so hard to make your dream come true."

This check explains everything. The insurance money must have counted toward my—what did Mr. Landibadeau call it?—Expected Family Contribution.

I'm filled with a chilling thought—did Papi do it on purpose so I could go to college?

I can't stop the tears springing to my eyes. "Mami," I start, "what I said to him junior year, about the college trip . . ."

Ma sees the darkness clouding over my face.

"Shh, mi amor, no, no, no," she says quickly. "You *cannot* think like that."

"But—I wish I could take it all back, Mami!" I cry out. "I never got to tell Papi I'm sorry."

"It has nothing to do with your . . . words with Papi. I promise you that."

Ma's pink-frosted lips make a tight line. "This check will *never* replace your father. *Nunca.* He's not coming back to us, and we have to accept that. But Papi doesn't want us to live inside the past. He wants us to live for the future."

Dream big, Aleja-ya. I'll always carry Papi's words with me.

"But I thought . . . you didn't want me to go to Whyder," I say. "You said I was making a 'big mistake.'"

"I didn't want you to go away, *punto*," Ma says. "Where I can't watch you and make sure you're safe."

"What made you change your mind?" I ask softly.

"I may have had a charla with your tía," Ma admits.

"Tía Yoona?" I say in disbelief.

Ma smiles ruefully.

I make a mental note to call Tía in the morning and thank her.

Ma gets up to put the kettle on. While she's gone, I look at the neatened paperwork. There's a letter from Jackson Heights Residential Services, announcing the fee structure for buyouts. Billy was right: we're going co-op.

I look at Papi's insurance check.

You're just like them. Billy's words echo loudly in my head.

But my own words echo back louder: *But I don't have to be.*

Ma comes back with mugs of tea.

"What are these letters?" I ask.

"Not your worry." Ma takes a sip of tea. "I want you to do what makes you happy."

"Ma," I venture. "Were *you* happy?"

You never loved him. Tía Yoona's words from the funeral.

Ma puts down her mug. I can see she doesn't want to answer. I can also feel her sensing this is her moment to come clean. That she knows I will see through her bullshit if she doesn't.

"I came to Mi-Guk all by myself. I was scared and homesick,"

Ma starts. "And when I met your papi again here . . . Juan was familiar. He reminded me of back home. He was so kind to me, showing me the city. He even took me to eat parrilla because I missed steak from Argentina so much! Juan taught me everything I know about Mi-Guk. Usos y costumbres, when no one else did."

I nod, understanding. My hands circle my tea mug, trying to hold in the warmth, trying not to let it grow cold.

Ma continues. "You have any idea how hard it is in this country, Aleja? Yanquis look down at you unless you speak perfect English." She switches to a nasally English: *"Huh? Ex-CUSE me?"*

I laugh at her neoyorquina imitation.

"Here, they treat you like mierda. But in Argentina, you don't speak perfect Spanish, it's okay. Todo tranquilo, tranquilo, nobody rushes you. ¿Acá? Everything is ppalli-ppalli, nobody has time for you. I would have been lost without your papi. Sometimes it felt like the two of us against the universe."

She shuts her eyes tight.

Ma never talks about her early days in Mi-Guk. I don't know much—if anything at all—about her immigration story. Everything I know about her past I gleaned from Papi.

It's the first time Ma's ever opened up to me.

"You remember Papi's music. His jazz, it used to make my loneliness feel less lonely. ¿Entendés? But he never got to live his dream." Ma cradles her teacup. "It wasn't true, what your tía said. I wasn't too good for Juan. He was too good for me."

Ma looks away. I follow her gaze to her city hall photograph in the hallway. I see her slipping into another time, another place. Young, beautiful—but also lonely. I realize now, Papi took Ma's loneliness away.

"Juan . . . he was such a gentle soul. And I—"

She strikes her chest. I grab her fist before she can strike herself again.

"*I* never got to say sorry to him!" she cries. "I was so hard on him. How can I forgive myself for his accident?"

But you know it wasn't an accident. I see the way the fading light touches her eyes as she looks into that photograph, at that faraway place and time. They are now shiny with tears.

Ma's not right about Papi's death, I know that in my heart.

Can't you just let me hurt in my own way?

So I do.

Ma's still fixed on the photograph, memories clouding her face. This whole apartment is still charged with Papi.

I cast my eyes past our empty cups of tea and unanswered paperwork and this too-big Formica table, where we'll never sit together again as a family. Past the worn couch, still sinking with the phantom weight of Papi's body, and the old hibachi rusting on the fire escape. I can see past the four walls of our illegally converted rental. It's the only home I've ever known. And even though our window affords only a slivered view of María Inez Montoya Park and Jackson Heights, of the setting sun and streetlamps that flicker off more often than on and the 7 train rumbling in the distance, now I can see a world far beyond.

Subway Music

FAST-FORWARD FIVE YEARS, and I'm still in Jackson Heights, still in apartment 2B, but my whole world has changed.

I never went off to Whyder College. It might have been the perfect school for freshperson Ally, but it was no longer the right choice for senior-year Ale. I chose to go to Hunter instead, where I majored in psychology. Dr. C was my academic adviser.

Since I graduated from Quaker Oats, a couple of other things happened:

Ma and I started therapy. Dr. C had some great recommendations. Honestly, I was surprised Ma was down for it. Therapy's not some overnight cure-all; it takes time. But I think we now have better language to talk about our feelings, if that makes sense.

I also have a home—a real home. I used Papi's insurance money to buy our apartment. Ma insisted on putting it under my name. I'm twenty-three, and I own my very own piece of New York.

If I had gone to Whyder, there's no way we could have afforded to buy our apartment when the building "went co-op." Home prices are going up like crazy in Jackson Heights; the waves of gentrification have arrived on our shores, so to speak, and we would have been washed out of our own home.

Also, if I had gone to Whyder, I might not have ended up at Columbia, where I'm starting a PhD program in clinical psych. I owe a lot to Dr. C. In college, I learned that what I really want to do is help people—people like the test subjects in the First-Gen American Testimony project, people like Papi, and also families of the deceased, like Ma and me.

APARTMENT 2B LOOKS NOTHING like it used to. Before, it was an ugly, depressing greige (gray plus beige). We've painted it a bright, cheerful yellow. Family photos are framed and displayed prominently on the wall. The picture of Papi and me at the Rockaways is no longer buried in my bottom desk drawer.

The bulky black leather couch is gone. Ma and I bought a new couch and put it together, together. You know what the real test of family is? Assembling Ikea furniture. If you can survive that impossible instruction booklet with the stick-figure man and the Allen key, you can survive *anything.*

Home is really looking and feeling like home. They're also doing work on improving the building, finally. Julio is sanding away all those oppressive layers of paint in the elevator.

A lot can happen in five years.

THIS IS ACTUALLY THE last Christmas Ma and I will be spending together for who knows how long. In three days she's going back to Argentina. Tía Magda, Ma's sister, invited her to live with her. Ma's trying it out for a year, but it could be longer. The US dollar is strong against the ever-inflating peso, so Ma can live like the reina she is back in Buenos Aires.

My whole apartment smells like fry grease, but I don't mind. The empanada oil is heating in the pan on the stove. The dining table, that giant hand-me-down from Tía Yoona that always felt so large and empty, is now set for eight. Papi's old hibachi is fired up on the fire escape.

Ma's outside, working the grill. "Ma," I call out. "Don't you need more charcoal?"

"¡Ojo!" Ma says, waving me off. "Never tell an Argentine woman how to grill her meat."

Fair enough. I get busy chopping parsley.

Tía Yoona and Michael Oppa are arriving any minute to help make the empanadas. Michael Oppa's fiancé, George, is coming later with the wine. They met at an arts nonprofit, where Michael Oppa is CFO. Michael Oppa left his soul-sucking job at Goldman the same summer I graduated Quaker Oats, and he's never looked back.

Billy is bringing the Díaz family's famous tres leches cake. I have not seen him since he came home from the Marines. Five years ago, I waited for him at Montoya Fountain. Five years ago, Billy never showed. Later that night, I found his note stuck in our mailbox:

Ale,

I said some things to you I'll always regret. I had no right to explode at you like that. Your pa would be SO PROUD of the woman you've become.

I know you have things you want to say to me. But I've got some things I need to figure out for myself. Things that have nothing to do with you, or your dad, or anyone else.

By the time you read this, I'll be on my way to basic training.

Good luck at Whyder. I know you'll do great.

love,
Billy

I was heartbroken. But what could I do? Billy was already gone. I'd been so tunnel-visioned on my own journey that I was completely oblivious to Billy on his.

Over the past five years, our contact has been touch and go. There was always a sense of unfinished business between us. I heard from gossipy Mrs. Sánchez that Billy sent his mom money for the down payment when our building complex went co-op. But now Billy's coming home, for good.

Claire Devereaux is bringing macaroons—sorry, macarons—from some Upper West Side macaronerie (yes, that is apparently a real word). I keep reminding her she'll have to say "so long" to all things bougie when she moves in with me next month, and she argues it's the Upper *East* Side that's "bougie" and the

Upper *West* Side is "boho," and I'm all, "same diff." Claire's starting work at Elmhurst Hospital while applying to med schools. Before Whyder, she thought she wanted to be a novelist like JBJ. (Well, *not* like JBJ.) But writing was more Grandmama's dream than her own. Claire fell in love with medicine, and she switched tracks.

That she roots for Los Cafeteros is a bit of a sore point in our friendship. Papi and I always thought they were a bunch of cheats crying foul on the soccer pitch.

If you'd told me five years ago that Claire Devereaux and I would become such good friends, let alone roommates, I would've said *no way*. But Michael Oppa says that's how it is with people from high school. Kids you barely knew, let alone liked, can end up becoming your closest friends after. Like how George *also* went to Stuy. But back then, George and Michael Oppa weren't on each other's radars.

Michael Oppa also says there are those high school friendships you think will last forever, but don't.

Laurel Greenblatt-Watkins and I don't keep in touch. She went to Princeton, and she really seemed to find her place there, her "home." Which, at least from the photos she'd upload—we follow each other online—was *not* her father's or her sister's place. Laurel organized peaceful protests on women's rights. Then she summered in Oregon to campaign for a local assemblywoman. Last I heard, she'd joined the Peace Corps, where she's helping build a school for girls in Ghana.

And Payal—Dr. C says I can call her that now that I'm no longer her student and will soon be her colleague—will stop by with some Indian sweets from her auntie, who also lives in the barrio. She always foists on Payal these sugary blocks of candy that are pretty to look at but will guarantee a trip to the dentist the next day.

YOU KNOW WHAT'S FUNNY? It took me senior year at Quaker Oats to admit I had imposter syndrome. Five years later, it feels like something we tell girls—women—like me, to explain why we feel we don't belong. Instead of examining the larger reasons *for* those feelings. Payal, for one, hates it: "It's just another term foisted on us that we didn't ask for."

CHRISTMAS WAS PAPI'S FAVORITE holiday. And I'd like to think he's smiling down on us from above. I don't know if I believe in an afterlife, but I truly hope that Papi has found his peace.

Over dinner we'll share stories of Papi. The greatest hits. After, we're all boarding the 7 train to Queensboro Plaza. Ma, too, had been avoiding that station since Papi died. I had no idea. A few Christmases ago, she and I held hands and faced our fear together. This Christmas, there'll be eight of us. We'll say a short blessing, then listen to the rush of trains coming and going in the station. Papi's Subway Music.

I know that sounds corny, but frankly I don't care. We're not saying *goodbye* to Papi. We're saying, *We still love you.*

***

YOU NEVER "GET OVER" the loss of a parent. It stays with you all day, every day, like a persistent shadow. But some days, you get lucky. The shadow kind of goes away for a little while. The sun shines brighter than usual, and all you feel is its warm glow around you.

MA AND I HAVE made the decision to not commemorate the day Papi died. For Ma, it's too painful to relive his "death-iversary." And therapy has taught me I should accept Mami's wishes, because we all have our own ways of grieving. As for me, I just go about my day like it's business as usual. I mean, of all the things to memorialize, why am I going to celebrate the day he left us? That'd be like giving power to Papi's death. Instead, I choose to celebrate his life.

Acknowledgments

I HAVE SO MANY people to thank. Too many.

To my parents, siblings, and the next generation. Especially to Umma, whose sweaters saved the family in Nam-Mi. To my late uncles, may you rest in peace. To Canada Tía, Tía Gladys, Tía Silvia, and Tío Silvio. Special thanks to my niece and nephew, to whom this novel is dedicated—I cherish our conversations about books.

Thanks to the following folks for lending their eyes, expertise, sensitivity, or all of the above: Lisa Borders, Mónica Cantero-Exojo, Alison Daniel, Coleman Dash, Brieana Garcia, Anna Godbersen, Carol Gray, Heather Hume, Lauren Kay, Jessica Landis, Rafi Mittlefehldt, and Denise Morales Soto.

On the publishing side, I thank Sarah Burnes and Phoebe Yeh. To Sophie Pugh-Sellers, Elizabeth Stranahan, Arely Guzmán, Daniela Cortes, Jessica Cruickshank, Ray Shappell, Melinda Ackell, Kris Kam, Adrienne Waintraub, Barbara

Marcus, and all the wonderful folks at Crown BFYR and Random House Children's Books.

Thank you to the Jerome Foundation and the Mount, the Edith Wharton Writers-in-Residence Program. Thank you to my colleagues at American University and to my students.

I'm grateful for the scholarship of Shinhee Han and David Eng.

And to Brett and Sally. Always.

About the Author

PATRICIA PARK is a professor of creative writing at American University, a Fulbright Scholar in Creative Arts, a Jerome Hill Artist Fellow, and the author of the acclaimed adult novel *Re Jane.* The Korean American reimagining of Charlotte Brontë's *Jane Eyre* was named an Editors' Choice by the *New York Times Book Review;* the winner of an American Library Association award; an *O, The Oprah Magazine* pick; and an NPR "Fresh Air" pick, among other honors. *Imposter Syndrome and Other Confessions of Alejandra Kim* is inspired by the author's own struggles to overcome feeling like an imposter at school, at work, and in life.

Patricia's writing has also appeared in the *New Yorker,* the *New York Times,* the *Guardian, Salon,* and others. She was born and raised in Queens and lives in Brooklyn, New York.

PATRICIAPARK.COM